THE COMET'S RETURN

Alma Chronicles V

Toby Fesler Heathcotte

Mardel Books

The Comet's Return is a work of fiction. Names, places, and incidents either are products of the author's imagination or are used fictitiously.

The Comet's Return ©2009 by Toby Fesler Heathcotte

First edition released in 2009 by

Mardel Books
6145 West Echo Lane
Glendale, Arizona 85302
mardelbooks.com

Cover design by Zanne Kennedy
Author photo by Dennis Habbershaw

ISBN: 978-0-9819961-4-1

In 2061 Arizona, Angela dreams of people she should recognize and events she should remember. With her career and her sanity in jeopardy, she goes to the trunk opening for Halley's Comet and finds her love from their previous incarnation. Connecting with her previous lifetime opens Angela to the great knowledge. Kegan yet walks the world, intent on ending the blood feud from Celtic times.

"This journey of rediscovered love and spiritual awakening will leave readers speculating on forces that impact their own lives, long after the last page."
Michael J. Murphy, Suspense Novelist

"Deep, tormented characters evolve through a succession of dramatic lifetimes. Celtic legends connect with known history, current and even future events, in a believable tapestry of karmic consequences, where good and evil intersect and sometimes even switch places."
Vijaya Schartz, Science Fiction and Romance Author

"I found this an exciting read about a crafty villain determined to keep Angela and Todd from their reincarnated destinies."
Cherie Lee, Novelist and Magazine Editor

"*The Comet's Return* is a most unusual book. It is replete with visions, premonitions, clairvoyance, reincarnated persons, and unusual thoughts about the reincarnated and their actions. The story moves rapidly and provides an enjoyable read. A most interesting sidelight is that it conjures up a number of thought-provoking ideas for contemplation about the unknown."
John H. Manhold, Fiction/Nonfiction Author

For my grandchildren

The Alma Chronicles

Incarnations of the Souls

50-10 BCE England	1700s CE England, Scotland, & Maryland Colony	1900s CE Arizona, California, & Afghanistan	2000s CE Arizona and California of Greater Hispania
Alma	Alison	Angie	Angela
Taliesin	Thomas	Ty	Todd
Lugh	Lainn	Luke	Luke (living)
Morfran	Mac & Megan	Melinda	Melanie
Caitlin	Catherine		
Kegan	Colin	Karim	Kendall & Kegan
	Henry	Hank	
	Emily		Euphoria
	Judith & Jeannie	Jillian	Janice
	Aaron & Donnie	Aaron	Aaron (living)
Emmons (in Afterlife)	Emmons	Emmons (in Afterlife)	Emmons (in Afterlife)

One

Vague Longings

Phoenix, Greater Hispania—May 25, 2061

In a dream, Angela huddled on hard ground. She heard a popping sound and looked up with a sense of dread. Yellow flames burst through the air. Something huge was on fire above her. Heat seared her skin. The stench of burning rubber sickened her. She felt the coarseness of the cloth in her dress.

Someone lay nearby. She reached out to help him. When she turned him over, his face was burned and blistered beyond recognition. Desperately she cradled him. She didn't want him to die, but it was too late. She screamed for help.

The scream rattled in Angela's throat and awakened her. She bounded out of bed then glanced involuntarily at the other side terrified that she would see the burned body lying next to her.

Her movement across the carpet turned on the lavender light recessed in the wall, allowing her to see and assure herself that she was alone in her bedroom. Her nightgown damp from perspiration clung to her skin.

The digital clock read two in the morning. What an awful nightmare. She'd never dreamed the same dream twice before that she could ever recall. And now for the past three nights this horror had been visited upon her in her

1

sleep. Why? She pressed her hand to her rapidly beating heart and feared bad dreams could cause her to have a heart attack. She had to calm down.

Too exhausted to remain awake and unwilling to go back to her bed, Angela headed into the white-carpeted living room, grateful for the pale blue lights that welcomed her. She didn't want to remain alone in the house. How comforting it would have been to have a man with her right now, the right man.

Her condo with its sleek styling and transparent furniture looked as lonely as she felt. The decision to remain single and focus on her career worked far better in the daylight than in the middle of the night. Intellectually she accepted herself as cool and focused and not at all needy. But beneath that persona seemed to dwell another, more passionate self, one capable of tremendous love and devotion, perhaps even obsession. Those feelings poured out of her for the dead man in her dream. That must have meant she could feel those emotions awake too.

Who was the man in the dream? Someone she fantasized? Maybe her intuition meant she would meet the man, but why would she want to meet him if she were doomed to experience such despair because of him?

Who was she in the dreams? Her clothes seemed old-fashioned and an ugly style she'd never choose. That detail present in all the dreams seemed important, but how she didn't know.

Nothing made sense. She felt like she had a bomb in her mind that went off when she fell asleep. She understood herself less with every passing day.

Her need to uncover the truth about things had prompted her to choose a journalism career. She felt the need even more now that the search had taken such a terrifying and personal turn.

Angela punched up the pillows behind her and flipped on the video wall, switching channels until she found a comedy show in progress. That would distract her mind and help her remain awake until time to get ready for work.

The next moment it seemed sunlight flooded through the condo windows. She had not realized she'd nodded off. She was late for work, again.

Dashing into the bedroom, Angela threw on her black skirt and blouse, grabbed her gold lamé blazer and makeup kit. She ran through the front door into the parking lot and climbed into her opalescent Bimi. The little car, with its sprays of pink and green feathery flowers reminiscent of a desert willow tree, had cost a year's salary, but she didn't care about the money. She felt proud to own such a lovely machine.

Angela sped down the boulevard from her condo through the Bradshaw Mountains. She steered the vehicle onto the beltway and edged it into the track of the moving electric grid beside a bright red Bimi with yellow and orange flames. She set the amethyst steering knob to autopilot.

A sucking sound indicated her car had slipped onto the hover field. Angela leaned up in the velvet seat to apply her makeup. At least that would save a few minutes after she arrived. She ignored the other cars and trolleys traveling in tandem with her at two hundred kilometers per hour. The fuel cell hummed as it recharged.

She opened the makeup kit. Empty. Damn. She couldn't stop her thoughts: Who were the people in the dreams? Always the same. Why did the horrors keep repeating? She had an odd suspicion that she ought to know. If she didn't get answers soon, she would lose her mind. Could losing sleep cause a person to become psychotic?

Once she arrived at the news bureau downtown, Angela hurried along the corridor, vexed with herself. The sliding glass doors into the news room opened for her.

The editor, Campbell, charged toward her along the row of cubicles between secretaries and junior reporters. "For the love of God, can't you get here on time?" His gruff voice exploded. "What's happened to you lately?"

Curious faces peered above work stations, no doubt eager to see a colleague dressed down, especially one promoted so fast.

"I'm sorry, boss." Angela held up the hem of her skirt and hurried toward the makeup room door. Six minutes until air time. "Can we talk about this later?"

Campbell folded short arms over a starched white shirt, which barely covered his girth. He stepped into her path. His heavy eyebrows bobbed up and down in that annoying way he had of letting her know she'd disappointed him again, after all he'd done for her. "Sorry won't get the job done here," he chided in a sarcastic tone. "Do the words Alpha Centauri hold any meaning for you?"

Surely he wouldn't send her four light years away to beam back news of wars among barely known civilizations. She preferred that he would banish her or put her in prison. Angela gasped, "You can't be serious!"

"I can and I am. You'll be here to get prepped on the news and get into makeup in a timely fashion, or I'll be looking for someone else to fill your slot, and you'll be on a space transport." Campbell sliced a pudgy hand in the air with the motion of flight. He appeared to enjoy her discomfort.

Tired and listless, Angela didn't blame him much. "I know I'm off my stride. I'll try to do better." She didn't want to lose her job. Avoiding her boss's eyes, she dodged into the makeup room and sat in the tilt-back, molded chair. She clutched her jacket in a death grip.

"Get that copy for me!" Campbell shouted at the assistant director and followed Angela into the room. He glared at her while the makeup man kinked the wavy strands of her long black hair into a tailored bob.

"Here, boss." The assistant director, a nervous young woman, said in a shaky voice and thrust her arm into the room.

Grabbing the disc-shaped copyreader, Campbell tossed it toward Angela. "Get busy."

To keep her head immobile so the makeup man could work his magic, Angela strained her eyes around his muscular, suntanned arm to read the news line traveling across the disc.

The makeup man brushed a dewy blue gel on her lids to bring out the color of her pale eyes. Standing back, he clamped a hand on one slim hip and surveyed her face. "Girlfriend, you really need an eye job. Only surgery could cover up these dark sockets. And whatever can we do with this cadaverous skin?"

Angela gathered up her belongings. "Thanks for the critique!" Normally she would laugh off his catty comments, but today under the cloud of such sorrow from the dream and exhaustion from lack of sleep, she felt offended by the makeup man's comments.

"Well, you look a veritable harridan!"

The caution light blinked *two minutes*. "Leave me alone. I look all right." Angela didn't like being called a witch, even in jest.

True, she often picked the right moment to ask for interviews or knew the most telling question to ask. She credited her promotion to that knack for synchronicity, although some jealous reporters attributed it to what Granddad called her porcelain-doll looks.

As a kid she'd thought everyone's intuitions came to fruition like hers did. As an adult she downplayed the source of her knowledge to avoid being singled out as weird. The religious wars in the twenty-first century with beheadings, suicide bombers, and other atrocities had sometimes included witch burning. Her intuition warned her to be careful so she wouldn't be accused of witchcraft even though she had never practiced it. No one had been accused in Greater Hispania, but it had happened in some mid-eastern countries. Insane cultists could rise up anytime, anywhere.

The sweeping trumpets of a classical march on the sound system announced the early edition as Angela dashed onto the set. Stars glittered and an occasional comet streaked across the midnight blue projected on the domed sound stage with its imbedded silver dollar sized cameras. Looking relieved, the assistant director sat beside the sync-master, the only humans among the holographic audience, which applauded around them.

While Angela slipped into her jacket, she hoped the events of the day held such high interest that no one would notice her weariness. Breathing deeply to calm herself, she tucked the copy disc inside her sleeve and slid into her side of the transparent desk.

Her co-anchor, Juan, nodded from the next seat. He adjusted the collar of his matching lamé jacket and smoothed the sleeve, cleverly calling attention to his model-perfect physique. He smiled with a practiced charm that Angela distrusted. She couldn't decipher why he tilted his well-sculpted chin. Juan's brown eyes flashed beneath plucked brows. What was he thinking? Probably whether or not he should have his eyes done! Maybe he could change the color. She found blue eyes ever-so-much sexier.

Angela set aside her thoughts about Juan. If she didn't watch herself, she could become as catty as the makeup man. Besides, Juan had such talent and potential that he didn't need to trade on his good looks.

The green light blinked on, the fanfare faded, and he smiled angelically. "Good morning, Phoenix and Greater Hispania. Juan Calderon reporting."

"And I'm Angela Brock." She smiled steadily into the monitor until the midnight sphere turned opaque, then she focused on the copy tracking across her field of vision.

Nothing must break the cameras' illusion that she and her co-anchor floated in the firmament.

"An hour ago the Inter-Planetary Council censored Venezuela for threatening troop movements in the Caribbean." Juan's solemn voice made him sound like the sincere patriot he probably was. "President Gonzales reminded our Venezuelan neighbors that continued aggression may result in trade restrictions. So far, there has been no response."

"In medical news," Angela began with a genuine smile at delivering good news, "doctors at the Cancer Institute are closing their doors. Recent progress in research has revealed that ninety-five percent of cancers are curable with over-the-counter medications. The other five percent of patients, according to Dr. Lester Weinstein, steadfastly insist on their right to die of cancer. Dr. Weinstein said, 'We must honor the patient's integrity in such decisions.'" She felt enormous satisfaction that cancer had finally been defeated. She shuddered at even thinking of having it.

The assistant director pointed toward the tiny barrel of the camera in the corner, and Juan shifted seamlessly to face it. "Halley's Comet has returned to circle the earth. Today for the first time in seventy six years, it has become visible without the need for a telescope. In a light-hearted celebration of the Comet's return, L. A.'s famed Griffith Park Observatory has announced June Fifth as the date for opening the Halley's Comet Trunk, a time capsule, sealed in 1986. Dr. Todd Williams will preside. Dr. Williams is the astrophysicist who developed the tachyon drive, the first weightless propulsion system, the discovery that allowed faster-than-light travel throughout the galaxy."

The viewfinder monitor rolled film footage of a sleek, new high rise in downtown Phoenix. An elegant looking man in a tuxedo stood beside Governor Goldman while she broke a champagne bottle over the cornerstone.

Angela's camera light came on and she read the tagline, "Phoenix welcomes the Psi Therapy Clinic, which has opened for business. Dr. Robert Kegan, the managing director, reports that full services will be rendered according to the English paranormal model, a first for Greater Hispania and in fact for all of the United States of North America." She smiled as the footage cross-faded with her image. "In further government news, the National Home Council will convene on Sunday evening, June Five for the culminating tally on this month's issues to be voted on by the electorate. Stay tuned following this important message."

When the familiar neigh of Tamale Tim's nag whinnied in the monitor, Juan leaned across the desk and laid a warm palm over Angela's. Startled, she withdrew her hand quickly and gave him a quizzical look. Holding conversations during commercials always broke her focus, so she didn't like doing it.

"I've got tickets to the Mozart concert tonight. Will you go with me?" Juan looked boyish, as if dreading her response. Not surprising, considering how many times she had refused him. "Don't say no. We can have dinner at the spaceport and watch the sunset. It will be fun."

"Please, I wish you wouldn't ask me. I'd prefer we have a professional relationship." Angela dreaded the idea of establishing a relationship with Juan, or anyone else for that matter. She didn't want to be part of a couple. Still she felt lonely for the love of a man.

"But why not? We're perfect for each other!" Juan scowled, distorting the handsome lines of his face. "It's not like you've got anybody else. If you did I'd understand. It seems you just refuse me out of spite, and I don't deserve that."

"Five seconds," the assistant director hissed from the midst of the hologram.

What a relief! Angela sighed.

8

Juan relaxed into a bland smile and fixed his eyes on the camera lens. The rest of the newscast passed uneventfully, but Juan didn't look at Angela again. Afterward, she felt fortunate to have a telecom interview scheduled and hurried out of the sound stage. Anything to avoid Juan's accusing eyes.

At the end of the workday, Angela drove her Bimi onto the beltway. Normally, she loved to watch the Phoenix skyline with its towering glass buildings in geometric designs, set against the cloudless blue desert vault. Depressed today, she ignored the view of the northern beltway on the fast track drive. She leaned against the magenta seat and closed her eyes.

Although she felt guilty for refusing Juan, she would do the same to any man who happened to ask for a date. She wondered at her overwhelming lack of interest in the men she knew or met. She had no homosexual leanings like her brother, but something was definitely wrong with her. At thirty, most women wanted a husband, home, and children. Most of her friends had already found relationships that would probably end in marriages. Her biological clock demanded a decision before long. Becoming a mother seemed a wonderful prospect.

Angela was too old to be a virgin. Well, almost a virgin, except for one summertime affair at twenty-two when her curiosity about sex overcame her wits. That worthy young man waited far too long for her to make a decision, but he finally gave up and married someone else. Angela wished him happiness and felt only gratitude toward him. Sex had been fun, but love and commitment to him? Out of the question.

Half asleep in the cozy Bimi, she entered a dream fragment.

Angela stood sobbing before a closed coffin then looked down into her own reflection in the glossy

wooden sheen. Did that mean she would die soon?
Her dress fell only to her knees, too old and short a
style. She had the eerie sensation of being in some
other woman's mind and feeling her despair.

"We've just passed the Anthem exit, darling," said the
baritone of the auto-pilot. Angela had chosen the voice for
its throaty quality that made her tingle. "You'll need to take
the wheel in five minutes."

Shivering, Angela opened her eyes and steered the Bimi
off the beltway. Soon, if Governor Goldman had her way,
the beltway would continue to Salt Lake City as it did to
Los Angeles and San Diego already. For now, Angela must
manually drive the last ten miles to get home, requiring as
much time as sixty miles on the beltway.

Cacti and fir trees sprang from a raked-pebble lawn,
and lights in small glass houses winked as Angela turned
west. The red sun set low, and the rock-faced Bradshaw
Mountains cast hulking shadows.

The darkness of her nightmares or these ridiculous
forays into the mind of some unknown other woman, if
that's what was happening, had to cease. She needed to
forget the dreams and focus energy on her real life. Mom
and Dad certainly had the right to expect grandchildren, a
fact they often mentioned. Angela sighed.

Duty to family seemed burdensome, but in the long run,
she must respond to it. Since her brother lived on Biosphere
Nine and hardly ever came to Earth for a visit, she had only
Mom and Dad with their soiled chemists' lab coats and
Granddad with his jokes and wise sayings. Her brother
might adopt since he was in a long-term relationship, but
that would never satisfy Angela's family. They counted on
her to do the procreation and give them biological heirs.
Certainly they loved her and wished her well, but they
wanted little ones, portals for souls to reenter the world, as
Granddad always said.

Disappointing her family haunted Angela's days like the dream woman haunted her nights. She'd have to take action. No one could do this for her.

Steering with one hand, Angela flipped on the holophone and said, "Juan Calderon's home." A bit self-conscious, she smoothed her rumpled hair before he had a chance to see her.

A tiny image of Juan in a silk dressing gown appeared on the dash. "Hello?"

"Juan, you were right. We have the same career goals. We probably have a lot more in common. There's no reason in the world we shouldn't explore a relationship."

"What? Is this a joke?" asked Juan's surprised-looking hologram.

"No." Angela laughed. "I seriously want to see you without cameras circling us. It's too late for dinner, but if the offer is still open, we can catch the concert, and I'll treat you to drinks at the End-of-the-World Café."

"Sure, okay, good. Uh, what changed your mind?"

"If I knew, I'd tell you."

Perhaps she should go on home and change into something sexier. Angela glanced at her working silk gown and jacket. The fabric always looked freshly pressed. Good enough.

Screeching the Bimi's tires, Angela turned and headed back toward Phoenix, determined to make the evening turn out well. Juan might not be the most interesting man in the world, but he was kindhearted and photogenic. They would make beautiful babies both the family and the press would love.

How would he be in bed? At the thought, Angela's heart thudded with guilt. She couldn't have felt worse if she had actually betrayed her beloved, but she had never promised her fidelity to anyone. Why did she feel as if she had? That emotion made no sense. She had to stuff it. And stuff it, she would.

When she arrived at Phoenix's Symphony Hall only moments before the overture, the stone plaza twinkled with lights in olive trees growing from squares of real soil, not the earth-colored nutrient chips gardeners normally used. Cooling towers with banks of spring flowers rose high overhead and made the grounds smell fresh. The water bubbled to the accompaniment of a recorded Mozart piano concerto.

Entering the lobby, Angela glided beneath the crystal chandeliers on heavy carpeting that muffled her high-heeled step. She'd not seen the place since its restoration to is 1970s splendor. A few last-minute arrivals hurried past ushers clad in eighteenth-century costumes in honor of the composer. Angela enjoyed seeing the charming George and Martha Washington look alikes.

Juan, dignified in a tux, stood in a circle of a dozen or more concertgoers, older women in long black dresses and bejeweled wraps. His smile revealed how much the attention of signing autographs please him.

"Hello!" Angela hoped her voice sounded engaging like a date's should, although she had little concept of what that meant. She was probably the only single woman alive who had not been on a date for eight years.

"There you are!" Juan shouted gaily and excused himself from his admirers.

"Oh, my goodness, it's her." One of the ladies nudged another.

"Who?"

"The female one, you know, his partner. I didn't know they were married."

"They aren't." The second lady rolled disapproving eyes. "What's her name?"

"Oh, I can't remember. Let's hurry. I don't want to miss the overture." The women scurried through the portal as the lobby lights winked off, then on again.

"Hello." Giving her a quick kiss on the cheek, Juan encircled Angela's waist possessively. "I can't tell you how glad I am you're here, darling."

At the use of that endearment a flush crept up Angela's throat. "Well, thanks." His familiarity made her uncomfortable. His heavy, musky scent oppressed her. She wished he smelled fresh and outdoorsy.

"Let's find our seats." Juan guided her through the doorway and into the center front section, some of the best seats in the house.

Practically every seat on the main floor contained a well-dressed occupant. Angela glanced up at the box seats nearest the stage and saw Governor Goldman next to an attractive older man. Her usual bodyguards sat behind them. Angela thought she ought to recognize the governor's companion. Oh, yes, the man from the news spot, the new director of the Psi Therapy Clinic. How interesting. Rumors suggested that the governor might reconcile with the husband she'd divorced after the election, but from the look on her face as she flirted with Dr. Kegan, Angela guessed the rumors to be false.

The musicians filed in and sat down to prolonged applause. As the performers on stage began the first movement of Symphony 25 in G Minor, Angela found herself drawn into Mozart's timeless music. Its power quelled all thought and worry. She dwelt in the fabric of the sound vibrating through her.

Between selections, Juan squeezed her hand and whispered about how lovely the music sounded and how beautiful she looked, but his words sounded empty. He treated her as if he already owned her, like the rights to a stage play—her only value lay in being seen.

At the intermission, admirers again surrounded Angela and Juan.

"Here she is," a woman said and thrust a program into Angela's hand. "Sign this, please."

From time to time, Angela had experienced some renown. Once in a while at market, someone recognized her and nodded or looked away embarrassed. Clearly Juan's presence enhanced the attention. They were public people. Television viewers identified them as a couple already, and seeing them at a concert together confirmed their notions. Juan reinforced their belief by behaving as if Angela were his constant companion. By other people's standards, she shouldn't experience any anxiety about the date.

Finally, the concert ended. In spite of Angela's earlier offer to buy drinks at the café, Juan insisted on seeing her home instead. That entailed his following her in his car on the beltway. During the ride, Angela fought conflicting emotions about Juan, a charming man, both on camera and off. Any woman in Greater Hispania would probably rejoice at the chance to have him visit her home, but the prospect made Angela shudder. A concert and public attention seemed one thing—spending time alone with him, quite another. What would he expect? A kiss, or more?

After she locked her car in the parking lot, Juan hurried to her and caught her in an embrace.

Angela felt invaded, afraid, and put off. She knew his behavior and his words did not warrant such a negative reaction, close to revulsion.

With the same familiarity that Dad often kissed Mom, Juan pecked Angela briefly on the mouth and whispered, "I'm so happy you let me into your life. You'll never be sorry!"

His forthrightness surprised Angela. "I'm glad, too," she said, although she didn't feel glad. She wished mightily that she had stayed home and read a book, exquisite as Mozart had been.

When they walked up the ramp to her condo, the computer sensed Angela's identity. The metal door etched with rosebuds opened. The recessed aquamarine wall light came on, casting an underwater hue onto the living room.

"Would you like a drink?" Angela hoped he would say he couldn't stay. She knew little about Juan, including whether or not he drank alcohol. She tried to stir up some interest in learning about him.

"Maybe later." Juan pulled her to him. "I'm very fond of you, Angela." He kissed her on the mouth before she could pull back. His damp lips and intrusive tongue tasted like stale popcorn. "I want you to care for me, too."

Extracting herself from his arms, Angela said, "A martini perhaps, or some wine?" He didn't seem like the beer type.

"I just want to taste you." Juan nuzzled her neck and pushed her toward the bedroom.

A shiver of dread coursed down her spine. "What are you doing?"

"I want to make love to you."

"Not so fast!"

A look of defeat creased Juan's perfect features. "How can we have a relationship if we don't go to bed together?"

"Maybe we can't, but this just feels all wrong." A sense of betrayal assaulted Angela. "You're a fine fellow, Juan, you're just not for me."

"But you said—"

"I'm truly sorry if I mislead you."

Once she convinced him of her sincerity, she asked him to leave. The door closed on a dejected-looking Juan. Angela regretted subjecting them both to the evening. He didn't understand her, and neither did she. She should want a relationship with Juan, or at least somebody. Kicking off her shoes, she wandered aimlessly around the condo. She took an open bottle of chardonnay from the refrigerator and found a goblet.

A wave of loneliness rolled over Angela. How mundane her life seemed compared to the bizarre quality of her dream life. She passed from the living room into the bedroom, and the lighting changed to muted lavender. She lay across the disheveled coverlet, drank all the wine, and fell asleep.

In a dream, Angela ran across hot pavement toward an antique airplane idling on the tarmac. Over and over, she screamed, "Don't go! Don't go!" But the plane took off, banked, and exploded.

Shafts of orange and red flames shot everywhere. The sky began to glow then pieces of the plane fell down around her, crackling and burning. Someone she loved was burning inside, but she could do nothing. Desolation engulfed her.

Angela thrashed on the bed, wrenching herself awake. The digital display on the bedside table read 8:00. She'd never make it to a nine o'clock broadcast. Exhausted, she dragged herself to a sitting position, flipped on her wrist phone, and said, "Campbell." When her boss came on the line, she asked, "Could you get someone to sub for me today?"

"What in hell? You should be here now!"

"Please, Mr. Campbell, I'm sorry."

"If you're not on the air in an hour, you're fired!"

"No, something's wrong. I'll get help. See a doctor, or something." Angela wondered what kind of doctor to call. One who surgically removed dreams?

Campbell shouted to someone in the studio. "Get Hannah in a show jacket. She's going on." He snarled into the receiver, "Angela, I'm permanently replacing you right now. Don't try to get back on the morning news."

Not even the threat of Alpha Centauri? Angela sighed. What choice did she have? Her emotional reserves failed her, but she couldn't afford to get fired. No other station would touch her after that. Campbell often had trouble finding reporters willing to take low-key assignments. On a hunch, she offered, "How about I fly over to L. A. and cover the Halley's Comet exhibit?"

"You're willing to take on a grunt job like that?" Campbell bellowed. "Let's see how you can fuck that up!"

After ending the call, she jotted down the date she recalled from yesterday's newscast then headed for the bathroom to find some aspirin. At least she'd remain employed until June Fifth.

Somehow she had to get rid of these nightmares.

Two

Stemming the Tide

Sedona, Greater Hispania

At home, Luke Brock hoped to spend an hour in quiet contemplation before meeting his students. In his private library, books as old as the 1950s lined the walls, carefully preserved behind sliding glass panels. He didn't want any interruptions. Just as he took the holophone off his wrist and dropped it on the lamp table, it rang with the tinny clink of sheep bells.

His granddaughter's adorable face appeared in the dial. Since she called less often these days, he couldn't afford not to answer, so he decided to skip his meditation. He laid the wrist phone on the arm of his ancient tilt-back chair and sat down. A tiny hologram of Angela hovered above the wristwatch. She appeared to be at home in her fluffy housecoat.

"Hello, sweetheart. It's nice to see you."

"Granddad, I need to talk to you. Remember those dreams I told you about? Well, they're not stopping."

"Did you write them down like I told you to?"

Her hair swayed with her animated movements. "I've got to do something fast if I don't want to lose my job."

Luke felt fairly certain she was glimpsing a past lifetime, and he thought he knew which one—his own mother's. Still, he refrained from saying so. One thing a hundred years of living had taught him was that he couldn't tell people the most important things. They had to discover

18

those truths for themselves. He considered that a flagrant waste of earth time, but unavoidable. "The dreams'll ease after a while. At least the nightmarish elements."

"I thought I'd go to the new Psi Therapy Clinic and see if I can get some help."

"You probably don't need that, but—"

"I can't wait." A worried expression furrowed her brow. At such times she looked just like his mother.

"Why did you ask my advice at all if you're just going to ignore it?"

"No, no, I...well." Angela grinned, obviously owning her own mischief. "What do you think of that place?"

Luke chuckled at the fact that she asked his opinion again. Without a doubt she would ignore this answer too. Such obstinacy more than any other trait convinced him Angela could be his mother reborn. He wished for the hundredth time that Aaron and Vera had not named her for her great-grandmother. It just muddied the psychic waters.

"I don't know. Who's the head of the clinic now?" Luke asked.

"A Dr. Kegan. Don't you watch the news?"

"Never heard of him, but I know the clinic. It originated in London and has a good reputation. London has diminished in importance in New Age circles since the Scottish revolution and occupation of England. Relocating the clinic to Greater Hispania sounds like a smart move on their part." Scotland's rise to dominance in the European Union pleased Luke at a soul level. He proudly remembered a previous lifetime where he was born Scottish and had to flee English persecution. He had devoted much time, energy, and love to insuring that the colonies' revolt succeeded after the Scottish one suffered defeat. He'd better respond to Angela's question. He didn't want her to think his mind had wondered even if it had and said, "You'll probably get some good counseling, but you'll have to pay a lot for it."

"That's all right. Money's not the issue." Angela looked and sounded impatient.

Luke knew she was beginning to awaken spiritually. He didn't know how effective he could be with his own relative, so he welcomed the experts at the clinic. At least she would be safe there. Still it was worth a try. "My counseling's free."

"Oh, Granddad! I'll let you know how it turns out."

Angela's image dissolved. Luke turned off the phone and settled into the contours of the chair to ease the achy back muscles that he ignored in public.

Luke loved all his living family members, Aaron and Vera, his grandson Harlan, his stepdaughter Psyche, her kids, even her assorted husbands. Yet, although Luke would never admit it in words, Angela was the dearest of all to him. He felt a joyfulness in her presence that he never felt with anyone else. It would be wonderful if the day came when she acknowledged her soul identity, but even if she never did, this relationship, grandfather to granddaughter, had been the least demanding and most fulfilling of his life. So far, anyway.

Nervous but hopeful, Angela entered the Psi Therapy Clinic. She smoothed the folds of a powder blue sheath gown and scanned the office names on the interactive kiosk—Telepathic Techniques, Clairvoyance Techniques, Regression Portal, Progression Portal, Cosmic Disks and Tapes, Metaphorical Mind Integration, and Dream Analysis. Amazing the range of techniques she knew nothing about. Maybe she would do a documentary on this place later.

Angela cleared her throat, stepped into the elevator, and whispered, "Dream Analysis." It shot up to the fifth floor.

Unfamiliar with any of the employees, she had made an appointment with the first available counselor and now wondered if perhaps she should have taken the time to investigate credentials. After all, she was about to entrust the secret she had withheld from everyone. Who knew what could happen? Anger tugged at her for having to go through such a procedure, her boss's hostility notwithstanding.

Just as Angela decided to forget the whole thing and go back down in the elevator, the doors opened, and a smiling middle-aged woman stood, small and trim, in the entryway of the Dream Analysis Office. Extending a warm hand, she clasped Angela's. "Miss Brock, I'm so pleased to meet you. I'm Janice Beatty and I want very much to help you. Please come in and sit down."

The counselor conveyed an easy hominess, and Angela liked her. "Call me Angela, and thank you for seeing me on such short notice." Once inside the dimly lit counseling room, she sighed with anxiety.

The walls glowed in a rosy hue. Live frangipani, fresh and spicy, decorated the small space and lent the comforting ambience of the outdoors. The fragrance reminded Angela of many a trek over the red rocks of Sedona with Granddad. The faint sound of a stringed instrument seemed to emanate from the faintly rustling leaves. Angela settled onto a micro-fiber futon.

Colored lights blinked on the top of a glass table with a video monitor embedded in the top. Janice sat down before it. "Let me familiarize you with the procedure we follow here at the clinic. First, I discover your symptoms and possible problems, then we evaluate potential treatments. Counseling alone suffices for ninety percent of our patients. Some are hospitalized for mind infusion. A few require neurosurgery."

"Surgery, oh, my goodness." Angela shivered at the prospect.

"But rest assured, Dr. Kegan does outstanding work, though it's highly unlikely you'll need his services. I merely wanted you to understand that we have effective treatments with a ninety-nine percent recovery rate."

"Ninety-nine?" Angela teased to cover her concern. "What happens to that other percent? Death from dream analysis?"

Grinning, Janice rose and took four tiny remote electrodes from the back of the futon then placed them carefully on Angela's temples and neck. "These help you produce theta waves." Soundlessly the futon reclined as Janice passed her hand over a red light on the desktop. "I'll be recording our sessions, of course. On the phone you mentioned a recurring dream. Let's begin there."

"Do you want me to describe it?" Angela felt a theta pulse at her temples. The stringed music rippled through her. In moments she relaxed and her mind drifted. She couldn't remember whether Janice had answered the question. Although startled by the sudden onset of the altered state, Angela found the experience surprisingly enjoyable.

"There's no need for words. I'll be monitoring you. Simply allow yourself to re-experience the troubling dream. I'll be here to help you through it."

The memory of the recurring dream filled Angela's mind. Again she ran across the hot tarmac, screaming. Once more the plane exploded, and bursts of flame shot out in all directions. Willing herself to awaken but unable to do so, she collapsed and cried, filled with despair at the certain death of her unknown loved one.

"You are relaxed and calm," came the voice of Janice as if within Angela's mind. "You have done well. Now, I want you to remember another dream, one closely associated with this one in meaning."

The pulse in Angela's mind quickened, and an image of herself flashed into her view. She gazed into the polished wood of a coffin lid where her own reflection sobbed back at her. She picked up a framed picture that sat on the coffin and felt she should recognize the person in the photograph. Against her skin she felt the horribly antiquated clothing, a short dress in some kind of ugly fabric.

"Awaken now," Janice said.

The music and the theta beat stopped. While the futon straightened, Angela opened her eyes and wiped away tears. "There's something about this dream image that seems wrong. It's me, and it's not me at the same time. Guess that doesn't make much sense, does it?"

"You have outstanding dream recall!" Janice passed her hand over an orange light. The rosy room faded to gray, and images began to dance on one wall.

Fascinated, Angela watched her dreams play out in full color. Seeing them so, as if they were productions of a film company, the horror diminished, and she could watch with a more open mind. She noticed as her dream image ran across the tarmac that she wore the old clothing in that dream, too. "Could I be dreaming someone else's experience, not my own?"

"What do you mean?" Janice answered a question with another in typical counselor fashion. "Computer: Freeze."

At her command, the wall displayed a still and haunting image of Angela lying on the pavement, her face contorted in terror.

"I'm not sure, perhaps some kind of trace memory of another time, or maybe a genetic memory? Perhaps one of my ancestors had this experience."

"Those are certainly possibilities worth investigating. You could also be having a past life memory, but I prefer to consider the symptoms in a more conservative way."

"I think I do also." All her life Angela had heard Granddad speak of past lives as if everyone experienced them, but she had never given reincarnation much thought except as a philosophical possibility. Instead, she had followed her parents' lead and focused on career and intellectual development.

Janice leaned back and tapped a long fingernail against an upper tooth. "The chances are very high that your subconscious mind has created the metaphors of both these dreams to give you the same message."

"The same one? What makes you think that?" Angela had not thought of that explanation before, particularly of linking the dreams to one cause. Giving herself a hidden message seemed quirky and unlike her logical approach to life.

"The question is more precisely this: who or what is dying in these dreams?"

"I don't know who, but I feel like I should." As the second dream played, Angela strove to make out the image in the photograph. "Do you think it's me?" A shudder passed through her. "Do you think maybe it's a premonition of my own death?"

Janice clucked her tongue as she walked to the wall and pointed to the reflection of Angela's face in the coffin. "To me, the metaphor is classic. Yes, you're the one dying, but not a physical death."

"That could be."

Faint images of Angela and the coffin crisscrossed Janice's face. "It's a part of yourself that's dying. Something that you have been doing no longer works in your life. You must create a new path for yourself. Does that make sense?"

"It makes enormous sense. My family wants me to settle down and have a family. My career is precarious. Things have got to change." Angela spoke of herself calmly, glad that she had come. It was good to get these worries out, to look at them, and to have the help of a mature person like

Janice. Somehow the counselor seemed like an old and trusted friend.

Returning to her chair, Janice asked, "Are you afraid to marry? Perhaps you've chosen the wrong person, and that's what the dreams are about."

"I'm not even seeing anyone."

"Why not? Are you afraid of change?"

"Not really. I find change exciting." Angela thought of growing up in the old Tudor house in a Los Angeles suburb. Aaron and Vera Brock were possibly the most predictable set of parents on the planet. How she had chafed for change as a girl. "What I need to do is find somebody, but—"

"Don't hesitate. Tell me why you don't."

"I feel guilty, but there's no reason to." Thoughts of turning Juan away flooded Angela. How foolhardy she had been with him. She had unfairly drawn him into confusion. He hadn't deserved her animosity, for merely caring about her.

Janice's face bore an indulgent smile. "My guess is those feelings will go away when you find the right man."

Relieved that the counselor thought the whole problem revolved around finding a husband, Angela rose and restlessly moved to the wall. "You're probably right." She ran her hand across the coffin image. "Who is in there? My old self?" The answer felt insufficient.

"Our time is up, but I feel we've made wonderful progress."

"So do I." Angela laughed. "In fact, I feel a bit foolish, like a teenage girl having a talk with her mom."

"Anytime." Janice squeezed Angela's hand in a friendly way. "Let's do a follow-up appointment in a week, but I think we've turned an important corner. If you have any problems, don't hesitate to call."

Angela left the Dream Analysis Office more optimistic than she had felt for a long while. At least she understood why she had experienced the dreams, and her appreciation grew for her own mental abilities and for what might be going on at deep levels of consciousness.

Once back in her condo, Angela called Granddad.

His tiny image fluttered on the marble coffee table. Clad in his gold teaching robe, he bowed and said, "Hello, dear girl."

"I just wanted to tell you that the dream analysis worked. I think I've solved the problem."

"Good, good. What did the counselor say?"

Angela plopped onto the teal and pink couch with its muted Indian print. She curled up her legs, happy to talk with him. "It's all metaphorical. I've got to change my life."

"Oh, how?" Granddad's voice sounded disbelieving.

"You know, find a man and get married and make you happy."

"Nonsense." Granddad brushed back tousled hair. "You always make me happy."

"You know what I mean... the baby souls!"

"Ah, yes, I do, but about these dreams. What explanation did the counselor give you?" After hearing Janice's analysis, Granddad paused. His small transparent face looked perplexed, and his tone carried doubt. "She could be right. Time will tell."

"I think she is!" Angela felt a sudden and powerful urge to spend time with the old man. He might not always be here. "Want to get together for dinner tomorrow night?"

"Sorry, I've got twelve new students coming in Saturday morning."

"So soon? You just finished a session."

"Hey, I'm old." His tone sounded naughty. "I've got to get in all the good licks I can with the Universe before I die...to make up for my wild younger days."

"You have to tell me those stories sometime."

"Here's something that will cheer you up. Want to see a new trick I've been working on?"

"Sure."

Luke's holographic image disappeared from the coffee table. Startled, Angela picked up the holophone and examined it. Perhaps she'd let her lease lapse or the service had gone down.

Faintly, the shadowy image of Luke materialized on the couch beside her, full size. He smiled and waved. He mouthed the words, "Love you. Bye."

As Angela reached out for him, he dissolved.

Angela laughed. She had no idea how he managed to create an apparition of himself, but found his playful spirit irresistible. She blew a kiss into the darkness where perhaps she'd seen his soul.

Three

To Know One's Place

Los Angeles, Greater Hispania

When the holophone rang, Todd Williams skinned his finger on a lug nut. "Damnation!"

Quickly wiping the blood on greasy coveralls, he slid out from under the rusty chassis of a vintage 2012 Mustang possibly beyond viable restoration. The face of his motherly secretary resolved in the crystal of his watch. He had great respect for her because she could make his life work better than he could. "What's happening, Ms. Lizbet?"

"Melanie called. She's furious."

"Oh?" Confused, Todd retraced his date with Melanie the past Friday. They'd seen a great interactive show, had better sex than usual, then parted on friendly terms—no reason for anger.

"You missed the meeting with the Planetarium Committee."

"The what?"

"You know, as in Comet. Return?" Ms. Lizbet's hearty laugh made him feel understood. "You also were supposed to participate in an intercontinental chat room on trajectories. What have you been doing all day? Playing hooky?"

"Yeah, I guess you caught me." Todd laughed, comfortable with the admission. "I don't want to do all this stuff. I want to think about physics problems. You know, temporal fluctuations? Super symmetry? And restoring this damned car so it can fit in with its high-class ancestors."

His secretary's green eyes glittered as she scanned the garage. "You still working on that dog?"

With a pride he'd long since given up trying to control, Todd gazed at a row of classic Mustangs—a scarlet 2029 with fins, a sleek black '01, a 1992 that had been repainted many times. Once he got it down to the bare metal he recognized the original canary yellow color.

His pride and joy, a virtually restored '73 Mustang, had cost him an embarrassing amount even for a multi-billionaire. It had an electrical top that still worked. The convertible gleamed on a raised platform in the garage. Todd had considered displaying it on a mechanical turnaround but found that too pretentious even for his collection.

He'd settled on allowing free public tours and enjoyed watching the intake of breath when people saw his rare cars lined up. Even though he seldom drove them, he had refused to convert them to hydrogen fuel, something many who called themselves collectors had begun to do. Gasoline had to be imported and could not be used in cars that locked onto the beltway.

Todd enjoyed spending time on his cars. What else did he have to do on Sunday afternoons, anyway? Melanie always had her spiritual roundedness events at that time.

"Send Melanie some flowers," Todd said. "Roses, maybe. I think she likes them."

"I already did. A dozen yellow ones. I knew you'd want to."

"Thanks. You're the best, Ms. Lizbet. See you tomorrow, for sure." The watch face darkened then displayed the time—five o'clock. As Todd hung up his tools, he dropped a wrench on the cement floor. The clank reverberated through him. Clenching his brow at the sound, he dreaded the onset of another headache that would likely debilitate him for several days.

Although not part of her job description, his secretary often took care of the courting details he had so much trouble remembering. Ms. Lizbet had told him she enjoyed the effort though he could tell from her guarded looks that she didn't think too highly of Melanie.

Todd felt anxious about her, too. The most beautiful woman he had ever known—and more accomplished—she could surf, dive, ski, windroll, hostess, hob. You name it. Melanie was physically and socially splendid, accomplished at all the skills of the rich. Todd had not been born to their activities. He'd had to learn, after the wealth from the discovery of the tachyon drive had aced him almost completely out of the intellectual community. It was difficult to claim a need to work with all the comforts and small pleasures of life so easily affordable.

After closing the door on the showroom garage, Todd sauntered through the arbor alive with passionflowers to the back door of his white stucco mansion with a red tile roof. He rode the glass elevator to his bedroom. Although he cared little for the fountain in the living room, the servants liked to keep it running. At least it recycled so he didn't have to waste any of his precious water allotment.

Todd hated the demands put on him by the business of being a scientist. Sometimes he wished he could go back to scholarship student status. There he had been free to think, to create, to explore. Now, with a multi-billion-dollar business in name-credits alone, Todd depended on his accountant, his lawyers, and his secretary to give him quality of life. Fortunately he had the Mustang collection. Soon, he wanted to begin an airplane collection that would rival the museums. How delightful to stick his hands up to the elbows in crankcase oil.

Stripping, Todd stepped into the shower and let the hot water batter his tired muscles and ease his restless mind.

He half-heartedly scrubbed his hands with a lanolin bar and chuckled at remembering Melanie's annoyance with the traces of grease under his fingernails. The stains reminded him that he lived in a physical world with laws that worked. He needed that grounding to counter his fairytale life.

Perhaps in time he and Melanie would come to love each other. Now, he knew she found him irresistible only because he had so much notoriety. Although she had a great deal of money, Melanie lacked fame, and she truly enjoyed the paparazzi who often snapped pictures of them in public places. Unfailingly, the tabloids carried their images the next day.

The mechanical voice in the water pipe squawked, "Your water allotment for the day has expired. Four minutes, eleven seconds. You went forty-nine seconds overtime yesterday."

Sighing, Todd turned the golden dial to off and toweled dry. He donned casual slacks and a cobalt silk shirt Melanie had bought him to match his eyes. He felt awkward wearing it, like a fashion model on display. Cotton shirts and jeans suited him much better, but Melanie would want to make an impression at Cicero's. Todd dared not disappoint her, mainly since he'd forgotten the stupid Comet meeting.

After a brief drive on the beltway in his new silver Mustang, Todd arrived at the restaurant. The maitre de, a chubby man in a toga with a crown of laurel leaves, led Todd to a secluded table in the crowded dining room. Patrons sat at tables or reclined on couches, eating and drinking. Many wore Roman clothing. Todd lay on a gold satin chaise longue and ordered a brandy. He didn't particularly like it but sought the feeling of relaxation from tension.

As he ordered the second brandy from a small toga-clad robot, Melanie arrived, her smile wide and tempting. She looked magnificent as always in a shimmering opalescent toga, so sheer and silky it revealed the faint pinkness of her nipples and the indentation of her navel as it clung to her body in a way any man in the room would aspire to cling to her. Todd grinned. "Bring the lady a gin martini straight up."

"Hello, darling," Melanie said in her public voice and folded her long legs onto the next chaise lounge, her head near his.

A quick kiss let Todd inhale her luscious scent, like a forest after a thunderstorm. "I'm sorry I missed the meeting, but...I've been over my head on the new propulsion package." He regretted the lie.

"Todd, you can't let the committee down." Melanie's smile dissolved, and her almond-shaped eyes turned to slits. "I told them *in your absence* that you would be delighted to participate in all their plans for the trunk opening."

"Well, I'm not delighted. I don't want to do it. The Laxy moon orbit is behind schedule."

"But you will, won't you, darling? For me?" Her delicate olive-toned fingers slid teasingly across the small table between them, toward his crotch.

Todd disliked public displays of sexuality, no matter how commonplace they were. He settled back out of her reach. "Damn it, Melanie. I don't want to get on television and take old trinkets out of a trunk. You knew that. Why did you get me into this?"

"For Buddha's sake, you sound like a kid. 'I don't want to do it.'" Melanie mimicked him. "Your career is going to suffer if you withdraw. Bad publicity won't do you any good."

"My career has nothing to do with it." Todd's head ached, a bad sign.

"Shhhhh." Her voluminous black hair flipped around her face as Melanie glanced toward nearby customers. They appeared uninterested in the spat.

"My career has nothing to do with Halley's trunk...or the damn Comet." Todd whispered. "Cosmically speaking, Halley's Comet is a meaningless dwarf. "For Buddha's sake,'" he mimicked her, "why can't you understand?'"

"Think about me for a change." A sharp edge in her voice left little doubt of Melanie's disapproval. "How is it going to look for me? I said you would do it. I'll look like a damned fool in front of the committee and the press."

Their drinks arrived, and they ordered a Mediterranean sampler with bouillabaisse, grape leaves, melon balls, and manicotti. Both sipped in silence. Todd knew Melanie didn't deserve that kind of embarrassment. After all, she had merely tried to set up a public service event. He felt a vague obligation. "All right. You win. I'll do it."

"Thank you." Softness filled Melanie's voice, something he seldom heard out of the bed. "And thanks for the flowers. That was very thoughtful."

"The what? Oh, yes."

"What is wrong with you lately? Your memory has disappeared along with your manners."

"I'm sorry." Todd sat up and rubbed his throbbing temples. "I've not been sleeping very well. My head aches, too."

"I saw an ad on television about a new surgical technique to relieve headaches. Maybe you should investigate that."

"Oh, of course," Todd grinned. "That's just what I need. Some struggling medic to laser my brain so he can pay his mortgage."

"Maybe he could laser out your ridiculous interest in old cars and other junk metal."

Before he could protest, the dinner came, and they ate ravenously. It took a lot of food to satisfy Todd's six-foot-tall, stocky body, but he wondered where Melanie fit hers. She ate like a street person but somehow managed to look sophisticated and remain slender.

The robot rumbled up and said in a pleasant voice, "Your bill is four hundred twenty-seven dollars." Todd waved his identity wrist tattoo at the red light beneath the robot's mouth. Momentarily, a green light flashed. "Thank you for dining at Cicero's." The robot raised a tiny, pin-jointed arm. "Hail Caesar."

"Let's get out of here." Todd squeezed her soft arm.

"I haven't finished my drink yet." Melanie raised the glass, her fingers delicately threading the stem, and sipped.

The dinner had eased Todd's headache. He felt sated and warm. He slid his fingers along her arm. "Why don't you come over for the night? It's warm enough to swim naked."

"Darling, I'd love to. Didn't I tell you? I'm going to Sedona on a retreat this weekend. I've got to pack and prepare mentally. Having sex will hinder me, keep me focused on the physical." Melanie pouted so prettily she might actually regret stranding him for yet another weekend. "You know what I mean? Of course, you do. You're so understanding. What would I do without you?"

"Oh, I don't know, fuck the cat?"

"Todd, what's the matter with you?" Her onyx eyes glowed ominously. "You know I need to develop spiritually. So do you. Why don't you go with me?"

"No thanks." Todd felt out of sync. Where were temperance and skepticism? Melanie merely followed the fashion when she immersed herself in one spiritual roundedness event after another. "The last thing I need is some airy-fairy guru telling me what's wrong with my attitude and charging me a thousand bucks a minute to do so."

"That's ridiculous."

The harshness in her tone suddenly made it all right to spend the weekend alone. That would give Todd the chance to fly down to San Diego to the Cessna exhibit and bid on the antiques. Maybe, the headaches wouldn't bother him on the auction floor. He wished he could believe that was a better plan as he watched Melanie amble across the tile floor with feline grace.

Men sat up all over the room and watched her. What a great ass! Todd got a kick out of the other men's attraction to her, but the thought of new men she might meet at the retreat gave him a pang of jealousy.

Four

Clear Seeing

Sedona

Clad in a white participant's gown, Dr. Robert Kegan rode the elevator to the twentieth floor of the Tree House and stepped into the round workshop room. Glass walls revealed the outdoors and the stately red rocks rising in grand patterns unobstructed by the buildings of the metropolis hidden below. Lilting orchestral music poured from the sound system.

Kegan spotted a gorgeous brunette across the room. "Excuse me." He threaded his way among a dozen or so gown-clad students either reclining on circular chairs or sitting on the thick nub of the carpet. "Excuse me." Many looked up with relaxed expressions and glistening eyes at the sound of his voice. He didn't want to disturb their meditations. Who knew where the next patient might come from?

Much of his clientele frequented such places, and he had made invaluable contacts each time he attended a roundedness event in England. No doubt he would find a similar experience in Greater Hispania.

Whatever happened, he wanted to get close to the brunette. Kegan nudged an old lady who snored and snorted. Her meditation had obviously devolved into sleep, she but moved aside. Kegan dropped down on the floor between her and the brunette. "Hi, where's the teacher?"

"Hasn't come in yet," the brunette whispered. She sat up gracefully and crossed her incredibly long legs in Buddha fashion. Nipples, navel, and shaved labia lips shuddered in and out of view beneath the fragile saffron silk of her see-through gown. "Don't worry. You aren't late."

"Good." Kegan inhaled the sharp scent of sandalwood she exuded and shifted his gown to hide his arousal. He'd not planned to attend this particular function, but his dead grandmother had come to him in a dream, her message unmistakable—All four of his enemies had finally incarnated in the same place.

The time had come for Kegan to fulfill his destiny. He had fought its control over him long enough. He had prepared long enough. Now he would assess the individuals. Later he would make his plans.

If such a delicious chunk of meat as this lovely would keep him company, he'd learn to deal with the obviousness of the events. He leaned close enough to mingle his aura with hers, tantalizing but not touching with their physical selves. "I've heard this teacher is better than most."

"He certainly is, and I should know. I've met them all." She flipped her long hair erotically. "I've never seen you here before."

"No, my first time." Kegan welcomed her flirty style and smiled, hoping to seem harmless and open. "I'm Dr. Robert Kegan. Perhaps you've heard of me? Experimental neuro-surgery?"

"No, sorry." The brunette traced the linked golden rings in the carpet with a sculptured orange fingernail. She seemed very aware of her allure.

The young man on the other side of her bent toward her and touched her arm. "Here he comes."

Perhaps the young man was her companion. That might prove an interesting obstacle, but nothing would stop Kegan. He would have this woman, hopefully before the night was over. At a loss to understand his overwhelming attraction for her, he felt compelled to join with her in an animalistic way. He must remain vigilant so she didn't subsume his psychic senses in the physical.

The students whispered and moved, many rising to their knees. "*Namaste*," they murmured, palms together, fingertips to chins.

An old man clad in a gold robe strode to the front of the room and stood before one of the glass walls against the majestic mountains outside. His fingertips touched his chin in the classic Hindu prayer gesture. "*Namaste*. The God in me greets the God in you."

It was Luke Brock all right. Kegan would know him anywhere. The bastard hadn't changed much in forty years.

The teacher bowed, gray-blond hair rumpled childishly. "Forgive me for keeping you waiting. My granddaughter wanted to talk to me. I love her very much." His voice and manner conveyed an irritating guilelessness.

"Can you guess how old he is?" the brunette whispered to Kegan.

"I don't know." Kegan played along, although he had a fairly good idea of the answer. Engaging her in conversation was very important, no matter the subject. "Sixty, sixty-five, maybe?"

Her throaty chuckle tantalized him. "Try one hundred. Can you imagine being born in the 1960s?"

"No! I'd say it took at least five reconstructions to give him that facial elasticity and muscular structure."

"Now," Luke spread his arms in an expansive gesture. "I want to give my total attention to the needs of you, my students."

Breathing in the sexy woman's pungent scent, Kegan inched closer to her so that, when he breathed out, his shoulder barely touched hers. She turned a rapt face toward the teacher, who droned on. She seemed infatuated with Luke, and Kegan wondered what it would take to turn that emotion toward him.

"Thank you for coming to my treetop sanctuary," Luke said. "We have much to share. Please form a circle around the room, and we will begin."

Murmurs accompanied the shuffling of feet as the students rose, formed a circle, and held hands along the glass walls. The view of red rocks and summer-emerald trees outdoors created a panoramic sense of freedom in nature, high above earthly cares.

Kegan held one of the woman's hands. The idiot beside her grabbed the other.

"Quietly, now," Luke called, and the room fell silent. He joined the circle between the young man and the old lady who had so recently been snoozing. Luke gazed up. "Om," he chanted.

All the students responded, "Om," and the rich tone rose up, lifting Kegan into its clarifying atmosphere. He usually required an hour of meditation to reach such a level of psychic attunement on his own.

Certainly Luke had retained his psychic abilities, but he had no way of knowing how Kegan's powers had grown.

Luke left his place in the circle and took the hands of the brunette and the younger man beside her. Luke chanted, "Om," and energy danced around him and through the room.

Kegan slightly averted his eyes and disregarded the lights in the room. That way he could plainly see Luke's aura and bring it into focus. Its colors swirled in patterns of bright yellow, brown, and green.

"One more time." Luke moved to the other side of the brunette.

When he held Kegan's hand, a charge shot through Kegan's arm.

"Om," Luke intoned, and the whole group imitated him.

Inhaling deeply, Kegan imagined charging his own aura with midnight blue energy. He visualized spreading it over Luke and all his pitiful students, enmeshing and paralyzing

39

them. Playing with his own strength, Kegan focused on dematerializing Luke. In thought the old man was gone, out of sight, nothing at all. Just as Kegan wiped the teacher's face off the field of mind, Luke let go of his hand.

Luke stepped back and studied Kegan, as if trying to figure out what had happened then walked to the center of the circle. The old man had always been slow witted, but in his youth Kegan had underestimated Luke's power. Luke had rendered an embarrassing defeat in their astral battle and caused Kegan to have to seek the Imam's protection. Such errors would never happen again.

In an apparent rebound from the psychic attack, Luke said, "We're going to do an exercise called 'clear seeing.' Choose a partner and sit across from him or her."

As the students complied, Kegan deftly intervened between the sexy woman and two other men. "*Ma chère,*" he intoned mockingly, "you simply must choose me as your partner."

"Oh, of course." She laughed and allowed Kegan to guide her to a chaise longue where the two sat and faced each other. "My name is Melanie Vanderson."

"Why don't you call me Rob?" With an air of ownership, he took her delicate bronze-tone hand and closed his own long fingers over it.

Luke strolled around the room, touching people on the shoulder while he gave instructions. "Your goal is to stay completely open as you look into your partner's eyes. Focus on learning information from the past that will help your partner overcome old karma. Say whatever comes into your mind without judgment. You must trust your own abilities."

"Let me start." Melanie said amid the murmurs of other students. She gripped Kegan's hands and gazed into his eyes, exuding conflicted and timid energy, grayish pink mingled with dark red. "You come from a very close family. Your mother loved you a lot."

"Actually, that could be true, but I'll never know. My parents were killed when I was six. My grandmother reared me."

"Oh," Melanie pouted. "I'm afraid I'm not very good at this."

"That's all right. I think there are other things you are very good at." Kegan rubbed her soft palm suggestively. A knowing smile filled her face. Fires began to dance in her black eyes as he gazed into them. "Let me try this," he murmured.

The music and other voices faded, replaced by the ghostly groan of bagpipes. Melanie's lovely, semi-nude body winked out, and in its place appeared the vague image of a warrior clad in a short tunic. Then another man drowned in a bog.

"I think you were a man in a former life, maybe more than one lifetime, and you wish to be again."

"A man?" Melanie snickered. "That's ridiculous. Have you taken a good look at me?"

When she leaned toward Kegan, the touch of her breast against his arm broke his concentration. He recognized the images of her past, but he wanted to concentrate instead on the wonderful possibility of tupping her. She seemed available, but Kegan recognized a very masculine rage barely concealed beneath her flirtatious manner, a fascinating characteristic. Perhaps that explained the pictures of the warrior and the drowning man. Regardless, Kegan felt an urge to own her physically and a sense of connection through a shared past. He didn't know which was the more powerful pull on him.

Pausing beside Kegan and Melanie, Luke touched their clasped hands and said, "Stay focused, and you will clearly see the past this woman fails to understand."

The older man's touch seared Kegan, who drew away and clutched his own wrist. Pain shot through his arm, but his psychic vision cleared.

Both Melanie and Luke were transformed into warriors, brandishing daggers. They hated each other and him.

Bad blood had existed among them for centuries, Kegan felt certain. He hated both, but at the same time his erection stiffened. He would have Melanie. Then he would determine whether her allegiance fell with him or against him.

A way to get even with Luke would occur to Kegan later, when he could devote his entire strength to it, free of the sexual tension the woman brought to the mix.

"Tell us what you see, doctor," Melanie murmured.

"Nothing. I see nothing," Kegan lied.

"Perhaps later you will remember more," Luke counseled. "That often happens." He moved on to students sitting nearby but cast back a glance that Kegan read as foreboding.

The bastard knew something had happened but obviously hadn't been privy to the same images Kegan had seen. Or had he? Kegan struggled to present composure while his wrist ached and his penis throbbed.

Melanie opened her legs and her labia lips trembled, inviting him. Kegan could see them plainly beneath her gown and longed to kiss her. In other circumstances, perhaps in a nightclub or park, he would stroke and kiss without regard to the public display. Yet no one else in the room appeared to be indulging. The spiritual in the air trumped the physical.

Melanie's glance indicated she approved of his erection.

Just now Kegan did not wish to draw attention to his need in the presence of his old enemy. It might look like weakness. Never could he allow that.

When Luke dismissed the assembly for the day, Kegan accompanied Melanie to her treetop hotel room. He had not asked. Apparently, she also assumed they would consummate the day in bed.

Their encounter, by candlelight, was the most robust and passionate sex Kegan could remember, far more frenzied than with his wife. Melanie brought more ardor and enthusiasm to the sex act than even Kegan's favorite mistress in her best years.

At the last, when they lay beside each other exhausted, Melanie asked him, awe apparent in her tone, "How did you know I wish to be a man?"

A scene played once again in Kegan's mind. Melanie became a tunic-cloaked warrior and planned with him to overthrow the king. Then, she fell to the ground, bleeding, a knife in her back. She had been murdered by the high priestess. With his companion gone, Kegan angrily challenged the king and fell to ignoble defeat—maimed, banished, and forgotten. If only he had died in the challenge, his honor would have remained intact. Now, shame goaded him. Only sweet vengeance could stamp it out.

"When we did the exercise, I saw you as a man." Kegan nuzzled her warm neck. "You were treated very cruelly. Murdered, in fact."

"Really, you saw it?" Melanie rose and paced naked at the end of the bed. "Why can't I? I've spent a fortune on these roundedness events, and I never remember a damn thing." She paused and placed her hands on her hips, her female contours luscious by flickering light.

"I think you intuitively know you need to get revenge, even though you can't recall details."

"You're probably right. Something's going on inside me. Demands and needs I don't understand. Who killed me? Anybody I know?"

"It's not all that clear to me either, but I'll help you. We'll figure it out together."

Kegan thought it prudent to withhold some details from her, including the identity of Luke. He would help Melanie gain her revenge. That would put him in the path of the treacherous others. Luke, the bastard king, would die. That was easy.

But who were the others? That news reporter, for one. Kegan had recognized her from TV. The high priestess herself reborn. He wouldn't rest until she burned, preferably at the stake.

Five

A Promise Kept

Angela's optimism lasted for several days. In spite of not having the TV studio to go to, she slept well and dreamlessly. Convinced that the counseling session had resolved her dream problem, she felt rested, and color had returned to her complexion. Too bad the makeup man couldn't see her. The beastly fellow had been right. But then, sleeplessness and depression would spoil anyone's appearance.

Angela wanted to believe a flesh and blood man would come along, one she could care for and with whom she could perhaps form a bond. Her desire for a husband and family grew each day. She divided her time between answering web ads guaranteeing to introduce her to the love of her life and replenishing the clay pots that stood empty on her patio. She loved to plant flowers and vines, deciding this time to bank them on tiered steps.

The temperature neared one hundred degrees in the daytime, even in the mountains. Angela looked forward to the trip to Los Angeles where at least the evenings cooled down.

Even though she had volunteered for the assignment to save her career, Angela felt impatient to cover the Halley's Comet ceremony. She wanted to interview the famous physicist and write his story. It seemed like a wonderful change, to go to Los Angeles and meet the physicist and other new people. She didn't even have the name of the cameraman assigned to her. All those unknowns gave her a sense of adventure. She had a good feeling, an intuition that it would turn out well.

The evening before the trip, Angela decided to reset the sprinkling system on her patio so the plants would thrive in her absence. As she knelt on the flagstone and threaded the tiny hoses through the plants, she shivered with dread. It felt like the experience of being watched by someone who intended her harm.

Angela placed a lawn chair near the wall and climbed up. She saw nothing except the neighbor's empty patio, other condos, and street lights in the distance. She searched the sky for someone flying an ultra-light personal plane or a Dial-a-Bike. She discovered nothing unusual but couldn't shake the feeling of being watched.

Laying down the remaining hose, she flipped the switch on the irrigation system, and hurried into the living room. After slamming the glass-paned door, she called out to the security system, "Lock up now."

The soothing masculine voice she had programmed responded, "You're safe now, darling."

Angela needed to get away. She packed an overnight bag, thinking she would stay over at her parents' house after finishing the assignment, although she kept a few things there anyway. She looked forward to seeing her parents and the ocean again. Perhaps a good story would come out of the trip, though no one at the TV station expected that to happen. At least she might gain some peace of mind.

Dropping onto the bed, Angela drew the comforter around her, dozed, and let herself envision a new life with a man she loved. What would he look like? Handsome, of course, with blue eyes. She recognized him and knew him intimately.

Suddenly aware in a dream, Angela couldn't breathe. Water poured over her, engulfing her. Her arms flew up as she struggled against a rush of fishy, salty water that gushed into her nose, her eyes, her mouth, her ears. A tangle of seaweed clawed at her feet. She didn't want to die. With enormous effort, she flailed the water, forcing her body to move upward for air. Finally, she broke the surface and wiped her eyes. All about her ocean waves crashed.

In a small boat stood a man, who shouted at her. His cobalt eyes riveted her. His graying hair fell across his brow as he stretched out a saving arm to her, like a lifeline. Gasping, she reached for him.

Angela awoke drenched in sweat. She fanned the clammy gown that clung to her skin and crawled out of bed. A shower would feel great, but the thought of water made her shudder.

Only two hours of the night had passed. Needing some rest for the long day ahead, she changed her gown, poured a glass of milk in the kitchen, and lay back down in bed. Why had she dreamed again of death? Undoubtedly her own, this time. Would these hours awake in the night again induce her to oversleep?

After worrying and checking the alarm at least five times in an hour, she fell asleep.

In a dream she ran across an airfield, stumbled, and fell in an agony of fear. An airplane exploded above her.

Her screams awakened her. The same nightmare had returned in all its terrifying intensity.

Shaky and tense, Angela rose and donned her uniform, a long black skirt, black shell, and gold blazer with KLOW embroidered on the pocket. At eight when the Psi Therapy Clinic offices opened, she phoned the counselor.

Feelings of guilt and embarrassment at Janice's potential reactions seemed too much to endure, so Angela didn't turn on the video function. When Janice answered, Angela explained that the nightmare had recurred along with a dreadful new dream.

"I'm so sorry." Janice sounded genuinely concerned. "I hoped we had resolved your issues, but clearly that's not the case. I'll send the doctor a transcript of your last session so we'll know where we are when you come for your next appointment."

"The doctor?" Angela felt nervous.

"Dr. Kegan will want to examine you, I'm certain. We might need to move you up to the next level of therapy." Janice's tone sounded placid, no doubt to allay Angela's growing fears. "We need to resolve your problems so you can live a normal life."

After the phone call, Angela fought the depression descending on her.

What a dreadful night! Now, Angela knew first hand how it felt to drown. She could have gone a long time without such awful details. The nightmares had recurred in such an insidious way. If genetic memory explained this experience, what other horrors might befall her if she were living out her ancestors' negative experiences? They could stretch out endlessly. Here she was, farther from a cure than ever.

Angela grabbed her overnight bag and sling purse then drove her Bimi to the high-speed subway station in Anthem. She flashed her identity card across the laser light to board and took a back seat in the commuter car, empty on Saturday morning. She mulled over the dreams and Janice's reaction. Consulting with the doctor seemed inevitable unless something drastic happened.

In an effort to redirect her mental processes, Angela scanned the data on her wrist computer to familiarize herself with the career of Todd Williams and the history of

Halley's Comet. She dictated a list of questions for the interview. With only one stop in Blythe, the subway arrived in Los Angeles in less than two hours.

A skinny young man, both photographer and pilot, met her and guided her to a KLOW ultra-light. He was on loan from the Los Angeles subsidiary. He yawned and dropped his arm loosely over the wheel as if bored already with Angela and the whole project. At least he wore a crisp blazer like hers. She hoped he would behave professionally when the time came. A lot depended on his technical abilities today. At least a lot for Angela.

Under an overcast sky, he flew above the buildings of the city while she prepped him to take candid shots of the people in attendance, the dignitaries, and anything else that might add meaning. "Besides the interview itself, I want as much footage as possible so I can edit a story that hangs together when I get back home."

"I think I can handle that, if I see anything interesting at all, which I doubt." With a smug nod, the photographer descended into Griffith Park. Because the parking lot was filled with buses, cars, bikes, and planes, Angela asked him to drop her off at the sidewalk directly in front of the observatory.

"Who was your slave this time last year?" He set the plane down despite his caustic attitude. What choice did he have with Angela in charge of the assignment?

"Thank you. I really appreciate it." Angela hoped her smile looked genuine despite the desire to make a smart remark in return. She wanted to establish a more positive relationship. All she needed was lousy footage to mess up the whole project. "I'll see you inside."

After she deplaned, she gazed up at the white, art deco building. It looked dramatic, as usual, with its three copper domes enormous against the blue brilliance of the sky. All the haze had vanished in the past few minutes and left the observatory etched against a sparkling California afternoon sky.

Angela remembered school field trips when she had come here to see the vault open up on the wonders of the universe. The huge telescopes and the people who built them awed her. She still felt amazed that people on earth could squint into a tiny lens and see the whole firmament, let alone travel around in it.

Families and groups of school children scattered about the lawn. Ice cream vendors, souvenir peddlers, children and adult visitors, many elegant in sleek sheaths or jumpsuits. All the activity created a festive atmosphere outside.

Walking up the sidewalk, Angela passed the Astronomer's Monument, the six famous scientists with arms folded like mummies buried standing up. A bust of Einstein stood near the main monument. It occurred to her that the man she was about to meet might qualify to become the eighth honoree. After all, he'd discovered a way to use weightless propulsion and turned space travel from a dream into a practical alternative.

That would make a good lead for her story. She stopped, read the names of the six, and spoke them into her recorder. "Hipparchus, Copernicus, Galileo, Kepler, Newton, and Hershel."

Angela went through the open double doors into the main rotunda. Many visitors stared from the railing of the golden pit at the pendulum swinging in perpetual motion. She couldn't get close enough to gaze down herself. Although she wanted to pause and admire the colorful mural painted on the ceiling, Angela doubted she could enjoy the place because of her increasing concern about how the interview would go.

The photographer entered the rotunda and found her. He leaned down and whispered in a conspiratorial way. "I got some shots of the vendors selling ice cream. That'll really punch up your film, won't it?"

"Thanks." Angela ignored his wise guy remarks and pointed at the pit where the gold pendulum swayed. "Let's get that."

The photographer pulled a camera from his jacket pocket and pointed it toward Angela. The camera expelled a flash of light around her, and she did a small intro, pointing out the pit and the crowd. Around them, people chatted and engaged in lively talk, children laughed, the massive whitewashed walls bounced the sound. Surely all of these people were not here for the trunk opening.

After she finished the intro, Angela hoped out loud that the quality of their recording today wouldn't be tinny.

"Don't worry. I can compensate with my camera." The photographer's angular face bore a scornful expression. "The question is *will* I?"

"Please do." As Angela accompanied him down the hall, she couldn't help worrying. Maybe her intuition had been wrong. The story might be her last. She had to get everything right to save her job. What wretched luck sent this smart aleck her way?

In the East Rotunda new displays of galaxies suspended at every level created the illusion of walking in space. Moving holographs depicted meteorites, stars, and comets.

Several dignitaries had already arrived, including a dark-haired woman in a too revealing green dress. She spoke with two gentlemen in official observatory blazers. Several old people, dressed up and clearly excited, moved around, looking at the displays and chattering as if they'd not seen each other in years.

Chiffon drapes swooped above the display in which the small Halley's Comet trunk sat. The key dangled from a chain tied to the railing. A sign above the wooden trunk read:

Sealed in 1986 When Halley's Comet Left the Solar System.

A tall man in boots, jeans, and a corduroy jacket, leaned against a pillar, his back turned to the assemblage. Out of place fashion-wise, he seemed fascinated by the display and oblivious to the crowd.

"There's the guest of honor." The photographer pointed at the unusual fellow and focused the camera on him.

Angela liked him already. She'd heard Dr. Williams was unconventional, but why not? He had all that money could buy. Why shouldn't he wear what he wanted? Do what he wanted?

"Dr. Williams? I'm Angela Brock." She reached out to shake his hand. "May I do the interview now?"

As he turned around, he said, "Yes, but please call me Todd." He stared down at her with a smile full of wonder.

His intense gaze transfixed her. Eyes the same cobalt color, the same gray-black hair, the same angst in his expression. He was the man in the explosion, the man reaching out to save her from drowning, the man in her dream, but that couldn't be true. She'd seen many photos of Todd Williams, even live footage. She had never recognized him before.

"Glad to meet you." Todd clutched her hand with both of his.

Todd's almost desperate touch drew Angela into a vortex of silence.

The people, the sounds, the smell of fresh plaster all faded away. She'd never experienced such a sensation before, of clarity somehow, filled with the fresh scent of cherry blossoms.

Angela and Todd stood together before the exhibit, dressed in the dumpy-looking shorts and knit shirts of the 1980s. Only a few visitors milled around. The galaxies had dissolved into old wooden display cases. All the bustle was gone.

The trunk sign had been transformed and now read:

To Be Opened in 2061.

"It's sort of a time capsule." Todd spoke in a rich, low baritone, familiar and adored. "To be opened when Halley's Comet comes again. Every seventy-six or seventy-seven years."

Angela laughed at the easy warmth of their companionship. They had come to the planetarium right after making love. He was her man, had been forever. "Did you know Mark Twain was born the year the comet came, 1835? He always said he'd die the year it came again, and he did. In 1910."

"Thanks for the lesson, English teacher."

Angela shrugged, amused. She enjoyed his bantering tone, knowing his sense of humor well. "When you've got thirty-five wriggling sophomores in front of you, you've got to keep them believing you're smarter than they are." She felt completely confident in her identity as a teacher, even recalled a rangy image of the high school campus in Phoenix where she taught. She was herself, Angela, in her other skin.

"How did Twain come to make such an odd prediction? I thought he wrote children's stories."

"He had a lot of psychic experiences. He believed in reincarnation too. Said he dreamed of his soul mate in many different bodies, but always the same sweet girl."

A grin crinkled Todd's forehead. Always the tease. "He's got nothing on us."

"What do you mean?"

"I'll meet you here for the trunk opening. In 2061."

Angela knew the power of his kiss, how it felt to make love with him, to love him, to be loved by him, with passion and reverence. "I'll be here. I promise."

She would do whatever it took.

"Oh, Todd, darling," a whining female voice intruded. "We're ready to begin."

"Ms. Brock, are you all right?" Todd's voice caught.

"Hey, Angela, come to, woman," called the photographer.

"Ooooh, they're going to open the trunk now," an old lady cried out.

The interfering voices brought Angela to herself with a nasty jolt. The galaxies winked back into view.

Todd cupped her face in his hands. "What happened to you? Can I get you some water or something?"

Angela longed for him to pull her close and kiss her. "Thank you, I'm fine." But she was definitely not fine.

The brunette in the trashy green gown tugged on Todd's arm. "Come on, darling. It's time to open the trunk." She had no right to call him darling. What an infuriating woman.

Todd stayed focused on Angela. "Ms. Brock, perhaps we should call the paramedics."

"I'm fine. Really. I'm sorry."

The photographer grabbed Angela's elbow and pulled her away from Todd. "Hey, come on. Let's get to work."

"See that she gets some medical attention!" Todd spoke firmly to the photographer. "Take care of her."

Angela let the photographer guide her to a bench where she sat, confused and embarrassed. She didn't know what had happened just now, but undeniably something extraordinary.

Not a dream, something much more. She had known herself as the woman of over seventy years ago. She had been her same self then as now. Even though she had no recollection of where she had been in the intervening years, genetic memory could never explain such an all-consuming self-awareness.

To experience the memories, if that's what they were, in the dream state had disturbed her enough. To experience them awake had a much more profound impact on Angela's heart and mind. She had either died and been reborn or she had gone completely insane.

Because she was still thinking rationally despite these bizarre events, she hoped she had retained her sanity. That left only one conclusion.

Angela had remembered a former life but didn't understand the repercussions. She must talk with Granddad. He would be thrilled, in any case. The counselor, Janice, had suggested reincarnation as a possible explanation. Angela wanted to discuss the subject with the counselor too. She felt overwhelmed at the prospect of processing of all of this.

The photographer brought her a glass of water. "If you're not going to work, at least I'd better, or we'll both get fired." He cocked his camera, and his light flashed over Todd, who reached into the trunk.

The shakiness subsided as Angela drank the water and watched fascinated while Todd began his ceremonial duty.

The old people who gathered around screeched out comments as Todd withdrew a red Frisbee from the trunk. "This is called a Halley's Hurler. It was used for some kind of game."

"That was mine." An old man grabbed the Frisbee.

"Here's a comet T-shirt." Todd handed the ugly garment to an elderly lady who stepped forward, giggling.

"I put that in when I was in third grade."

Todd pulled out a scarf and a book called *The Comet and You*.

Another woman in the crowd claimed the scarf. "Oh, that takes me back."

Although Todd smiled graciously at the reaction, he glanced at Angela. She wondered what he might have experienced while he held her hand. Had he seen the same images? Heard the same words?

Retrieving a newspaper, Todd held it up for everyone to see. "It's the *Los Angeles Times* for January 29, 1986. The headline read 'Shuttle Explodes: Crew Killed.' A sad reminder of the sacrifices our forebears made in conquering space flight." He turned toward Angela. "Perhaps you as a reporter would like to see this, Ms. Brock." He handed the newspaper to her.

That Todd thought of her touched Angela. She was so moved it was difficult to pay attention, but she needed to stay focused on the here and now.

"These were the First Timers Club." Todd handed a stack of photographs to the three oldsters, who began to flip through them.

After much applause, thank you's from the officials, and champagne toasts to the comet, Todd left with the floozy clinging possessively to his arm. She had not made eye contact, treating Angela with disdain.

Jealousy twisted inside Angela. She longed to hold Todd's arm and leave with him.

They probably both thought she had lost her mind. She knew for certain she had lost her heart. And probably her job too.

The time apportioned for the interview appeared to have gone through a time warp. How she would square this with her boss Angela had no idea.

That problem fell second to figuring out how to see Todd again.

Six

Trials of the Flesh

In robe and briefs, Luke settled into his tilt back chair where he often managed to reach a profound state of meditative consciousness. Tonight he would settle for quiet reflection.

The weekend's roundedness session had left him agitated. Usually Luke enjoyed his students, but this had been a most unpleasant group of people. That on top of his worry about Angela, who seemed to be struggling with her ability to open up. She probably had fears of the spiritual ramifications of her dreams and so stopped confiding in him. It irritated him that she considered his status as grandfather insufficient for helping her with her problems. *A prophet is without honor in his own country.*

"I draw down the white light. It fills my body with love and health."

After waiting an extraordinarily long time without producing any alpha waves, Luke thought a message to Euphoria, his second wife and greatest love. She had sometimes whispered to him in the years since her death, though less and less frequently. Emmons appeared more often instead, so Luke called on his guide, who also refused to appear.

Why had the other side abandoned him? Annoyed, Luke decided to force his mind into theta waves scientifically. He rose and grabbed his state altering glasses with a brain entraining chip. "Celestial Bells," he barked. A harp concerto combined with gently ringing bells played through the sound system. He fell back in the chair, groaning as his lower back protested.

To be honest with himself, he knew but didn't wish to face the reasons for his inability to meditate or commune with a spirit guide. He set the glasses to deep alpha and donned them.

"Where are you today?" Luke squinted and tried again. The glasses pulsed against his temples causing his eyes to move rapidly beneath his lids. At length the familiar lethargy of deep alpha encompassed him.

"I am here." An ancient voice spoke with great clarity into Luke's mind.

Without physically opening his eyes, Luke used his psychic sight to see the fragile image of his guide.

Attired as an eighteenth-century country gentleman of considerable years, Emmons often wore the guise of his last earthly life. Luke had been with him then, when the entire soul group had incarnated together.

Emmons stood by the mantle with a riding crop in hand. "What's troubling you tonight?"

"There's not a chance that Angela's dreams are metaphorical. I don't care what that counselor says."

"We've always known she's dreaming true, but you have to let her discover that in her own way."

"I know. It's a flagrant waste of good earth time, but what can you do?" Luke echoed the sentiment his guide had often uttered when he became impatient with his wards' progress.

"That's not all. What else is bothering you?"

Luke shifted restlessly but didn't open his eyes. "This last batch of students. Their vibrations reeked of greed, anger, and self-indulgence."

"And what's new?" Emmons's insubstantial visage bore an understanding smile. "But that's not the point either. If you can't be honest with your own guide, you're in a lot of trouble, here and hereafter."

"That Kegan fellow. I recognized his energy field, but not his face. I don't know whether from this lifetime or another. Who is he?"

"It will come to you in good time."

"In other words, you're not going to tell me."

"And the woman?"

Emmons read Luke's mind as a matter of course. How could he not since he resided at some level within Luke's soul? One definition of enlightenment was never to be able to keep a secret, complete transparency.

"That Melanie," Luke sighed, glad to finally admit his thoughts. She looks enough like my first wife to be her twin, but she's been dead fifty years." Luke felt frustrated all over again. "I got an erection just holding her hand."

Emmons chuckled. "Thank the Divine for long robes."

"I conquered that response years ago. But if this Melanie is my first wife reborn..."

"Nothing happens by chance."

"But I'm too old," Luke moaned at the intensity of emotion even memories of his first wife stirred up.

"You're still attached to a body. You have something to learn here."

"But what?"

The silence brought Luke to wakefulness. He glanced at the mantle, but Emmons had gone without answering the question, cryptic as usual.

Years ago, even before his first wife, Melinda, died on Nine Eleven, Luke became disenchanted with sex. In his marriage to Euphoria the sexual act had become a beautiful dance of love and commitment. Never did he hope to experience such ecstasy again until he could sustain cosmic consciousness.

Considering the effect this student had on him, she probably was Melinda reborn. If so, he had better watch out. The last thing he needed was a flirtatious indulgence with some young thing. Why had the Melinda look-alike shown up in the roundedness event? He had a feeling he would find out. So much for ethereal thoughts. "Oh, Euphoria, my darling, how I miss you." His inability to identify the hostile man bugged him. "And where do I know that Kegan from?"

Shifting in the chair, Luke glanced at the clock and set aside his state altering glassees. With a groan, he protected his back as he turned to face the video wall. "Channel nine four nine on."

The screen resolved into the image of Governor Karen Goldman in an elegant gown. A map behind her showed Greater Hispania, what used to be Southern California, Arizona, New Mexico, Utah, Baja, and the northwest section of Mexico down to Mazatlan.

"Thank you for attending the culminating count of the National Home Council," the governor said with a smile. "To vote Yes on the funding of Arctic Sea Research, punch one. To vote No, punch two. Now, punch."

Luke fumbled around himself in the chair, retrieved the tiny remote that had slipped down in the cushions, and punched one.

A line of text crossed the bottom of the screen: Forty two million eight hundred twenty seven thousand twelve citizens vote yes. Eighteen million nine hundred fourteen vote no.

The governor squinted as she read the results. "Final tally. We will fund the research."

"Get some eye implants, woman." Luke called to the image on the screen. He had to admit that talking to people on television was the biggest indicator of aging he'd noticed in himself. Unless it was talking to himself. So what? He would have his one hundredth birthday just this month. With male life expectancy at eighty-five, he had nothing left to prove.

"Now for the vote on Council Person-at-Large, vote one for Walton, two for Garcia, three for Bills, four for Pierson, five for Navarro, six for Perez, seven for Smith. Now, punch."

Luke punched five.

"Jennifer Smith has been elected. And now the last vote of the evening, the Western Waterworks Act. Utility fees would rise approximately two hundred dollars per household. To vote Yes, punch one. To vote No, punch two."

Luke punched one.

The governor's shoulders slumped as she read the results. "The Waterworks Act fails."

"Damn cheapskates!" Luke glanced up at her image. "Monitor off. Nightlight on."

The wall screen went midnight blue, and a panorama of tiny lights shot across the wall, creating the illusion of a night sky. Luke loved the nightlight. It reminded him of Sedona when he was young and a person could still see the stars, before urban sprawl obliterated them.

Lumbering into the bathroom, Luke brushed and flossed his teeth in the semi-darkness created by flashes from the nightlight in the study. He splashed his face and took a sponge bath to save on water. He'd been allotted only one full bath a week.

Luke donned a white sleeping shirt because he'd given up sleeping nude after he hit ninety. If he became ill or died in the night, he believed a spiritual teacher should be found clothed in a dignified way. How lovely were the days when he and Euphoria slept nude, sprawled across each other.

As he headed to the bedroom and lay down on the silky duvet, his memory clicked.

"Well, I'll be damned. It was that asshole Kendall Roberts!"

After all these years, over forty, he's shown up again. Little remained of the lean and haunted youth Kendall Roberts in the graying, distinguished-looking Dr. Kegan. The aggressive, hostile energy had been the clue, not the physiognomy.

61

Floored at his own dim-wittedness, Luke wondered how he could ever have failed to recognize the man who had tried to murder Euphoria. Such forgetfulness was unforgivable. He must get a prescription for a nanobot ingestion to monitor his ginkgo intake.

Luke saw no point in continuing to chastise himself. Done was done. Now he'd have a look at this rotten individual who had wormed his way back into Luke's life. He went into the study and found the enrollment forms for the roundedness event. The infamous Dr. Kegan had listed the Psi Therapy Clinic as his only address. Luke cringed at remembering how blithely he had responded to Angela's suggestion that she go to the clinic. He should have investigated this new company personally. With such a dishonorable man at the helm, all kinds of bizarre things could be going on. A good reputation in England didn't necessarily translate to one here.

Although Luke taught astral projection in some of his seminars, he hadn't gone out astral traveling himself for a long time. Remaining alive in the physical body seemed equally as miraculous to him now as leaving it to travel in the astral plane once had. He did of course always sleep with his head in the north to align his body with the magnetic force of the earth to help him sleep better.

Settling into the pillow, he relaxed and dropped into alpha waves and from there into theta with ease. His breathing slowed and reversed into diaphragmatic, yet he remained alert. As he dropped into delta waves, he imagined his astral body as a shimmering silver sheath above him. Once he had it clearly in mind, he imagined his mind slipping into the sheath.

With barely a blip, Luke turned and saw the familiar bluish tinge of the astral plane around his bedroom. Spreading his arms, he soared through the ceiling and out into the midnight sky high above Sedona. Although he would enjoy flying up high enough to see real stars, he focused on the business at hand, turned south, and headed down the mountain. The nifty thing about astral projection was the ability to squeeze physical time. He arrived at the Psi Therapy Clinic in Phoenix after only a few moments.

When Luke flew past the glass structure, he found the offices closed and empty of humans. He focused on the thought: *I want to see Kendall Roberts wherever he is.*

Turning onto his back, Luke allowed himself to be pulled by the force of his desire. He saw others out astral traveling in translucent bodies, but he paid no attention to them.

Soon he found himself in the very posh condominium district of downtown Los Angeles with personal planes parked on the rooftops. Luke wondered if he had fallen asleep and begun to dream because he found it so improbable for Kendall to live here when he worked in Phoenix.

The penthouse unit of a circular tower attracted Luke's attention and he hovered outside the window. There indeed sat Kendall Roberts, or Dr. Kegan, as he called himself now, lounging on a sofa with a drink in his hand.

Before him stood Melanie in a bright green evening dress. She smiled, pulled down the gown, and let it drop to the floor. Totally nude with the draperies wide open. She looked more like Melinda than ever without her clothes.

Astounded to find these two in such an intimate scene, Luke refused to eavesdrop or window peep. Melinda, Melanie rather, might be in even more danger than Angela. He headed for home and his physical body so he could warn both women.

Luke's old enemy had returned intent once again to cause harm. Kegan or Kendall or Karim, whatever name he went by in whatever lifetime, when would he learn that revenge always turned back on the perpetrator?

Luke had to protect Melanie and Angela from Kegan. And evidently Luke had to also protect Kegan from Kegan.

Melanie wore crystal stilettos and a cocky grin. Her hair, threaded with sparkles and swept high, made her at least six feet tall. She looked stupefying. Kegan remembered well what that delicious body could do to satisfy him. That he still wore his business suit and tie made her nudity even more erotic.

So as not to appear too eager, Kegan glanced down at the pile of green satin lying on bright red carpet. He would never treat expensive clothing so. Growing up poor and having to earn and budget his money had taught him the worth of material possessions. Only a person born to money would fail to value it. Melanie thus showed her breeding, or lack of it. "That's a very nice gown. It might get damaged on the floor."

"Doesn't matter. I'll never wear it again. Too conservative." Melanie kicked the dress out of her way and strode to the black and white tile bar. She managed to show him a side view of tits and ass while she fixed a drink.

Melanie obviously enjoyed displaying her body. No reason why she shouldn't. Kegan raised his glass in a toast of appreciation and gazed at her through the amber of his Scotch and water. Her distorted reflection reminded him of the warrior she had been in their previous life, a powerful man with broad shoulders and rippling pectoral muscles.

Sipping the Scotch, Kegan wondered if they had been lovers then. Although he had no conscious recall of going into battle naked, he knew the Celts did. Kegan must have done so in his previous lifetime. The idea tantalized him, abject vulnerability or total domination. The Celtic warriors often had homosexual liaisons before founding a family with a woman. Kegan had never experienced a male lover in this life, and he felt curious about how different that might be from a female. Any exploration would have to wait until he became bored with Melanie, something not likely to happen for quite a while. Part of Kegan's attraction to her stemmed from the masculine aggressiveness she still possessed.

Picking up her martini goblet, Melanie returned the toast. "To you, darling, and our new romance." She downed the drink and made a refill.

"How was the...uh...what did you call it where you've been?"

"Trunk opening."

"Oh, yes, with the famous astrophysicist."

"A deadly bore, but it's important to Daddy that I do some kind of charity work. The observatory was my choice. Maybe I'll learn something about science." Melanie laughed as if she doubted the probability of that last remark and sat beside Kegan on the black velvet couch.

"Which is boring? The astrophysicist or the trunk opening?"

"Both."

Kegan adjusted to accommodate her against his side and put his arm around her. "Well, *ma chère*, let's see if we can't make life a little more interesting."

Just as he reached for her breast, Melanie pulled back. "I want to enjoy my drink." She spoke in a teasing tone and took a gulp. "I'm not going to see Todd anymore."

"Oh, why not?"

"I found somebody much better suited to me." She nipped his lip then pulled the olive out of her drink and popped it into her mouth.

"How'd he take it when you told him you were calling it off?"

After several chews, Melanie finally swallowed. "I didn't take time to mention it because you were here waiting for me. I'll tell him next time he calls."

The day they met, Melanie had shown Kegan a press photo of her with Todd Williams in some five star restaurant. Kegan recognized the bastard, and immediately he knew fate had come to bid him attend to his affairs. No coincidence like that could ever happen. It must have been Divine intervention to reveal the last of his enemy quartet—Todd Williams, Angela Brock, Luke Brock, and Melanie Vanderson.

Intuiting that this moment would come, Kegan had made a plan, one not without risk because he didn't know Melanie well enough to predict her reaction to his marriage. She might bolt like a silly girl. If so, he'd have to make a different arrangement. She might form a loyalty to him and help him kill the others. If not, she'd have to die too. Her fate was in her own hands.

"Perhaps you'd better not tell Williams just yet." Kegan spoke in a measured tone to play it as low key as possible. "It would be better for us if you had a cover relationship."

"A cover? What do I need a cover for?"

Kegan set his drink on the glass coffee table and squeezed Melanie close to his side. "Well, I'm married so we can't be an item in a public way. But we can have the most exciting private life any two people ever had." He pressed his tongue deep into her mouth, which tasted like pine needles smell, and he ran his tickling fingers along her thigh.

Melanie grasped his hand and stopped its forward movement. "Where is your wife?"

"In Phoenix."

"You live with her?" Melanie sounded curious but thankfully not angry.

"Yes, but that's nothing for you to concern yourself with. She and I have an understanding. I take care of her very well. In return she attends public events with me and keeps her nose out of my business. Have you been married?" When she shook her head, he asked, 'Do you have a child out of wedlock?"

"Of course not. Why would you think that?"

With a movement of his head, Kegan indicated a stainless steel bookshelf loaded with stuffed bears in a multitude of colors. "Whose are those?"

"Oh, that's my Care Bear collection. I've got three thousand and forty two. Daddy buys them for me every year on my birthday. Some of them are packed away in boxes though. I don't have all of them out."

Kegan tried to frame an appropriate response but couldn't. What kind of immature quirk did this represent? When he returned to Phoenix, he'd ask Janice Beatty about the possible psychology behind it. Probably neurosis. He hoped to hell he wouldn't have to get into bed with a Care Bear. He decided not to take the chance. He would take Melanie here on the couch. If he didn't have so much at stake with his other three enemies, he might just take off.

"How long have you been married?" Melanie cocked her head. She sounded as casual as if she'd asked how long he'd owned his suit.

"Forty years."

"That's fifteen years before I was born. Not that I care. I like older men much better."

Yes, I had a child older than you. A son I'll never be able to acknowledge. Kegan thought, but he said, "A lot happened before you were born. In this lifetime and in our previous ones."

"And you remember?" A look of unabashed envy crossed her face. "Tell me more."

"You and I were companions, friends then, like we are now. We fought on the same side in a war, but we weren't strong enough to win. This time it will be different. We will stick together and triumph."

"How will we know who to fight? What will we fight with?" Melanie seemed fascinated by the possibility.

"Don't worry. I'll take care of that. About the astrophysicist. Will you keep seeing him, at least for a while?"

"For you, my soul mate? Anything." She guided his hand to its moist destination.

Kegan felt confused about Melanie. Would she turn out to be friend or foe? What did Providence have in store for them? He didn't know whether he was supposed to keep her or kill her. Luckily, he didn't have to decide tonight.

As Kegan explored her femininity, Melanie's features relaxed, and the smiling face of the warrior swam into view. Kegan longed to join with him and possess her—to conquer her maleness and dominate her femaleness. The urgency of Kegan's desire swamped him.

Seven

The Perils of Candor

The dull throb in Todd's head last night had developed into a migraine-strength ache this morning. He needed to stop letting Melanie's rejection get to him. Sometimes he thought she liked to see how far she could push him. He hated to think of sex as a tradeoff, but damn it, she owed him, after that ridiculous Halley's Comet duty. On the other hand, he had enjoyed watching that cute little reporter lose her cool. She piqued his curiosity, for sure.

As Todd walked toward the office, his secretary waved from the other side of the glass doors that slid open before him. "Hi, Ms. Lizbet. Damn well got a..."

Her Hawaiian print caftan swirled around her chubby figure as Ms. Lizbet placed a forefinger to her lips and nodded toward the opposite wall. "Someone to see you."

As Todd turned, a small woman rose from a transparent chair and shifted her shoulder bag nervously from one arm to the other. "Dr. Williams?" Her voice quavered.

"Hello, Ms. Brock. It's nice to see you again." Todd shook her sweaty hand, trying to recall when he'd ever had such an unsettling effect on a woman. "I hope you're feeling better."

"Thank you very much for your kindness yesterday. I assure you I'm in possession of my wits today." Angela did not release his hand, instead clutching it more tightly. She gave him a nervous but charming smile. "I wonder if you could answer the questions I intended to ask."

"Intended to?"

"For the interview? The one we didn't get to have?"

"Oh, I did agree to that, didn't I?" Because she looked so vulnerable, he fought an urge to tease her about spacing out at the planetarium. He definitely wondered what had happened. Maybe he'd ask a question or two of his own. "I'm certain I can make the time, can't I, Ms. Lizbet?"

"You're due at the think tank in half an hour. I'll call and say you'll be a few minutes late." Ms. Lizbet sounded unusually obliging. Normally she fussed at him to make his appointments on time.

Todd wanted to open the door for Angela but felt awkward about moving. He suppressed an irrational urge to take her in his arms and reassure her. He glanced down at their hands, hers pale and warm against his reddish skin, scrubbed clean of grease spots.

"Sorry." Angela pulled away as if she'd just learned he had smallpox. A flush traveled above the neckline of her lavender gown to her pretty throat. She bowed her head, probably to keep him from seeing her embarrassment.

With a smile that he hoped would set her at ease, Todd pressed the button that opened the wood panels to his inner office. He made a sweeping gesture for her to enter. "Milady."

Angela stepped inside in front of Todd, and he closed the doors. Despite high heeled pumps, she moved gracefully across the thick carpet. The folds of her gown flowed like waves around her ankles as she gazed at the built-in bookcases and photos along his walls. "Oh, my."

Todd enjoyed the impact his office had on people. Such a contrast to the sleek design of the rest of the building. He wondered what she thought. Maybe she would consider him eccentric. That shouldn't be a problem. She seemed rather eccentric herself. Of course it didn't matter what she thought of him personally. He wasn't available.

His couple status with Melanie had more to do with his desire to keep her from seeing other men than with enjoying her company. The fact that she already had all the money and social influence she could ever want reassured him. Finding another relationship seemed like a lot of work, especially to avoid women who were only attracted to his money and fame. Did Angela have an agenda other than her news story?

"You must really like to read." Angela grinned in a genuine way, for the first time. "You've got more books than anyone I know, except maybe my grandfather."

"Yes, and I also collect them." Todd picked up a physics textbook, enjoying the rich texture of its leather binding. He flipped it open to the publisher's page. " Copyright 2022. You know how hard these are to find?"

"Not exactly, but I can guess." Angela moved to a display of holographic pictures of airplanes, helicopters, stealth bombers, and spaceships.

Todd wondered what her interest in aircraft might be. "I call this my history of flight." He pointed to a photo of an old Cessna. "I've been restoring Mustangs, but if I can find one of these, I'll get into restoring them."

Her eyebrows furrowed down, crunching their pretty black arch. She looked momentarily angry or maybe even frightened. "Why this one?"

"No particular reason. Just an interesting machine." Todd guided her to one of four overstuffed chairs that surrounded a table with a holographic portal. "Sit down, please. What did you want to ask me, Ms. Brock?"

She perched on the edge of a chair as if its heavy maroon nub would gobble up her delicate presence. She turned on her holophone, acting very professional. "Do you mind if I record our conversation?"

There was something Todd didn't understand. He might have offended her in the conversation about the planes. How could a simple comment about restoring a plane upset her? An intriguing puzzle. Should he ignore the subject or ask her about it?

"Dr. Williams?"

Todd came to himself and realized Angela was giving him a sidelong look. "Excuse me." Feeling sheepish, he dropped into the chair across from her and shifted his weight to balance his arms along the top of the chair. He hoped he looked relaxed. "Please, Ms. Brock, what is your first question?"

"What would you say is the significance of the comet's return?"

Todd wanted to avoid saying on tape what he really thought of this cosmic dwarf. Not worth the time spent on it. "You mean scientifically why it returns?"

"No, the impact of 1986 on our time, that's the focus of my story."

"Oh, then I'd say the people of 1986 reached out in a peaceful way toward our time. I guess people want peace in all times. Maybe we'll have it by 2136 when the comet comes again. We're a long way from it right now."

"Should we create a trunk for the America of 2136? Institute a tradition?"

"I believe that is being done, but I don't know what trinkets are going into it. I hope something more meaningful than Frisbees. Maybe we should have a contest."

Scowling, Angela consulted the screen of her phone and ignored his attempt at lightening the mood. He wondered whether she had any sense of humor at all. Even so she looked very sexy in an elegant, understated way.

"What do you think should go into the trunk?" Angela asked as if she cared about his answer.

"News story disks are a good idea, like they did with the Challenger newspaper. Maybe a disk that explains the rationale for moving the capital from D. C. to Phoenix. Maybe one on the latest weapons of mass destruction. We're establishing a legacy of living in fear that I find disturbing." Todd also disliked the commercialization of the trunk event, like an ad for the planetarium, but he had the good sense not to mention that.

"Dr. Williams…"

"Todd.

"Thank you, Todd." When she said his name, Angela's face and posture took on much greater vitality. She looked like she did on the news—smart, sophisticated, and honest. That look made viewers in Greater Hispania trust her as an anchor.

"Don't mention it." Todd grinned, hoping to get her to smile.

Angela looked serious. "Many would say that your contributions to weightless propulsion constitute the most important change in people's lives since the comet's last visit in 1986. Would you agree with that assessment, or is something else more important?"

As always, Todd hated this turn of the questioning. Not that he harbored any false modesty. He felt great pride in his contribution to science. No one ever believed the ease with which he had discovered the key, immediately on graduation from college and beginning his work at the government lab. The facts had been obvious to him, something mankind had struggled to learn for years. As if he'd been born to make the discovery. How could he explain without sounding conceited?

"Weightless propulsion is important," he said, "no doubt about it. I built on the work of many other scientists, so I don't want to take all the credit or the blame. That ability could turn sour fast if we don't figure out a way to keep Earth out of interstellar wars."

"What will the most important changes—" Angela's holophone began to emit the sound of a Tibetan bell. "Excuse me while I disable this." She waved her hand over the face of the phone with frustrated exuberance.

Her expressive face made her seem capable of many emotions. Todd thought she could probably attract any man she wanted. He wondered whether she was married and glanced at her hand. It bore several rings so he couldn't tell. "Go ahead and take the call if it's important."

"Just my grandfather. I can talk to him anytime."

Todd felt an unexpected relief at learning the identity of the caller.

"Now," Angela asked, "what will be the most important changes between now and 2136 when the comet returns?"

"I wish I knew. I'm certain illness will disappear, but we'll have to face an incredible population explosion. Solving one problem always creates another."

Her knowing smile indicated she saw the irony in his comment. "What problem is your think tank working on solving now?"

"It's called the Seagull Project, but it's off the subject of your story, and it's my turn to ask questions." When Angela seemed amused, he decided to plunge ahead. "Would you mind telling me what happened to you at the planetarium? You seemed very distressed. Are you ill?"

Sinking back into the chair, Angela sighed and glanced away. Her eyes appeared out of focus as she scratched at the upholstery. Perhaps the question had undone her. Todd thought he should treat this woman with special care. She could go off again right here in his office. Then what would he do?

"I don't really know you well enough to trust you, but I feel compelled to confide in you anyway." Angela slid forward and laid a trembling hand on his. "I saw you and me in the clothing of the 1980s. I think we knew each other then. Knew each other very well. I might even know how you died." She took a quick look at the hologram of the Cessna. "In one of those."

"You mean to tell me that you actually think you visited the other time?"

"No, not really. I think I'm remembering myself. And you. We were…engaged to be married." The flush rose along her throat once again, but she did nothing to conceal it.

With a slight squeeze, Todd set her hand off his. He climbed out of the chair and strode across the room. For several moments, he studied the Cessna photo then turned back .

Angela gazed at him with eyes the blue of a robin's egg. The expression on her face transfixed him. Todd forgot what he was about to say. She was looking at him as if she loved him with great devotion. She must believe that she did. He longed to respond to her. He wished he could be the object of such adoration. Todd wanted to hold the loopy, lovely Angela but dared not.

What could he be thinking? This woman's craziness was infectious. He'd better watch out. He ought to be thinking of Melanie. After all, they were most likely the lead item in the morning's tabloids.

When in doubt, logic usually served Todd well. "It's possible that you've experienced time displacement. Some type of temporal fluctuation. Or perhaps a projection of consciousness. The twenty-first century you, I'm speaking of, displaced time and became conscious momentarily in the twentieth century. Is that what you felt? That you were alive in that time, not this one?"

"For a few moments I did." Angela seemed to want to say more but didn't.

"Theoretically, there's no reason why you can't travel through time as well as through space. In the Seagull Project we're working to prove projection of consciousness. Some Buddhist yogis can project an image of themselves to a second location. We're trying to lock down the physics behind that behavior, understand it, and put it to use scientifically."

"But I recognized you as the man I've dreamed of, too, and I've seen those dreams exteriorized and projected onto a wall. I know you're the man."

"Dreams?" Todd chuckled. "Please, Ms. Brock, you mean to say I'm the man of your dreams?" He blurted out the words. He'd meant to tease her but may have sounded too desultory.

Shooting out of the chair, Angela grabbed her bag and slung it over her shoulder. "I should have said nightmare. How could I be so foolish as to expect you to understand? Thank you for the interview." She hurried across the room and stopped before the closed doors.

"I was just teasing, Angela. I shouldn't have. I really want to understand what happened. Come back and tell me."

When she turned and glared at him, her gorgeous eyes narrowed to slits. "Open the doors and let me out of here." Angela's rigid posture revealed great anger as she walked past Ms. Lizbet and spoke evenly. "Thank you for your help, ma'am. It was very nice to meet you."

The glass doors to the hall closed on Angela. As she walked away, she cast a look back at Todd, one so forlorn he felt more confused than ever.

"Hey, hey," Ms. Lizbet gave him a thumbs-up sign. "Now, that's a lady who could be worthy of you. We had a chance to get acquainted while she waited for you. Angela Brock is as warm and sincere in person as she is on TV."

Nodding his agreement, Todd expelled a great breath that emptied his lungs. He'd not been aware of such tension in himself. At least his headache had gone away. "Maybe you better send her some flowers."

"You've not messed it up already?" Ms. Lizbet's tone conveyed her disapproval and indulged his blunder at the same time. "What kind does she like?"

"On second thought, I'll take care of that detail myself. Did Ms. Brock leave a calling chip?"

"Coming right up." Ms. Lizbet pressed a tab on her computer console and the words from the chip raced across the wall.

"Just her business address in Phoenix? No personal info?"

"Sorry, boss." Ms. Lizbet didn't sound sorry at all. She sounded entertained by his disappointment.

Todd memorized the address and phone and headed toward his office, closing the doors firmly behind him. He'd be damned if he'd provide any more entertainment for his under-worked, over-nosey secretary.

Immediately, Angela returned to Phoenix and locked herself in the editing room at the TV station. As she added Todd's interview answers into the original piece of film, she had to force herself to focus. She'd rarely felt more distracted or less interested in her work.

Such a fool she was. She had made a total mess of the entire visit, the one and only chance she might get to create a good impression on Todd. Today she'd intended to induce him to forget her crazy winking out act yesterday. With that accomplished, she had hoped to convince him of her honesty and forthrightness. Maybe he'd see her as a worthwhile person and develop an interest in her.

Todd had even obliged her by asking about the incident. Had given her the chance to say the truth. His reaction of disbelief had been completely predictable. She should have accepted that and understood.

But what had she done instead? Got pissed at the man for merely trying to tease her. For God's sake, that impertinent disposition was as much a part of Todd's soul as his unruly dark hair or his handsome appearance. How Angela loved him. She wanted him to care for her.

If there had been any doubt at all of her feelings for Todd, they would have dissolved when she saw him in his office, his natural habitat, with old books, old cars, and a photo of the very plane in which he had died in her dreams. The man was a walking testimonial to their past life together, even if he didn't seem to remember anything.

All of her need for Todd might have to go completely unexpressed. As she reviewed the footage she recognized his companion, the outrageous Melanie Vanderson, a subject of the exploitive media ever since her debut at sixteen in a see-through gown. Angela refused to dignify the publications by calling them newspapers or magazines.

Why Angela had not recognized the heiress at the planetarium remained another mystery. What might the brazen woman mean to Todd? Certainly they were lovers. It galled Angela that Melanie knew Todd intimately.

The way things stood, Angela had no right to her beloved. Hateful though she found admitting it, Melanie had the prior claim on his affections. Angela refused to dishonor herself by flirting with someone else's man.

Because of the late hour, hardly anyone remained of the regular staff so Angela ducked into Campbell's empty office and set the disk of the finished story on his desk. She left a note to thank him for giving her another chance.

Would Todd be willing to do the same? She ached for him. Already she had discovered that loving someone could be equally as painful as the loneliness of having no one, maybe worse. Angela needed to confide these extraordinary emotions. She looked forward to the next appointment with Janice. Perhaps the counselor could offer fresh insight or some idea on how to make amends. Angela had to come to terms with the fact that a real romance wasn't possible now. No one else but Todd would do.

Because she had ridden the subway from Anthem to Los Angeles then back to Phoenix, she knew her car was not parked in the garage. Regardless, she followed an intuition to go to the garage level on her way out of the building. Once there, she looked around at all the parked Bimis and personal planes, wondering if she'd lost what psychic ability she possessed. She had no idea why she had come to the garage or what to do while there.

Just as she gave up on finding the answer and headed for the elevator, she heard a woman call her name. The night watch woman hurried up, gun clanking against her lanky legs in her regulation jumpsuit.

"Oh, Bernice, hello."

"Glad I caught you, Miss Brock. Come on back to headquarters. I got something for you."

"What on earth?"

"A delivery. That's all."

Once they arrived at the guard station, Bernice handed over a huge basket of live sunflowers to Angela and giggled. "Got an admirer, do you, ma'am?"

"Maybe." Angela tried not to blush. "Thank you."

Once inside the elevator, Angela surveyed the petals and the leaves. She found a plastic button in the brown center of one flower.

When she pressed the button, a miniature hologram of Todd appeared on a yellow petal. Like a cavalier of olden times, he bowed and said, "Please forgive me, milady."

"Done," she whispered and wished he could hear her. She pressed the button again and watched him in wonder. "Lobby."

While the elevator carried her body to the main floor, his words took her heart to the pinnacle of a roller coaster—from the depths to the heights in moments.

As she rode the subway home, she wondered if she could bear this experience of being in love. She had new respect for her unwitting wisdom in avoiding it so far in her life.

But she believed instinctively that she had something to learn from all this. Otherwise all the memories would not have broken through into her dream life. She had to trust her previous self, the one who had provoked all the memories in her subconscious. Angela hoped she could rise to the challenge. She thanked her intuition for sending her to the garage level.

Any more excitement in her life would have to wait until she replenished herself. At her condo, she retrieved a veggie lasagna bake from the freezer and set it in the convection oven while she showered. Donning aqua silk pajamas, she set the flower basket on the patio table, started the aerator and sprinkling system, then sat down and ate her meal with some Chardonnay. The mist cooled the air to a comfortable level now that the sun had gone down.

With the idea, too obvious to be an intuition, that she could be making more trips to Los Angeles in the near future, Angela thought perhaps she should consider purchasing a personal plane. Of course, that would necessitate taking flying lessons, but she really should know how to fly. Everybody did these days.

"Angela, Angela, are you in there?" The unmistakable tremor of Luke's voice called over the repeated ringing of her doorbell.

"I'm out here, Granddad." Angela set a chair beside the wall and climbed on it. In the glow of the amber security lights, she could see Luke hurrying across the pebbled lawn toward her, wearing trousers and a light shirt.

"Is that you?" Luke's face creased in a worried frown. "Where in hell have you been?"

Angela laughed at his ludicrous question. "Hey, I'm a big girl now. I don't have to answer that."

"Either come over this wall or let me in the front door right now." With his arms on his hips, Luke looked and sounded angrier than Angela had ever seen him.

Vowing to erase the amusement from her voice, Angela rushed through the living room. It wouldn't do for him to think she was laughing at him. She could never hurt him in any way.

"Okay, okay." Angela said, "open" to the locking code on the front door, which swung toward her. "Come in, please."

She grabbed Luke's arm, pulled him into the living room, and tried to put her arms around him to kiss him, but he resisted. "What is this all about?" she asked.

"You tell me. I've been trying to call you all day."

"Yikes. I was doing an interview when you called, and I forgot to turn my phone back on."

"I hoped it would be something like that." Luke grumbled but let her lead him to sit on the couch.

"I was having some wine. Let me get you a glass."

"Got any beer?"

"I think so."

In the kitchen, Angela popped the top on a beer, carried it to Luke, and headed for the patio door.

"Where you going?" Luke barked his question.

"To get my wine. Is that all right?" Angela could hardly believe her grandfather's abrupt behavior, so contrary to his usual mellow, supportive way with her.

"Oh, okay." Luke took a long drink of the beer.

Shrugging in what she hoped was a humorous way, she retrieved her glass and the wine bottle from the patio.

When she returned he was talking on the phone with no holo image. "She's okay. Go on to bed." Luke paused momentarily. "Yes, I'll tell her."

"My folks? Are they worried?"

"Naturally. Your father says he loves you."

"I'm sorry you felt you had to call them. It was nothing." Angela sat beside Luke and poured herself another glass. "I'm also sorry that I worried you. I didn't mean to. I was just...involved." She considered whether to tell him about Todd. Why shouldn't she?

"You need to keep your phone on at all times." Luke sounded far too stern for the situation. "We've worried about you all day. We feared the worst."

"The worst? What on earth could happen to me? I'm just fine. I took the subway to L. A. Big deal."

"And you didn't even let your folks know you were there?"

"I was going to, but I got...caught up. In work, of course. And some other things." Angela hesitated, feeling like a kid again. "Granddad, I've got good news."

"It can wait." Luke swilled down the rest of the beer, set the can down, and folded his arms. "There's something I need to tell you. You could be in danger. I mean your life could be in danger. I already told your parents."

Angela choked back a laugh. "Danger from what?" She glanced around the room to indicate that she saw nothing to warrant concern. "What are you talking about?"

"You never know when someone might want to harm you, kill you even."

His assertion seemed completely preposterous. Angela had heard stories of old people suddenly becoming delusional, but she didn't believe it could ever happen to her beloved grandfather. "No one wants to kill me."

Luke leaped off the couch, laid one hand on his brow, the other on his hip, and paced back and forth across the room. He'd always had a lot of energy for his age, but not like this. He seemed so agitated Angela feared he would have a stroke.

"Angela, I've told you before that I had two wives that died."

"I know. Grandmother Melinda and your beloved Euphoria."

"I never told you how they died. They were murdered. By the same man." Luke spat out the words.

"How can that be? Melinda died on Nine Eleven."

"Her murderer was the pilot of the plane, and just as surely as he lived then he reincarnated and killed Euphoria. I can't prove any of this in a court of law. But I know in my heart that he caused her death. He tormented her in the astral plane and she died of a heart attack. His name was Kendall Roberts, in fact he was your mother's teaching assistant at the university. I don't know where he's been all these years, but now he's back with a new name and a plan to kill again, as surely as we're in this room together. Now he calls himself Robert Kegan."

"The doctor? The head of the Psi Therapy Clinic? But why? He doesn't even know us." Blaming that Englishman who had just come to town seemed completely insane.

"What reason does anyone have to kill? There is no reason. He has a vendetta against me. He killed my wife because he wasn't strong enough to kill me. Now he's after you and...someone else. I intend to warn the other woman, and I hope she believes me. Do you believe me? Angela, do you?"

"Yes, of course." Angela felt so worried about her grandfather that she'd say anything to calm him down. She would call her parents in the morning to discuss what could be done. Maybe he needed a rest. Living alone and working as he did. At a hundred years of age, he had to slow down.

"Stay away from the Psi Therapy Clinic." Luke demanded.

"All right, I will."

Angela had all the more reason now to speak with Janice. She could no longer confide in her grandfather. He had become fixated on this story. How much of it was his concoction, Angela didn't know, maybe a mixture of fact and fantasy. He had grieved so much over the deaths of his mother and his wives. It may have finally overwhelmed him. Something had caused him to start hallucinating. Maybe her parents could arrange for him to go on a retreat. They'd have to make the decisions, but Angela hoped they would honor her judgment in this.

Luke clutched her shoulders and looked into Angela's face. "Promise me that you will keep your doors locked." Clearly he believed passionately in his story.

"Yes, all right." Angela remembered many times when she had just walked into his house because he'd neglected to lock the door. He'd acted far more casual on this subject than she ever had. "You need to do the same."

Looking sheepish, Luke said. "Okay, I will. And I want you to remember not to go anywhere alone. Call Nine One One at the first sign of suspicion."

"Okay, Granddad. I promise."

"Good, then. I feel a little better." Luke headed for the door. "I'll call you in the morning."

"Please don't go. Tell you what. You can sleep in my guest room, then you can fly on up to Sedona tomorrow. Okay?"

"That's not necessary. I'm fine." His haggard face belied his words.

"I know, but I would feel better if you stayed." Angela edged close to him. A short, stocky man, he only stood a half head taller. She nestled her check against his chest, still broad and protective. She squeezed him as she had done ever since her childhood. "Please stay, for me?"

"All right. I am rather tired tonight." Luke kissed her cheek and patted her back. He always smelled so wonderful, sandalwood and beer. "What was it you wanted to tell me, honey girl?"

"Oh, never mind. I'll tell you tomorrow."

Eight

Best Laid Plans

Early the next morning, Angela called Todd's office and left a message, thanking him for the flowers. Not caring that she might have acted too forward, she left her holophone number. Hopefully he would ask to see her again. If not, she'd know his relationship with Melanie was genuine. Angela dreaded to have to give Todd up before really knowing him, but she wanted him to have happiness. If that meant Melanie's love instead of her own, somehow she would learn to adapt.

When Luke awoke, he warned her again of the supposed danger to her life. His notion that her life was in danger because of some man she didn't even know seemed preposterous. Sadly, Luke must need medical attention. She wanted her parents' viewpoints on Luke's condition, but she feared Alzheimer's or mental illness.

Over breakfast of French toast and juice, she convinced him to take her to Los Angeles. He agreed so Angela called her parents and suggested they all get together for lunch. She didn't prejudice them prematurely by sharing her fears about Luke's new, paranoid-seeming behavior. That way they could make their own judgments. With a pang, Angela realized she'd have to forgo any chance of seeing Todd on this trip. Her duty to her grandfather took precedence right now.

"I've been thinking I might buy a personal plane if I get my old job back. Maybe you could teach me how to fly the plane on the way, Granddad."

"I will on one condition," Luke eyed her floor-length skirt, "you wear something suitable for a cockpit."

"I hadn't realized I'd have to forfeit style to do this." Grinning, Angela went into her bedroom and changed into white jeans and a red tank top. She'd bought the garments many months before on an uncharacteristic impulse but had never worn them because she felt uncomfortable in sporty fashions, too sleek and revealing. Now she wondered whether her dreaming self, or the 1980s self, had influenced the purchase.

On the other hand, she wouldn't see anyone but her family, who cared little about what she wore. After drawing her hair into a pony tail, she considered her attire perfect for a hot day. Maybe she'd become too fashion conscious for personal comfort.

Back in the living room, she twirled around for Luke. "So what do you think?"

"You look great. You're a dead ringer for your great-grandmother. Except she would have worn shorts."

"Oh, I've got something to tell you."

As she locked up the condo and walked with Luke to the parking lot, Angela related the scenes of the 1980s she had witnessed when she met Todd at the planetarium. She added portions of the conversation that she could recall.

As she finished her tale, they reached Luke's personal plane. On the outside, it resembled a Bimi with wings, beautiful décor with pale blue feathers painted on the darker shade to suggest a bird in flight.

Luke laid his knob-veined hand on the housing and studied Angela's face. "What do you think happened to you?"

"I'm not positive. I felt like I really was that other woman in that other time. Not some time displacement like Todd tried to claim. He is the same man, the one I've dreamed about, the one who crashed in the airplane. It's

Todd and it's not Todd. That's not a very clear explanation, but it's the best I can do."

A look of pain crossed his face, and Luke turned away. His shoulders hunched as if he were trying to get control of himself. When he looked at Angela, his head trembled and tears stood in his eyes.

She'd thought he might respond to her story with surprise, maybe interest, or even excitement that she alluded to his pet theory of reincarnation, but not sadness. She regretted having told him and wondered whether to apologize. Luke's reactions about everything seemed off.

"Well, let's do that first lesson." He swiped his tears, pressed a button on the starboard side, and the housing opened.

Worried, Angela climbed into the passenger seat. She had ridden in planes many times, but she had never piloted one. Could she trust him to fly the plane in his condition?

"Might as well do this the right way." Luke motioned her into the pilot's seat then pressed a button that closed them inside the cozy cabin. He gave her a quick explanation of the instrument panel and the fuel cell light. After they'd strapped on their seatbelts, he said, "Okay, starter."

Up till now Angela had been so focused on Luke and the story about Todd and the memory that she'd not realized what she'd opened herself for. Suddenly tense at the prospect of actually controlling the plane, she pressed the starter and the fuel cell began to hum.

"Vertical thruster." Luke pointed to a handle the size of a ball point. "Engage."

Confused, Angela scanned the instruments.

"Pull up on it, honey girl."

Her hand shook as Angela grabbed the handle and followed instructions. The plane lifted straight up above the parking lot. She'd not thought to look for other planes. Now she did. Her first mistake. She'd better take caution. A plane might be less forgiving than a car.

Evidently Luke had checked for traffic because the sky appeared empty for her maiden flight. They ascended high enough that her home looked like a toy condo complex with miniature trees and matchbox cars and planes in the lot. The altimeter read forty-nine hundred feet. Angela felt giddy, dizzied by the different perspective.

"Set your directional dial for L. A.," Luke said.

"A dial? How quaint."

"I've had this model for a lot of years. It doesn't have all the latest conveniences on it, but it runs great. It's a Mercedes. They don't make them any more."

Angela fumbled with the dial and finally managed to turn it. The word Phoenix disappeared. It passed through Yuma, San Diego, then showed Los Angeles. She stopped, uncertain what to do next.

"It's preprogrammed. Now press the dial."

When she did, the plane veered to the west. Angela's nerves escalated into fear. "Now what do I do?"

"Nothing for now. The automatic pilot will tell us if we're encountering traffic. Otherwise, we can relax."

"Relax. You're kidding me!" This was about the same amount of work as driving the Bimi onto the beltway and engaging its wheels in the hover field. Angela felt a trifle disappointed. She'd wanted more adventure at learning to fly, instead of suffering from beginner's jitters.

"It's a beautiful day." Luke gestured out the windshield. "I love the desert."

"Me, too." The sky looked clear and the day bright. Visible in the distance, other personal planes headed in a patchwork of directions. Sparkling lights and shadows adorned the mountain range below. With nostalgia, Angela realized her grandfather might not be with her much longer, in body or in mind. She felt lucky to share this time with him and kissed his cheek. "Thanks for teaching me."

"Angela," Luke grasped her hand and gazed at the floorboard for a long moment. "There are some things about our family's past that I've never told you. Now's the time."

Something trembled inside Angela. Somehow she knew Luke's words would change her world. Life itself seemed out of her control. If some force greater than herself had charge of her life, and intuition made her believe so, she hoped the force was benevolent. Perhaps she should pray, but she had no notion how to. It seemed odd that she even thought of prayer as a solution at all.

"Before I reveal facts about your great-grandmother that you don't know, I want to ask you something. Do you remember anything about the time before you were born into this life?"

"You mean like being in...uh...heaven?"

"Or here. Can you remember anything?"

"All I remember is what I told you about the planetarium, and Todd, and the dreams of the plane crash."

Luke sighed as if he were disappointed. At what Angela didn't know.

"My mother, your great-grandmother, was engaged to a Navy commander. He died a week before the wedding. A Cessna exploded with him and his pilot inside. To make matters worse, Mom had seen the crash in a vision and tried to stop him from getting on the plane. She never recovered from the grief and guilt surrounding that tragedy. In a way it killed her, though actually she died of cancer a few years later."

"I knew some of this. Dad told me."

"What he didn't tell you, nor have I, was that she and her fiancé had made a pact to reincarnate together."

"A pact?" Angela remembered the words she'd thought Todd had said. To meet in 2061, and she had promised. That could be interpreted as a pact. She glanced at her grandfather's earnest face, with his gray brows furrowed down. An urge to self-protection made her resolve to keep a tight grip on her sanity. Luke's assertions, if true, made her less and less certain of her identity.

"And you know where they made that pact? When they went to see the planetarium exhibit of Halley's Comet."

"Dear God! How do you know all this?"

"Mom told me. Nobody forgets a thing like that. I didn't want you to know before now. I didn't want to prejudice your memories or influence you in any way because I've thought all along this day would come and you would say these things. That you were named Angela, after her, is the least of the similarities."

"Dear God." Angela felt too overwhelmed to say anything else.

"In all your thirty years, I've never heard you profess a belief in God. Why do you use that phrase?"

She shrugged that she didn't know. Actually Angela had never thought about God or heaven except as an awareness of generic religious practice. Now the thought of praying or calling on a deity seemed right. Why? "Was your mother religious?" She whispered the question knowing the answer already in her heart.

"It was my mother's favorite expression. She believed in a Divine Spirit that lives in all of us and directed our path, just as I do."

Perhaps that spirit had sent the dreams to Angela so she would dream of her beloved and recognized him again in Todd. Luke's words felt right. They jived with her intense reaction at the planetarium, yet intellectually she struggled to grasp the import of the knowledge. She longed to discuss all this with Todd. His confirmation would mean everything. But if she told him, she had no idea how he would react.

A sudden updraft caused Angela and Luke to strain against the seatbelts. A mechanical voice squawked, "Vehicle approaching off the port bow."

Out the window beside her, Angela saw a purple Dial-a-Bike heading straight toward them, its noisy engine chugging. Inside a young man bent over, probably kissing his companion, who sat in the sidecar. Obviously neither was paying any attention to navigation.

Luke reached across Angela and nudged the directional dial. They turned to the right just in time. He shouted back, "Watch where you're going, punk!"

The roar of the Dial-a-Bike diminished as the distance between the vehicles mounted. The other people's carelessness might have gotten everyone killed. Angela felt angry with them for causing her to feel such fear, but Luke looked very much in control.

"Whew, a close one. Thanks, Granddad. You saved our lives."

"Hey, you're welcome." Luke kissed her cheek. "Move over." They switched seats, and he leaned back with a satisfied grin. "Now that was fun. Want another lesson?"

"Maybe later." Angela inhaled and exhaled slowly to calm herself.

"Now what were we talking about?"

Angela didn't remind Luke of the revelations about his mother, maybe herself in another life. It seemed too much to process, and she had no idea how to begin. Certainly not aloft in a plane that could crash at any moment. Dealing with Luke's failing mental capacity had a much higher priority today. "How long before we get there?"

Whatever Luke answered she didn't hear because her holophone emitted the sound of classical trumpets, the fanfare from the TV station. She pressed the view button, and Campbell's tiny, rotund figure floated atop the crystal.

"Hey, Angela," Campbell bellowed, "I've scheduled the screening for your comet show. We've notified the astrophysicist and the head of the planetarium, so they can sign off on it if they want to."

"Great. When?"

"Two this afternoon."

"Two? I'm on my way to L. A. I'll never get back in time." Why in hell couldn't he have given her more notice? The man got ruder every day he lived.

Campbell's tiny form shrugged. "Attend or not. It's your choice."

However much she wanted to be there, Angela had to visit her parents, for her grandfather's sake. His well being was more important. Still she couldn't stand the suspense. "Tell me. What did you think of the show?"

"Good enough to get you another special assignment. Not good enough to get you back into the anchor chair."

"How about a piece on why couples remain childless. I've always wondered why anyone would want to."

Campbell's image dissolved as if he had not heard Angela. She'd pitch the idea to him again when she returned to work. Having children was an important priority for Angela, right after finding a father for them.

All right, she could miss the screening without jeopardizing her job, but Todd might be there. What would he think if she didn't even make an appearance? She would call him tomorrow and say that she had family obligations. That explanation seemed insufficient.

Leaning toward the console, Luke turned the directional dial to Phoenix and started to press it.

"Wait. What are you doing?"

"You've got to go to the screening, and I want to see it too. You'll take me, won't you?"

"But we told Mother and Dad we'd be there. They'll be disappointed if we don't show up." Aware of the weakness of her argument, Angela didn't have the temerity to say the real reason. She wanted to see Todd more than anything.

"They'll get over it." With a shrug and a silly smile, Luke pressed the dial and the plane made a hundred and eighty degree course change.

Angela could feel the pressure on her body from the stark change in direction. "No, turn the plane around. I don't need to see that screening. It's nothing. I'll see the show when it airs."

"What's gotten into you? Of course we're going back." Luke sounded impatient. "Your job's not that secure. And Todd will be there. How many reasons do you need?"

Although unaccustomed to Luke's bossy, erratic behavior, Angela could not come right out and admit her fears about senility. That would be far too painful for both of them. "Okay, but we'll go to L. A. tomorrow, all right?"

"Don't you mean the next day?"

Luke hunched his shoulders and grinned as if they shared some secret. Angela assumed he referred to his surprise birthday party and decided not to ask. He might go off on another tale like the one about danger to her. Perhaps his comparisons of her to his mother were wishful thinking too. She couldn't blame that on old age because she shared the desire to understand her experiences in a larger context. She found something haunting and compelling about the whole business. Maybe the dreams had been nothing more than a bizarre coincidence or genetic memory. Who knew?

While Luke piloted the plane, Angela sank back in the seat and closed her eyes. She wanted to blot out her thoughts because she found them too confusing, but she couldn't.

With only minutes to spare, they arrived at the TV station, parked the plane, and took the elevator to the viewing room. The moment Angela stepped inside, she saw Todd. He lounged in one of a dozen recliners in candy cane colors, arranged in a semi-circle.

His gaze slid down her length and back up to her eyes. A wide smile dimpled his chin. She read in his expression how sexy she looked to him. She blushed, embarrassed and pleased at the same time. The jeans fit too tightly and the blouse revealed more cleavage than she felt comfortable about. She wished she'd worn clothes more appropriate to the work place.

"Hello." Angela hoped her voice sounded calmer than she felt. Did he notice the flush rising along her throat?

"There you are," a woman's voice called from the circus-style snack dispenser behind the chairs. "We were afraid you wouldn't make it in time." Stephanie handed one soft drink cup to Todd and one to an older man in the next chair. "Anyone want popcorn?"

"Granddad, this is Stephanie." Angela tried to remember the woman's last name. "She's legal advisor to Campbell's staff. Stephanie, this..."

"Oh, you don't have to introduce me to Luke." Her pink shift swished as Stephanie moved toward Luke. She placed her palms together, fingers touching her chin, and moved toward Luke. Her face had a look of sturdy belief. She tipped her bright red head of hair. "*Namaste.*"

"Why if it isn't Stephanie Burke." Luke imitated her gesture. "*Namaste.* It's good to see you again." He took both of her hands in his, and they smiled at each other in an unabashed way as if they were alone, evidently heedless of the awkward silence that filled the room.

Angela found it more and more difficult to account for Luke's behavior. She wondered whether he was flirting with the legal assistant or trying to read her mind. She needed to dispel the moment and reassert good manners. "I'm Angela Brock." She approached the large bearded man, who rose and engulfed her hand in his.

"Henry Kline. Volunteer at the Planetarium."

"And this is..." Angela began.

Todd raised an eyebrow as if she should remember. "Kline and I met at the trunk opening."

"Oh, of course." Angela hesitated to acknowledge that she didn't recall all of the events and people of the time at the observatory. She moved toward the dispenser. "Would anyone like some candy?" She extracted a chocolate bar and unwrapped it, certain it wouldn't abate her hunger.

Finally, Stephanie broke out of the staring match and said to Luke, "You know those astral projection techniques you taught? No luck. They didn't work for me. I might take another one of your workshops."

"Naturally I'd enjoy having you," Luke said, "but don't waste the money. Just review the literature I passed out and keep trying. Some people take longer than others."

Todd straightened in the chair. "What exactly do you do when you consider yourself to be astral projecting? What do you teach your students?" His tone indicated real curiosity.

Luke turned to Todd with a smile of recognition. "I exteriorize a portion of my astral substance then send my consciousness into it. Those two aspects of myself go traveling in the astral world while my physical body remains behind. That's what I teach my students to do."

"What does the exteriorized substance look like?"

"It's milky and bluish. It's pliable and can be molded into a likeness of a human body."

"Interesting." Todd rose and moved to Luke, shaking his hand. "Since energy becomes mass at speeds greater than that of light, we can potentially create forms at will. Thus, at least theoretically, bi-location could result. A person could be in two places at once."

"It's not theoretical. I can teach you if you want to learn."

"I'm working on a scientific model."

"Indeed!"

Stephanie coughed in an artificial sounding way. "We need to get started because we only have the viewing room for an hour. Sit back but don't relax too much. If anyone actually falls asleep during the sign-off screening, we know the show's a dud and won't air it at all."

Everyone chuckled and seemed to relax, as Angela did. Odd the way Luke and Todd had immediately struck up a meaningful conversation. They acted friendlier toward each other than the moment provoked, as if they knew each other and felt comfortable together.

Angela settled into the chair next to Todd, and Luke lay back in the one between her and Stephanie. As Stephanie aimed the remote, Luke leaned toward Angela and mumbled something like. "It's him. All three."

The room lights went dark. Angela didn't have a chance to ask him what he meant. The viewing wall glowed with deep blue light. From its center a tiny white dot began to expand, quivering to the strains of violins. The blue dissolved as the white grew into a snowy mass of star stuff and the music built to a crescendo.

As the music faded, Angela's voice began the narration. "On May 25 Halley's Comet streaked across Earth's sky, visible without a telescope for the first time in seventy-six years. Twenty five days from now it will depart for another seventy-six years. A rare, once-in-a-lifetime event for humankind to witness." Her voice pleased Angela, more contralto than when she heard it inside her head, knowledgeable and calm. She felt proud of the documentary and wondered how the others would perceive it, especially Todd.

At the end of thirty minutes, the screen went dark, and the room lights came up. Kline sat up and folded his arms. He looked angry.

Luke patted Angela's arm. "Good work, dear girl. I liked it."

"That was fine," Todd said. "Just fine. Congratulations, Angela."

"Thank you all."

With a look of satisfaction, Stephanie took out a clipboard and handed it to Todd. He signed his name and she offered it to Kline. Everyone glanced at him.

"Forget it." Kline spoke stridently. "I'm not going to sign off. That was a piece of trash."

His rude tone annoyed Angela. She would willingly concede the film wasn't the most profound piece she'd ever done, but it worked reasonably well. Even Campbell liked it. How dared this clown call it trash!

"As you wish, Mr. Kline." Stephanie assumed a cocky lawyer posture. "Your agreement isn't required by law. If you don't sign off, the station can still air it as a news story. If you do sign off, it can be aired as a repeating documentary and get you lots more publicity for the planetarium."

"Not good enough." Kline hauled his heft out of the chair and headed toward the door.

"What do you see as a problem, Mr. Kline?" Angela would address his concerns if they were only cosmetic and not substantive. It would be much better to have it air many times than only once although she didn't intend to lower her professional standards.

"Why, the whole film is far too slanted toward the comet and toward Dr. Williams and his career and thoughts. The planetarium barely got two minutes of air time and we paid for the whole event."

Todd rubbed his temples. "What do you propose, sir?"

"Maybe I could add two or three minutes of footage," Angela said. "I'll be happy to do some additional editing. I'll have to get my boss's permission to do so, but I'll ask him. Would that help?"

"I'll just talk to Campbell myself." The sliding door opened, and Kline barged through it.

All four gave each other worried looks that relaxed immediately at the swoosh of the closing door. Then they broke out in laughter.

Angela wasn't worried any more. "Campbell will eat poor Mr. Kline for dinner."

Taking Luke by the arm, Stephanie dropped her cockiness and looked more feminine. "Speaking of dinner, may I offer you some? I'd like to repay you in some small way for the many insights you've given me in your workshop and in your books." She gazed at him with a look bordering on reverence.

"That would be very nice, but I have to fly my niece home tonight. Let's do it another time." Luke looked as if he truly regretted his refusal.

"May I relieve you of that obligation?" Todd sounded sincere, no teasing in his manner. "I'd be honored to escort Angela home." He stepped close to her, laid his hand lightly on her shoulder, and smiled down at her. "You don't mind, do you?"

The warmth of him, so natural, excited Angela. More than anything she wanted Todd to take her home. She might never have another chance to be alone with him. On the other hand, Luke's trying to act like a young man again worried her. What could he be thinking, going out to dinner with a woman fifty or more years his junior? Such behavior constituted more evidence of his declining mental abilities. He'd never been irresponsible about women before, but maybe Angela should go with him. Not a chance!

"That would be fine. Enjoy your dinner." Angela said to their backs as Luke and Stephanie went through the doors.

Todd held out an arm in the same grand gesture he'd used in the hologram when he sent her flowers. "Your pleasure, my lady," His voice rang with cheerful mockery.

This might be her chance to show him she was a viable option to Melanie Vanderson, hooker slash socialite. Angela resolved not to mention anything about the past life memory or Granddad's ideas. She wanted to get to know Todd Williams, the present life man himself. The only one of all the incarnations in the flesh.

Nine

Once a Lover

The next morning, weary but resolved, Luke flew his plane to Melanie's penthouse in Los Angeles. He bribed the concierge to let him in and knocked at her door.

He had not enjoyed his evening with Stephanie, the red-headed lawyer, nearly so much as her charming personality warranted. Going with her had seemed fortuitous last night because it allowed Angela and Todd to spend time together, something Luke hoped to encourage.

Under ordinary circumstances he might have tried to get to know the lawyer better. He found her an industrious student and a desirable woman. If he were twenty years younger, she might have tempted him. Instead he had bid her an early farewell and gone home to a restless night.

Angela's speculation about reincarnation on top of Melanie's appearance at the roundedness event had been a one-two punch for Luke. Todd Williams's handshake delivered the knockout jolt.

In Todd, Luke had recognized the soul of the man betrothed to his mother in the 1980s as another companion soul. Todd's blue eyes looked more than familiar. In the young man of 2061, Luke recognized the loving wisdom of a father many times over.

Luke understood his mother's words, the original Angela's whispered prophecy:

We're coming back. All three of us are coming back.

She had returned as his granddaughter and she had brought her fiancé and Luke's first wife back as Todd and

99

Melanie. With that knowledge came renewed worry. Angela had not believed that Kegan presented a danger to them. Maybe Todd and Melanie wouldn't either.

In truth Luke understood why they might not believe him. His warnings probably came across as ramblings from a rattled old man. He would protect them all regardless of whether they believed him or not. At least he intended to try.

Luke vowed to remain alert to any sign, either physical or psychic, that Kegan intended harm. At the time of Euphoria's death they had exchanged barbs of supercharged astral energy. Luke's power in the astral had subdued Kegan, but who knew how powerful the asshole had become in the intervening years?

Why was it taking Melanie so long to answer the door? Luke rang the bell repeatedly, his concern mounting.

Finally, a muffled female voice yelled from within. "Okay, hold on a minute."

At least she was still alive.

Melanie opened the door with no click or command or tumbler unbarring sounds from within. She leaned against the frame and yawned. Wrapped in a yellow robe, she glanced down at Luke. With rumpled hair about her face, she looked like an overgrown child. "Why, Mr. Brock. Hello." The robe fell open, revealing bare flesh, as she placed her fingers beneath her chin. "*Namaste*, I mean."

"May I come in, Ms. Vanderson?"

"Sure. I mean, please do. Have a seat."

Embarrassed for both of them, Luke pulled her robe lapels together. This woman might need protection from herself as well as from Kegan. Everything about her presented problems.

Luke noted the red carpet and black and white tile bar, colors his first wife had loved and used for interior decoration. He sat on the sofa. "You know you really should keep your door locked at night."

"That's not necessary. The concierge is very strict."

"How do you think I got in? You never know who might try to gain entry. You're a beautiful woman, and I'm sure you have valuables. You could be a target."

"You think I'm beautiful?"

"You know that you are. You don't need me to tell you, but that's not why I'm here."

"Well, then, why are you?" Melanie buttoned the robe and smoothed her hair back with little impact on its disarray then sat beside Luke, their legs touching.

To keep a polite distance between them, Luke edged over to the arm of the couch. "During our phone conversation, I sensed that you didn't believe me when I said Dr. Kegan presented a threat."

"Oh, you mean the gentleman who sat beside me at the roundedness event?" Melanie raised an eyebrow with an exaggerated sense of confusion, a poor job of pretending ignorance.

"I think it's a mistake for you to see him…socially. He's a dangerous man."

"I'll keep that in mind. If I ever see him again, that is." A look crossed Melanie's face that showed she'd become enthralled with Luke. "How do you know this? Did you have a psychic intuition about me?"

"Maybe you could call it that."

"Oh, tell me about it. Please."

Luke wondered how much to confide in her. She didn't seem too bound by truthfulness, considering she was denying her affair with Kegan. Maybe she didn't want Luke to know because he might think less of her. Luke wasn't certain he wanted to dwell on the chaos she had brought to their previous lifetimes together and how deeply they were bound to each other. She seemed enamored of him. That could definitely lead to no good. He resisted an impulse to take her hand.

"I assume you believe in reincarnation, Ms. Vanderson."

"Call me Melanie, please." Her face bore an expression of expectancy. Like a kid about to be read a story, she gazed at him.

Her nearness disconcerted Luke. He wanted to cross his arms but he'd appear too defensive if he did. To give himself energy and composure, he rubbed the inside of his wrists together, stimulating the acupuncture points. The technique worked immediately and he felt relaxed. This girl needed his maturity and wisdom, as well as his protection, whether she realized the fact or not.

"Okay, Melanie, here it is. Do you know that you look a great deal like my first wife who died many years ago? She was a few inches shorter, but you both have the same black hair and eyes, the same...uh...figure, the same... I can't express it any other way. You look exactly like her."

"You've lost me here. Why is this important?"

"I believe you are the reincarnation of my first wife."

"You do? Wow! That's exciting."

"Do you remember any previous lives?"

Melanie shook her head, sorrowfully. "I've tried, but *nada*."

"Do you think people live multiple lives anyway?"

"I believe it because you say it's so. You're my guru."

"And I also believe we were together in another time, a couple of hundred years ago. Dr. Kegan was with us too. I remember—even if you don't—what evil he is capable of and beseech you to be on your guard."

Melanie scooted toward Luke and grabbed his hand. The robe fell open, revealing her breasts and lovely, long legs. "Where did we live then? What was I like? Were we married?"

"I'll leave that for you to discover. One of these days you'll remember on your own. I've got faith in you."

Melanie had died young in several incarnations. Perhaps that accounted for her immature reactions. She needed time to develop spiritually, and Luke intended to help her. He remembered his mother's assertion many years ago that Luke owed his first wife a debt from a previous life where he had misused her. Doubtless his mother had been right. He felt absolutely certain that Melinda lived again as Melanie and he would repay the debt. He intended to arrive at the end of this lifetime with a clear karmic slate.

Luke had to guard against succumbing to her allure. He stood up, glad that his knees popped. Maybe she'd realize how old he was.

"What was I like in bed then?" Melanie sprang up, grabbed his arms, and brought them around her waist, on bare skin beneath the robe. "Did I feel this good?" She cupped his face in her hands, and her tongue flicked inside his mouth.

Surprised, Luke backed away, unconsciously extending his hands to ward her off. Melanie smirked as she laid his hands on her breasts. "Admit it. You came here because you want me." Her voice took on a mocking tone. "Saying we were married in a past life. Kegan is trying to kill me, and you'll save me. I've never heard such an outrageous line, and believe me I've heard some."

"I'm telling you the truth." Luke extracted his hands from her grip. "Someday you'll realize that. Good day, Ms. Vanderson." Turning, he strode to the door as fast as possible without appearing to run. This had not gone well at all.

With a wicked laugh, she called, "Watch out. Somebody from your past life might kill you."

Obviously, Melanie had been playing him with her innocent routine. He had never even imagined that she would expect sexual attentions. Maybe he really was getting old. He dismissed her words as an idle tease to mask her embarrassment at his rejection.

Luke felt certain that anyone who had married him twice wouldn't want harm to come to him.

Just as Kegan knocked on Melanie's front door, she opened it. "There you are, darling. You're late. Now, hurry." Carrying a martini glass, she crossed the red carpet barefoot, her olive skin visible beneath the tissue-paper thin white negligee. "Fix yourself a drink and come in the bedroom. There's something I want you to see."

"Gladly. What's up?" Kegan thought he probably would be up himself soon. This woman kept him on an edge of sexual excitement. What a find she was.

"Todd called a few minutes ago." Melanie went through the open bedroom door.

Kegan fixed a drink and followed her, removing his tie. They'd had sex in the living room last time, so he'd not seen the bedroom.

Its décor confirmed his fears. The only modern feature in the room, the wall TV, illuminated a bed with a twentieth-century style headboard, more junk than antique. Ugly black and white checked sheets and pillows lay scattered about the huge bed. He wondered where she could have purchased such tasteless items but supposed Daddy's money could reproduce anything. Worst of all, rows of disgustingly cute stuffed bears in various colors lined the headboard, the bureau, and corner shelves.

Sitting on the bed, Melanie switched the channel, and a long shot of the planetarium filled the wall. "It's starting. Sit down."

"What is?" When Kegan sat, the bed sloshed beneath him. A waterbed? He should have guessed. He held his posture rigid in an attitude of meditation. He didn't want to get seasick.

"The program about the Halley's Comet exhibit. Todd said it was a one-shot deal and that I had to watch it tonight because it wouldn't run again."

"That's hard to believe. Every show runs scores of times. TV has gotten so boring I never watch it. If it weren't for the news—"

"Shhhh. This is the news."

Angela Brock's abrasive voice rose above the music.

That bitch, Kegan thought, as he slugged down the scotch. He enjoyed the burn from his throat into his belly.

When he saw Angela's image on the screen, he imagined her lying on a funeral pyre. How he would enjoy watching her go up in flames. He could almost smell the acrid odor of scorched flesh. The image of Todd Williams, cocky and cool, enraged Kegan even more. The two of them had stood in his way for the last time.

The fact that they could reincarnate, even though he killed them, galled him, but there was nothing he could do about that. He would decide when they lived and when they died, at least in this lifetime. He had that power, and they would know it. Then what would become of him in his next incarnation?

Was he trapped psychologically along with his victims? Kegan feared he could do nothing but kill them, over and over again, down through the centuries. It was his destiny. His doom. How he had protested his grandmother's declarations of his fate as a youth. He had not wanted to admit his being born to do murder.

His destiny's caul hung over his soul just as the membrane had hung over his eyes at birth. The gift of second sight carried a great burden.

Kegan closed his eyes in search of solace. His mind shut out the sounds and flickering light of the TV. As his British master teacher had taught him to do, Kegan breathed deeply and sank into himself to the place where he generated his self-control and the psychic power to manipulate physical reality.

"Dr. Bob, oh, Kegan darling!" Melanie's voice came to him as if from afar. With great effort he opened his eyes to find her standing over him, freshly filled drink glasses in her hands, and a teasing grin on her face. "You've not heard a word I said, have you?"

"Guilty, as charged. Just tired, I guess." Kegan took a glass from her, unwilling to confide any weakness in his will. "But I'm listening now."

"I thought the documentary was fine. It showed the planetarium off well. Todd hogged the spotlight more than I think he should have, but he was sort of the star, so that's understandable. I looked too matronly in my green dress, didn't you think? That's why I threw it out." She sat against the headboard, propped up by pillows.

Amused by the idea of Melanie's looking matronly, Kegan eased up with her, trying not to slosh the bed or the drink. He slipped one arm around her. "You looked fine. You always do." He held up his glass in a toast. "All the fellows say so."

"Oh, speaking of the fellows, guess who tried to date me." Her voice cracked. Her bright laughter almost kept her from spilling out her words. "Luke Brock, that old fogy. Can you imagine him and me...you know...I told him no, of course." She gulped the martini.

"Where did you see him?"

"Why he came to the door. Got around security somehow."

"He was here? What the hell did he want?"

"A date...duh...that's what I just said."

"Stay away from him." He hoped his stern voice would persuade her.

"Do I have a sign on me that says Kegan's property? I'll do exactly as I please. If I want to see him, I will. Or anyone else for that matter."

"Not that old has-been psychic." The sight of Luke tupping Melanie even in imagination disgusted Kegan. "His powers are shot to hell."

"Why, I think you're jealous. Are you jealous?"

Melanie was enjoying his discomfort far too much. Better she think it jealousy than what it really was, barely controlled fury.

"Stick with me, baby. And here's why you should." Kegan gazed at half a dozen teddy bears arranged on a corner shelf near the ceiling. "Pick one of those."

"What?"

"Which one do you like best?"

Her face expressed confused fascination. "The green one, Lucky Bear."

"Watch a master, my dear." Kegan visualized a tiny pellet of his astral substance arising from his solar plexus. It hovered momentarily before him then shot up on a diagonal line to the shelf. The green Care Bear toppled off the shelf and plummeted to the floor.

"What the hell?" Melanie set her glass on the bedside table and scrambled over to the stuffed animal.

Just as she reached for it, Kegan said, "Don't touch it. Stand back."

Wild-eyed, Melanie stared at the Care Bear and backed up against the wall.

By an act of Kegan's will, the green bear flew up, lodged on the shelf, and fell against its pink and orange mates.

For a long moment Melanie remained still, her hand pressed against her abdomen, then she sighed and perhaps whispered something Kegan could not hear. He felt proud of how well he had impressed her. At least she knew now where the power lay.

In silence, she padded across the carpet, reached up and adjusted the bear, then left the room. He slipped out of his clothes, ready to change the subject.

Momentarily she returned, an open fifth of gin in her hand. "How in hell did you do that?"

"Trade secret."

"What trade? Don't be glib, Bob, tell me. Who taught you that?"

"Actually, I was born with the power, but I've had a couple of teachers along the way. My grandmother was a witch herself with considerable power. Then later, in England, I joined Aurum Solis. That's where I found my true spiritual teacher, the one who taught me how to control my powers and manipulate matter." Kegan intentionally left out his brief, unhappy venture into Islam. It was none of her business, none of anyone's business.

"What else can you do?"

Kegan touched himself, and his voice became gruff. "I think you know." He felt awkward teasing about sex, but she had seemed to respond to it. When in America, do as the Americans do.

This time Melanie ignored the sexual allusion. She tipped up the fifth and drank like another person would swallow water. "You know what I mean. What else?"

"Astral travel."

"You can do that too?" Melanie's shoulders slumped. "I took two classes in that, but I never had any luck. I think I'm a psychic boob."

"I don't think so. Not that kind." Kegan caressed her breast, but she seemed not to notice the pun. He wanted to change the mood before she drank herself into a stupor and was no good to him at all.

"Do you suppose you could teach me to move objects with my mind?"

"I don't know. I'll try." Kegan seriously doubted she had any psychic ability. "Focus on a Care Bear up there." He pointed to the shelf and described the process he used to formulate astral substance.

"Okay, the orange one." Melanie focused her attention on the stuffed animal, but it did not budge. She tried again and failed, took another drink, and tried many times more. Tears stood in her eyes. "Damn it. I'll do this or know the reason why..." She slurred her words.

"You can do it. Try one more time." Annoyed with her and wishing he'd stayed at the office, Kegan focused on the orange bear and knocked it to the floor. "You did it! Good work, Melanie. Good work." Fortunately his lie sounded convincing.

A look of surprised pleasure crossed Melanie's face. "I did it. Thank you for showing me. You are my guru, my spiritual master." Her kiss was wet, and her breath smelled sour.

"Will you do something for me?"

"Anything you say, master."

"Call Todd and tell him how you enjoyed the show on TV. And make a date for tomorrow, if you can."

"Why do I want to do that? I forgot." She giggled.

"Cover, you know." Kegan settled back with his arm around her.

"Oh, yes, cover." Melanie reached for the holophone.

"Don't forget to turn off the video capability."

Melanie looked confused.

"So he won't see you naked in bed with me!"

"Right." She snickered as she pressed off the video then spoke to the phone, "Todd."

Kegan worried that she couldn't pull off the deception.

After a brief ring, Todd answered.

"Darling, the documentary was brilliant. Didn't you think so?"

"I did. Glad you liked it." Todd sounded polite but distant.

"I'd really like to treat you, as a thank you for doing the planetarium thing. I know you weren't that keen on the whole business, but you did it for me, and I appreciate it. Can we have dinner tomorrow?" She ran her words together.

"That's thoughtful of you, but I'm going to be busy."

"Then when?"

"I think maybe we should take some time off from each other. Maybe for a few weeks."

Melanie paused for a long time. Her face worked as if it took a great effort to control herself. Kegan wondered if she were about to cry.

Kegan wondered what had changed in Todd's life to turn his interest away from Melanie. It would have to be something stellar. Or somebody rather.

"If that's what you want, Todd." Her voice sounded soft and feminine. "Good bye for now," Melanie whispered and clicked off the phone. "Goddamn it." She sprang out of the bed and paced at the foot of it. "The nerve of that son of a bitch! When do you want to get rid of him? The sooner the better."

"You may be psychic, after all. You read my mind." Kegan climbed out of the shivering bed, aroused for the first time. He grabbed her ass and pressed against her. "You are so hot. I want you now."

Her kiss bit into him, and he dragged her down to the floor.

Much later, Melanie fell asleep, sprawled on the bed beside Kegan. Although her bite marks still stung, Kegan felt a kind of satisfaction from the sex act that was new to him. Pleasure and pain had slid into each other, so that he could not tell which was which. Melanie's ability to combine female submission with male dominance thrilled Kegan. Her past lives as a male added to her erotic appeal. Fascinating.

Kegan had much yet to learn about Melanie. Even though he had not confided his ultimate goal of killing his enemies, she had intuited something of his agenda. Maybe she wasn't quite the fool she appeared sometimes. For that he felt relieved. Perhaps she would be helpful to his plans, after all. He had thought it would be easy to track Todd Williams. Something had changed if the scum didn't want to see Melanie any more.

Once he relaxed into a meditative pose, Kegan formed an astral sheath that looked like his own naked body. His consciousness slipped into the sheath. As he floated up to the ceiling, the air became faintly blue, and his eyes adjusted to the astral world. Perhaps he could manage to take Melanie for an astral stroll. He stretched out a hand to her, but he couldn't rouse her. He floated through the closed window and willed himself to find Angela Brock. He needed to keep track of his enemies so he could formulate a plan for doing away with them, one that would not jeopardize his career or throw his integrity into doubt.

In a moment he found himself floating above Angela's condominium in Anthem. He recognized it from a reconnaissance trip he'd made a few days earlier. It amused him to recall how fearful he had made her feel. Hoping to do so again, he floated down through the ceiling.

Wrapped in an afghan, Angela lay curled up on a couch asleep. Kegan looked around for that slug of a grandfather of hers, but she appeared to be alone. He offered his hand on the chance that he could entice her into astral travel, but she didn't respond. She did not seem aware of him at all. It was good to know how soundly she slept. He could drop in on her anytime on the astral level and lower her energy as he had done to Luke's wife Euphoria before her death.

Kegan glanced around to familiarize himself with Angela's home. In case he got inside while in his body, he wanted to know his way around. He noticed a basket of flowers sitting on the coffee table. A hologram of Todd Williams stood above it. Now Kegan knew why the bastard had thrown Melanie over. He was after this piece of ass. That knowledge might prove useful soon.

Ten

Dicey Encounters

Even though the comet documentary received good reviews the next day, Angela's boss growled about having to listen to complaints from the planetarium administrator. She kept busy, updating her computer files, skimming news bytes for possible leads to a story that could get her back into his good graces, and generally staying out of his way. Nothing promising occurred to her on the childless couple idea. Those activities left Angela restless and concerned about her career, but unwilling to give up. She would find a way to return to her anchor slot or get a better position. She had to trust that all would work out.

The whole business about Todd and the origin of her dreams remained uncertain. Some moments she felt certain she had lived before and had brought the consciousness of another lifetime into this one. Whether she had lived as one of her own ancestors, genetic memory might be the more likely hypothesis. She didn't know how prescient such memories could be.

That Todd had a picture of a Cessna in his office seemed significant but might be a coincidence and not a telling one at that. No explanation satisfied her, so she decided to keep her appointment with the counselor at the Psi Therapy Clinic.

At four in the afternoon, Angela rode the elevator down to the parking garage level. As soon as the doors slid open, she felt a strong impulse to avoid her car. It had been running well when she drove in to work. Silly as it seemed and with no notion of why, she hit the lobby level button, rode up, and hailed a taxi, which took her the several blocks to the Clinic building.

Once Angela entered the Dream Analysis office, the counselor exhibited her previous warmth, and Angela felt glad she'd come. She looked forward to talking through some of her feelings and settled onto the futon.

Janice sat in a chair beside her. "The last time you were here, we concluded your nightmares were metaphorical, dying to your old self, so to speak."

"Not even a possibility that's true." Angela gave a wry laugh. "A lot has happened that might make you change your diagnosis. Could you bring up the tape you made of my recall?"

Deep crow's feet creased Janice's face as she pressed a button on her console. She looked perplexed or worried or both. The lights went out, and Angela's dream images spread on the wall, side by side.

"Look at that one." Angela pointed to the image of herself in the old clothes, holding a photograph. "I met that man last weekend. The one in the photograph. When he shook my hand, I had a vision of some kind. I was transported back in time to when he and I made a pact to meet again."

"Ah ha. We'd not considered prophecy." Janice sounded amazed. "Do you then have a pattern of precognitive experiences in your life?"

"From time to time I've had intuitions or impulses while I was awake that panned out. I've never dreamed the future, though, if that's what you mean, and it scares me to think this might be a dream of the future."

"What are you afraid of?"

"You're kidding, of course. Of seeing someone die in a plane crash? That would be horrible!"

"Oh, certainly, I was thinking more of the wonderful quality of the gift for prophecy, not of the particular dynamics of this case." Janice's motherly smile softened the coldness of her reply. Not exactly an apology but better than nothing.

Frustrated that she wasn't conveying her excitement to the counselor, Angela tried a different approach. "What would you say is the time period here?" She pointed to the clothing her image wore.

Janice shrugged. "1970s or 80s."

Determined to lay the ideas out, Angela plunged ahead. "One of my ancestors, my great grandmother, was psychic. She had a vision of her fiancé's death in a plane crash. Then he died in one. The year was 1986."

A shiver ran through Angela, a shadow of the great sorrow her great-grandmother must have endured, a grief that nothing could quell, not even time.

"So you think genetic memory accounts for your dreams?"

"I don't know the answer. Either that or reincarnation. One thing I do know is that the man is the same. He looks just like the image in my dreams."

Janice peered again at the wavy image on the wall. "Who is he? He looks very familiar."

"Todd Williams."

"The astrophysicist?"

Hopefully, Angela had engaged the counselor's interest if not enthusiasm. "The same. Remember you suggested to me that the nightmares would end when I found a man?"

Rising, Janice strolled along the wall, clicking a fingernail on a tooth and studying the images. "And you've had no reoccurrence of the dream since you met him?"

"No, but I have seen the living, breathing man since." Angela remembered how Todd's flying her home thrilled her. "We talked easily together. I felt curious about the details of his personal life, but they really didn't matter. What mattered was the profound regard I felt for him, like no emotion I've ever experienced. I already love him and will continue to do so, no matter whether a relationship develops between us or not." Maybe she had gone overboard, but if Angela couldn't explain her emotions to her counselor, then why continue the appointment?

"You liked Dr. Williams, of course. I can't imagine that you wouldn't. He's quite charming. I've seen him on TV."

"He's a very special man." Angela felt a flush rising along her throat. She supposed she must learn to deal with embarrassment as a response to mention of Todd's name. "So what do you think? Reincarnation? Genetic memory?"

"Maybe neither. It's too soon to tell. I think the psychological dynamics are quite complicated, and I would like to consult on your case." Janice sat at her console and pressed a button. "Doctor, could you come in and meet our patient?"

Why didn't Janice accept Angela's theory of events? "You think I'm worse off? I thought I was cured. Or maybe in love."

"It can't hurt to be cautious. There's also a possibility that your subconscious mind created the whole scenario as a way to gain access to a person of high station."

"High station?" Angela murmured. Janice thought Angela was star struck?

The notion had never crossed Angela's mind. Neither had she ever thought herself of lower station or class. She had a good bit of fame herself. Probably every adult in Greater Hispania knew her by face if not by name. At least they did before Campbell benched her.

Maybe the populace didn't know her at all. Angela recalled the night she went to the Mozart concert with Juan. Everyone had recognized him, but they couldn't remember her name. In point of fact, she seldom got stopped and asked for an autograph while alone.

Yes, Todd made a lot of money, but her emotional reaction to him had nothing to do with that. Did it? She'd not dwelt on anything to do with Todd's life at a conscious level prior to meeting him, but perhaps something transpired beneath the surface. Had she wanted a man so much that she concocted the vision? Or could the reason have been a desperate effort to save her job?

If Janice had interpreted correctly, Angela might have cause to distrust her subconscious mind even more. The whole thing just seemed to get murkier.

A tap on the door announced the entry of the doctor into the room. "Hello, Ms. Brock. I'm Dr. Kegan. It's very nice to meet you."

In a white coat over a dark silk suit, Dr. Kegan appeared very professional, a dignified sort of man. He was near the same age as Angela's own father, and very intelligent looking with high cheek bones, clear eyes, and graying hair. He shook her hand then sat across from her in the chair Janice had vacated. "Have the dreams stopped then?"

Angela nodded.

"The dreams were prophetic," Janice said. "At least to the extent that they signaled an occasion to meet someone famous." Her tone had become more formal, less warm.

Dr. Kegan addressed Angela. "What do you think accounts for your experience?"

"I don't know." Angela feared the possibility that she had fabricated the whole experience out of shameful need. "Is there any way we can know for sure?"

"There are some useful techniques that may enlighten us. I'll need to review your file. Then Janice and I will make a recommendation for a counseling intensive or a mind infusion."

"Not surgery." Angela felt uncomfortable. She'd come in thinking she was all right. Now she didn't know what to think.

"Surgery is not indicated by the present circumstances," Dr. Kegan said, "but we won't rule it out as a possibility in the future."

"I shall make a follow-up appointment." Janice smiled reassuringly then consulted her computer monitor. "How will next Tuesday do? The fourteenth?"

Her granddad's birthday and Angela would be in here having her subconscious mind corrected instead of celebrating? She'd have to arrive late for the party and might miss it completely? That would never do.

Angela agreed to return on the following Friday. She thanked them and headed for the door.

Dr Kegan called after her. "Don't worry, my dear. We'll find a way to make you better."

His kind voice and smile didn't hearten Angela. She felt depressed at the possibility that she might need psychiatric treatment. Maybe she took after her grandfather in more ways than she realized. It seemed probable that he had some mental problems himself, considering this nice doctor was the same one Granddad swore was out to kill Angela.

During the return taxi ride, Angela felt dumb for not driving her car. How gullible of her to follow aimless impulses that cost her time and money?

Outside the TV station a police car sat with engine idling. Angela walked into the underground tunnel. In the parking garage two policemen engaged in conversation with Bernice, the security guard.

"There she is, officer." Bernice pointed toward Angela.

"What's happened? Is someone hurt?"

One of the policemen asked for Angela's identification. When she turned on her holophone and flashed the identity chip, she saw that she'd missed two calls while in the counselor's office. One from the police and one from her grandfather.

"It's your car, ma'am. Somebody set off a bomb in it."

The other policeman held a tiny metal device in a gloved hand. "Actually, someone set a timer. Looks like they expected you to be in your car at..." He glanced at the device. "4:15. That's when it went off."

117

"I would've been if..." Angela decided she'd not confide her premonition just now. "I took a taxi to my appointment."

Stunned, she hurried past many cars, bikes, and planes. One of the policemen followed her along with Bernice, who spoke on her holophone. They all rounded a corner and arrived at Angela's parking space.

There in her stall sat the singed and hollow shell of her beautiful Bimi, the object of a fire bomb. The tiles on the floor beneath were scorched. Fortunately the bomb had failed to damage any of the nearby vehicles.

Angela told the police where she'd been for her appointment and who the people were that she worked with in the building. "Who would have done such a thing?"

"Maybe a terrorist." Bernice appeared to enjoy herself. No doubt a relief from the boredom of the life of a security guard. "I've notified Mr. Campbell that you're here. He should arrive any minute."

"Did anyone else know you were going to that appointment?" the policeman asked.

"Campbell, my boss. Well, actually I told his secretary."

At the beginning of the day Angela had held the optimistic thought that something felicitous would happen. Was there any way the bombing of her Bimi could be interpreted as such? She hadn't thought she had any enemies in her personal life.

"We'll do a full investigation." The policeman frowned. "Could you call your husband or your brother, Ms. Brock? Get somebody to pick you up?"

"I don't know who I would call." The last thing in the world Angela intended to do was alert her grandfather to this situation. He might implicate Dr. Kegan. The fact that the doctor and Janice had been with Angela at the time of the firebombing spoke to their innocence. Who would set themselves up in such an obvious way? Besides, Luke might appear more rattled than necessary under the circumstances, and she wished to protect him from public embarrassment.

"Is there some place you can go?" the policeman asked. "For a few days while we do the investigation? Not your home. Just to be safe? We've got to assume someone wants to harm you."

"You can come stay at my apartment, if you want to." Bernice nodded enthusiastically.

"It's very nice of you to offer." Angela squeezed Bernice's arm. "Thank you but I don't want to risk endangering you. Besides, there's a story here. I'll be damned if I'll let somebody else break it. I'm the one who lost my car. I'm not leaving town."

The elevator doors opened, and Campbell rushed out. "Angela, are you all right?"

"Sure, boss. Thanks for asking."

"Mr. Campbell." The policeman nodded. "We've suggested to Ms. Brock that she go into seclusion, at least for a few days."

"Looks like we've got a story here that only I can deliver to you."

Campbell laid his pudgy hands on Angela's shoulders. "That's a story I want to see, but it won't happen if you're dead."

The realization settled on Angela that someone might actually have tried to kill her, but she couldn't believe it. Why had the culprit struck only her car? She might have survived had she been in it when the bomb went off. The damage didn't look that bad. She'd have to check out that detail with a forensics expert.

Maybe someone tried to scare her away. Surely not Juan. Maybe that mouse of a replacement, Hannah, the one temporarily in Angela's anchor chair? "Nope, sorry. I'm not going."

Offering his sternest frown, Campbell barked, "You can have the scoop, but you'll have to do the investigation from somewhere else. I'll assign a liaison here to stay in touch."

"That's really not necessary." Angela had difficulty with the notion that anyone would try to harm her. She couldn't recall ever mistreating anyone in all her life.

"You need to get out of town." The policeman looked exasperated. "It's the most prudent course of action. We don't have the staff available for a bodyguard."

"You've got to go, Angela." Campbell folded his arms over his belly.

"What about my job?"

"It will be here waiting for you, but only if you follow the policeman's advice."

"Okay. I'll go. It would probably be better if I went to…Should I tell anyone where I'm going?" Angela had an overwhelming urge to go to her parents' home, to feel the safety of their love and support. To safety, she hoped. To Todd, she wished.

Maybe the bombing was a felicitous event in more than one way.

"We'll take you where you need to go, ma'am." The policeman spoke into the receiver he wore on his head and called a squad plane.

Nervous but determined to discover the culprit, Angela set off with the police pilot on her way to her parents' house in Los Angeles.

At the same time Luke headed down the mountain in his plane. He'd had a most unusual experience, something akin to the visions his mother used to have.

A short while before he had been reading a delightful new poetry book and eating a favorite dinner of crab cakes at home in Sedona. He had stopped mid-bite, struck by a vivid scene that filled his mind. A pretty little car exploded, a static image that refused to leave his imagination.

Luke had recognized the car instantly. Angela's Bimi. He feared she was in danger. His attempts to call her failed. She'd turned off her damned holophone again. He wrapped the crab cakes in a napkin, grabbed a glass of milk, and finished eating as he flew toward Phoenix.

As a young man, he had become suspicious of his mother's visions, in part because his first wife feared them. For his own part, Luke had considered them an impediment to the smooth conduct of his life, they rained on his parade, so to speak. Later when he married Euphoria, he gained true respect for his mother's abilities, many of which his second wife shared. Euphoria had been best at psychic healing and communicating with the deceased. His mother at visions and premonitions.

For what reason Luke didn't understand, his own psychic abilities never had lain in the area of visions or clairvoyance, perhaps because of his early doubts but probably because people had different gifts by nature. He had easily learned to recall past lives and to trust the feelings they provoked whether he remembered every detail or not. As he became proficient in meditation, he learned to communicate with his departed loved ones and with his guide Emmons. Luke also excelled at astral projection and, the greatest blessing of all, he'd become a skilled teacher of all of the techniques, whether he could demonstrate them himself or not.

Glad for his vision of Angela's car, Luke never questioned its validity or the guilty party involved. He arrived in Phoenix and flew straight to the TV station parking garage where he knew Angela's car would have been parked.

A rather officious but engaging security guard recognized Luke from his bus ads for roundedness events. She assured him that Angela was physically unhurt as she had not been in the car. The police had flown her to an undisclosed location for her personal safety. The security guard didn't consider it appropriate to tell Luke his granddaughter's whereabouts. He understood her reticence, thanked her, and left, certain he could find Angela later. Right now Luke had more urgent business before him.

After parking his plane on top of the building which housed the Psi Therapy Clinic, he searched the kiosk for Kegan's name and took the elevator down to the seventh floor. Luke entered Kegan's office without knocking.

In the semi-darkness, Kegan rose from his desk and walked around in front of it. "What the hell are you doing here?"

"You leave my granddaughter alone."

"I'll treat her however I see fit. I'm the doctor here." Kegan smirked as he held out the lapels of his lab coat.

"Treat her? You? Fat chance." Luke ignored the six-inch height deficit and wagged a finger. "I'm warning you. Don't touch her or any of her possessions, ever again. After I report you to the police, they'll have even more evidence. Don't think you can get away with a thing."

"You're really becoming senile now, old man. I've not done a thing to harm anyone, and that includes Angela."

"How many lifetimes is it going to take for you to learn to take responsibility for your actions? I'm surprised you don't have a priest or imam around to cover for you now."

Kegan reached under the desk momentarily. "You've got a lot of nerve to lecture me on morality. Considering that freak show you run and call spiritual training. All I have to do is say the word to the governor, and she'll shut you down as a charlatan."

What a bizarre, over-the-top threat. Luke had no notion of whether Kegan could make good on it. Luke held his clenched fists behind his back to keep from ramming them where they wanted to go.

"You okay, doc?" came a male voice from the doorway.

Livid, Luke turned to see a stocky security guard wearing a holster.

"My guest was just leaving," Kegan sported a cocky grin. "Would you see him out?"

The security guard grabbed Luke by the elbow. "Want to press charges, doc?"

"Not this time, but if you ever see him back here—"

"Coward." Luke spat at Kegan but feared he was spitting into the wind.

Luke allowed the security guard to escort him to the rooftop and waved good-bye as he took off. The security guard proved he had no sense of humor by not waving back.

Finally, Angela answered his call on her holophone, and Luke confirmed that she was all right and safely home with her folks in Los Angeles. Relieved, he turned his plane toward Sedona.

The comment about reporting to the police had been a bluff that Kegan probably understood. Even in this enlightened time, police only took psychic evidence as corroboration of material evidence. Luke would make a trip to the police station later after they'd had a chance to do their investigation.

In the meantime, Luke needed to get a grip on his perspective. Kegan had feigned innocence and probably always would. He had also failed to use any telekinetic power in Luke's presence today although he displayed some potential at the roundedness event. That might mean he was stronger or weaker than when he had visited Euphoria in the hospital and killed her. What had this old enemy learned about life in the intervening years? Kegan, or Kendall as he had been called in the earlier years of the century, had been the vehicle for Luke to learn a valuable lesson he had forgotten today—he could protect no one, not even himself.

Each soul incarnated to learn lessons, and it was Luke's job to facilitate the learning, not protect them from it. At the moment he doubted his ability to stand aside and let Angela fall into harm's way. Or Todd. Or even Melanie.

Eleven

Always a Lover

Standing alone in his living room, Todd gazed at water droplets as they plopped on the rocks in the fountain. The sound usually comforted him but not today. He waited impatiently for Angela to answer his ring on her holophone and felt a bit guilty about juggling two women. He'd tried to be honest with Melanie and hoped she understood that he needed some distance. Even though they'd been seeing each other for almost a year, they'd never spoken of a committed relationship. At least, he hadn't, but he didn't know what Melanie assumed.

Once he'd decided to call Angela and take the chance that she might go out with him on a real date, he kept remembering her intense way of looking at him, as if he single-handedly set the sun glowing and the planets whirling.

The woman would not stay out of his mind. She was as addictive as cocaine, a substance he knew something about first hand. He'd wasted a year of his life on it when it first became legal and he'd discovered that it eliminated his headaches. Three years out of rehab, he still preferred the migraines, at least until the events of the past few days had given him a new perspective.

Certainly he had the right phone number. Maybe he had chosen a ring she couldn't identify and so didn't answer. *The Marine's Hymn* might be too martial for her. He switched to *Mustang Molly and the Merry Maids*. No more innocuous tune existed. He thought it hilarious because the cleaning ladies traveled around the galaxy in a red Mustang.

When Angela's phone clicked on, Todd did a sweeping bow. "Good morning, my lady."

"Todd, is it you?"

He could see her fumbling to sit up in bed, her hair tousled and pretty above the sheets. Her movements caused the sheets to drop and give Todd a momentary glimpse of boobs, not very large but perfectly round and inviting.

"Oh good heavens." Angela pulled the covers up to her chin. "I didn't expect it to be you."

Who did she expect? None of Todd's business. "Please forgive the intrusion. I didn't mean to..." Damn he wished he could think of something to say to redeem his blunder. Instead he laughed in embarrassment. "Uh...I'll call back later, if that's all right."

"Okay." Angela gave a self-conscious laugh. She sounded small and vulnerable.

When Todd broke the connection, he mentally kicked himself. She probably considered him the rudest bloke in town. He didn't recognize her location. Although he hadn't seen her bedroom when he took her home after the TV screening, he had enough architectural knowledge to realize that her tile-roofed, Spanish style condo didn't lend itself to gables and a brick chimney like the room where she'd been sleeping just now.

Todd wandered around his own living room, unwilling to sit on its ornate upholstered furniture. His decorator had called them pieces. He didn't want to sit on pieces. He wished he had some cozy chairs and couches to relax on and maybe someone cozy for company. Sometimes he wondered what he'd missed by not having a wife and kids.

Melanie's always-on flirtatiousness and flighty disregard for his needs wore him down, like her leaving him at Cicero's to go to her roundedness event. He'd cooked up the story about needing space because he didn't want to tell her that her style annoyed him. That would be too cruel to a woman who was fun sexually. He might someday regret distancing himself, but he wanted to get to know Angela better. He wondered whether he and she might have the potential for a more fulfilling friendship.

Sitting on the fountain's railing, he trailed his fingers in the water and wondered what Angela would be like in bed. Might he ever find out? Would Angela even answer when he called back?

After a few minutes his phone played *Fur Elise,* Angela's ID. He wouldn't have guessed her the Beethoven type, but he didn't know much about her. Yet. He pressed the on button and noticed that she'd shut off the video.

'Hi. What did you want to talk about?" Angela asked.

"Actually I was hoping to wangle an invitation to that...uh...what's the name of that suburb you live in?"

"Anthem, but I'm not there."

"Where are you?

"In L. A."

It pleased Todd to know she was nearby. "Are you visiting someone?"

"Staying with my folks for a few days. They live here." She was making this easy. "Guess you could say I'm hiding out."

Todd laughed even though he didn't understand her remark. "In trouble with the law, are you?"

"Someone firebombed my car, and the police thought I should stay out of sight for a while."

People in the public eye like Angela always had to deal with crackpots, just as Todd did. They might make an even bigger target together. Something about that idea pleased the in-your-face part of his soul. He could afford all the bodyguards they'd ever need. Todd realized he might come off as self-serving, but he asked anyway. "Who would do something like that? A crazy fan? An old boyfriend?"

"I have no idea who did it."

"Do you have police protection?"

"No. Not here, anyway. The Phoenix police flew me over last night."

"Does your father have a weapon in the house?"

Angela's laugh sounded bright and easy. "My folks march for the Department of Peace every year. They would never own a gun."

Somehow that description of her parents didn't surprise Todd. Their daughter seemed a gentle person, gently brought up. That trait made her more appealing. "I intended to invite you out for lunch today, but from what you're telling me you're not safe in public."

"I want to go to lunch with you. Very much."

Todd loved the way she said *very much*. That meant she'd already forgiven him for his earlier foolishness. "You shouldn't go out with me or anyone else. How do you know I'm not the bomber?"

"I just know. You would never hurt me." Angela sounded as if she were speaking to a trusted friend instead of a person she'd only met twice.

Her sincerity touched Todd and made him want to protect her. "I'll be there at noon." He asked for her address and ended the call.

Although Todd had never had a daughter, he'd had a mother and a sister and more than a few women friends. He would stand in the doorway and risk his life before he'd ever let one of them go out with a person he didn't know. He assumed Angela's father felt the same way, despite her protestations. A firebomb, for God's sake? Damned if he knew what perversion could drive a person to do such a thing, especially to someone like Angela.

Todd made arrangements for a private luncheon and for a limousine to pick him up at his front door. While he waited for it to arrive, he phoned Pinkerton's and hired two detectives. At five minutes before noon, the chauffeur pulled into the Brocks' street with Todd and the two detectives inside the plush lounge on wheels.

The two-story Tudor home was a twentieth-century imitation of a sixteenth-century English manor house. Its thatched roof and stonework would have looked out of place except for its location in the Citadel, the old section of the city that had remained untouched by earthquakes over the years. That structural tenacity made the homes highly prized despite their gauche architecture.

What kind of man would buy such a home? Todd found himself very curious about the Brocks.

The chauffeur opened the door and waited by the curb. The two detectives in dress suits and Stetsons took up stations in front and in back of the car, glancing around at rooftops and down alleys.

After a detective signaled the okay, Todd pulled on his corduroy jacket and climbed out of the car. He took the steps two at a time and rang the bell.

Immediately the voice of an older man called from inside. "Are you sure this is the man you know?"

"Yes, Dad. It's all right." Angela opened the door with a big smile for Todd. Her hair fell in waves around her shoulders above the royal blue of a silky, summer gown.

Her father, a tall, angular man with hair as black as hers, stood behind her and gazed at Todd with worried eyes. There was a Hispanic look to Mr. Brock's features. Todd could see no resemblance to Luke at all and wondered what the family connection was, if not father and son.

Todd didn't waste time on pleasantries. He offered his hand. "Mr. Brock. Todd Williams here. I've taken the liberty of hiring two Pinkertons to travel with us. Your daughter will be as safe as if she were in your care."

Her father gave a brisk, sturdy shake and peered outside, nodding at the detectives. "I see them."

"How very thoughtful. I'm Vera Brock." Angela's mother motioned Todd into the hallway.

128

Todd could see where Angela got her short stature and pretty eyes. By contrast, Vera looked well fed, chubby, in fact. She had a genuine smile like her daughter's. Over the mother's shoulder Todd could see into the living room and make out overstuffed couches, a fireplace, and a rocking chair. Angela's parents and her home seemed cozy and entirely lovable at first sight.

"Glad to meet you." Todd shook Vera's hand. "Would the two of you like to come along? I have a reservation at Lu Chan's."

Angela's father appeared about to accept the invitation when her mother said, "Thank you, but Angela has confidence in you, and so we do, too."

"Besides," Angela said with a laugh. "I'm a grown woman and I said I'm going out with you alone." She walked downstairs toward him.

"Shall we then?" Todd held out an arm, which Angela took, and they stepped onto the stoop. The Pinkertons glanced up and down the street then gave an affirmative nod.

Todd couldn't remember having more fun in a long time as he escorted the gorgeous reporter to the limousine. She even wore his favorite color. How lucky could a guy get?

To hear Todd's delighted laugh sent a thrill through Angela. Between times of seeing him she forgot how incredibly handsome and charming he was. She felt glad to be on his arm, despite the fact that a firebomb might have precipitated their serendipitous meeting. She definitely approved of the two well-dressed detectives. Without the hats, they'd looked just like businessmen. Angela felt even safer with them along.

The chauffeur stood by the door of the stretch limo and held his cap against his chest in a quaint way, reminiscent of stagecoach drivers.

Angela stepped inside onto a cinnamon carpet that looked like doeskin. The vehicle's plain black exterior had left her unprepared for the spectacular interior. A peach-colored divan ran out from the door on either side the length of the cabin and circled the ends. On the opposite wall were a long window, a bar, and an entertainment center, all done in polished walnut. Daylight filtered through the sun roof, casting a rosy warmth on everything.

After Angela sank onto one of the velvety divans, Todd eased onto the seat beside her. The two detectives stationed themselves like bookends at the far edges and set their Stetsons on the seat with the same respect, a part of their training no doubt. They stared out opposite windows

"Would you like some champagne?" Todd pressed a button on the entertainment center.

"Sure." Angela hoped she didn't seem uncouth but couldn't resist the desire to touch the carpet. She took off her sandals and rubbed her feet in the downy texture. The carpet felt like doeskin too.

Through the sound system, the tremulous notes of a saxophone played a ballad she thought she recognized, but the title didn't come to her.

"Make yourself at home." Todd grinned and did a double take at her feet. "Oh, I see you already have."

"This is lovely." Angela indicated the whole interior.

"Yeh, maybe I should buy it." Todd rubbed his dimple with a thumb as if seriously thinking of doing so. There was not a trace of boasting in his tone.

The limo slid into gear and glided away from the house. Her parents waved from the steps. Angela waved back with a smile and accepted the champagne glass Todd offered. She felt like a girl again, going out, knowing her folks would worry about her, but she couldn't stay imprisoned in her room. She guessed some things never changed.

"To you and your fine parents." Todd raised his glass.

Angela wanted to respond with "to you and your fine handsome self." Knowing the detectives could hear every word, instead she said, "Thank you for inviting me."

As she sipped the tart champagne, prickly bubbles filled her nose and throat. She repressed a sneeze. Todd settled back beside her. His leg barely grazed hers, a respectable distance, but Angela tensed with longing. The man set her on fire inside.

A second, unfamiliar ballad played. The same mellow saxophone gave a perfect accompaniment to the view. The neighborhood of old-fashioned houses faded into the distance, replaced by tall, wide-based, earthquake resilient office buildings. Sexy Malibu and the ocean front appeared in the window.

"What is that music?"

"The album's called *Sax at the Movies*." Todd gave her a naughty grin, but his voice remained polite. "It's one of my favorites. Movie themes. Do you like it?"

"Not a movie I've ever seen."

"It's re-mastered. *The Rose*. I can show you the film sometime."

"I'd like that." Angela liked anything to indicate a future date in the offing.

They sipped champagne and listened to the sax play yet another old song, one Angela should have been able to identify.

When the limo pulled up at Lu Chan's, the two detectives picked up their hats and exited first. One leaned back in and said, "Okay."

Todd took Angela's glass and set it down with his on the bar. "Put your shoes on, Lucy."

Even though Angela blushed, she didn't really care. His teasing held a reassuring quality of permanence. Todd acted completely unpretentious despite the opulent surroundings. She liked that about him. As she stepped out of the car, she noticed the parking lot empty of planes, cars, or any other vehicles. "Are you sure this place is open?"

"Oh, I think so." Todd seemed to regard her question as humorous. He gestured toward the chauffeur. "Come in with us, pal. Have lunch on me."

"Thanks, sir." The chauffer stuffed his cap in his pocket and followed them.

When Angela and Todd entered the pagoda-shaped restaurant, she understood the significance of the empty parking lot. The main dining room held at least forty tables with bamboo barrel chairs. Strangely there were only two people in the room—Chinese men standing beside the door. The gleam of stainless steel appliances, visible from the kitchen, made an incongruous contrast with golden dragon chandeliers and red, floral carpeting.

One of the restaurant men called out, "Welcome, Dr. Williams."

"Hello, Lu Chan."

One detective and the chauffeur sat at a table at the far end of the room, near the kitchen. The other detective chose the table closest to the front door.

Lu Chan hurried toward Todd and Angela and ushered them into an alcove. "Madam." He held a chair out for Angela then set menus on the tablecloth. "I'll return to take your order."

"Great," Todd said. "And thanks for arranging this."

"Glad to, for a special customer like you." Lu Shan returned to his companion by the door.

"Arranging things?" Had this man bought out the restaurant so they could be alone? The idea dumbfounded Angela. Was he playing her? She didn't know whether her lack of experience with men accounted for her feelings of distrust or whether Todd was laying it on too thick, especially after the stretch limo and the bodyguards.

Kicking back the other chair, Todd dropped down gracefully for a man with such long legs. Elbows on the table he rested his chin on his fists with a dour expression on his face. "Over the top, was it?"

Angela dreaded to appear to criticize Todd and set them off to a bad start. She'd learned something important about him. He read body language very well. He had sensed her shock at what seemed like excess. She mustn't lie at all, something she hardly ever did, although she sometimes left out subjects that might become troublesome. She'd try to be completely sincere with Todd.

Maybe the counselor had uncovered a disturbing part of Angela's psyche, something akin to hero worship. It seemed illogical for her to harbor any feelings of class consciousness. Her parents, scientists, her grandfather a spiritual leader, she'd grown up without thinking of class at all. But something within her soul understood the struggle to be treated like an equal, the powerlessness of second-class personhood, and the fear of abandonment. How that might play out with Todd she couldn't imagine.

"I don't understand. Why did you buy out the restaurant?"

"So we could be alone." Todd glanced at the table where the detective and the chauffer were talking and laughing. "Well, almost alone. And I wanted you to feel safe with me."

"I do already, even without bodyguards. All of this wasn't necessary."

Todd shrugged like a boy who'd been caught ditching and didn't care much about getting punished. "Oh hell, I just wanted to impress you."

"Well, you've definitely done that." Angela laughed as she reached for him.

Todd enfolded her hand in both of his. "Then you're not put off?"

"Not at all. A little excess is good for the soul. That's what I say."

"Good then, let's order something excessive." Todd beckoned to Lu Chan and said to her, "Tell the man our order."

Angela ordered an Emperor's Feast—garden vegetable spring rolls, gorgonzola salad, wanton soup, lobster yu choy, stir fry vegetable mélange.

"Will that be all, madam?"

Unable to fathom how they would eat all of that, Angela shook her head.

"Sake and wonderful cheesecake," Todd said. "We have to have dessert." He was clearly in the mood to splurge.

"Indeed we do." Angela couldn't wait. "Cheesecake's my favorite."

Lu Chan conveyed the details to the other Chinese man. They both dashed into the kitchen.

Angela excused herself and rose to go to the powder room. As she did so the detective at the table by himself nodded to the other one and followed her.

Turning back to Todd, she asked, "Do you think this is necessary?"

"Absolutely."

"Don't worry, Ms. Brock," the detective gazed at her with no suggestion of a smile. "I won't embarrass you. Wait here."

The detective pushed open the door to the powder room and stepped inside. He returned almost immediately to face her.

"No bombers in there, huh?" Angela asked.

"Not at the moment." Perhaps the detective did have a small sense of humor, after all.

Once inside the powder room, Angela refreshed herself, gave her hair a quick brush, then took advantage of the moment alone to check her messages. Nothing from the newsroom. She'd hoped for some clues to turn up about the firebomb. She spoke into her search engine, "Sax in the

Movies." The title sounded just as suggestive as when Todd said it. Too funny.

The phone whirred momentarily and presented the songs on the CD, circa 1993. She read through the play list. *Somewhere in Time.* 1980. That was the haunting song she didn't recognize. And *The Rose,* the one Todd had mentioned. 1979. He certainly had a healthy interest in things from the late twentieth century.

Angela returned to the table just as Todd closed his videophone and glanced up at her. "Good news. I got the bid on a Cessna. Late 80s, I think. It's in storage in Beijing, but it will be shipped soon. I've been wanting to try my hand at restoring one of those for a long time."

The horrible images of the plane crash from her dreams filled Angela's mind. He couldn't want to fly them again? "What fascinates you in particular about those planes? The past?"

"Not really. It's more the intricacy and complexity of design. There's a lot of satisfaction in bringing out the original glory of a perfect machine. It's actually very relaxing to sink your hands into crankcase oil. You should try it."

"So you want to rebuild them, not fly them?"

"Not for transportation. Just for sport."

Angela's fears for his safety were only partially allayed. "You speak of restoration so poetically, you make me want to try it."

Sliding onto the chair beside her, Todd glanced at the men at the other tables, then pulled her close as if he were about to kiss her. Angela felt breathless at the prospect because she thought she knew what his kiss would feel like.

Lu Shan arrived with a cart and set white porcelain dishes filled with salad on the table.

"I'd like to show you my car collection sometime," Todd whispered. "I've got a 1973 Mustang. Almost as beautiful as you."

There was that word again. *Sometime*. "I'd love to see your car collection."

Angela felt happy and bit into the gorgonzola. The cheese's bitter tang fell away in her mouth to a mellow sweetness. She watched Lu Shan take food to the detectives and chauffeur and wondered idly what they'd ordered. Nothing could be better than this salad. She didn't care how much she ate. The food was delicious, a lot better than the Chinese takeout she normally brought home and ate alone.

"How long do you think you'll stay in L A?" Todd asked. "Until the bomber is found?"

"I'm still on the story. Working with another reporter. We'll find out who did it or keep after the police until they do."

"Who do you think is responsible?"

"Probably somebody who hates my telecasts."

Despite her attempt at a joke, Todd frowned as he sipped sake. He set the tiny glass down and stared at it for a moment. "That surprises me a little. It would be a lot less dangerous to let someone else do the story, but I have to say that I admire your independent spirit. Of course, you'd want to do the investigation yourself."

His response surprised Angela since he'd acted as her rescuer today. With the detectives and private dining room, he seemed very much at home in the role of rescuer. Although she was having fun with him, she would not want to play the damsel in distress to his Galahad for very long. Games could become ways of living. She wanted none of that. "It's kind of you to say so."

"No need to thank me. I owe you."

"What for?"

"This is a secret, but I've not had a headache since I shook your hand in the planetarium. You're a good omen for me."

"Headaches aren't a very big deal, are they?"

"Mine are. I'd rather be in a plane wreck than have another one."

"A Cessna wreck specifically?" Angela felt absolutely convinced that his metaphor came straight out of his memory banks. And hers.

"What? Oh, you're talking about that vision—"

"I'm talking about you and your interests." Angela cut him off before he had a chance to say anything negative. "Stop and think with me for a minute. You love old cars, 1973, you said." She ticked the items off on her fingers. "You're going to restore a Cessna from the twentieth century. You collect old movies and music produced in 1993."

A startled look crossed Todd's face. "How did you know that?"

Angela tried not to blush. "I looked it up...while I was in...Look, Todd, I'm telling you this as a friend and an interested party—"

"A friend and interested party? Is that all you think of me?"

Deliberately, Angela ignored his attempt to get her to say her feelings for him. She needed to make him understand his complicity in her dreams and memories. "The late twentieth century holds great allure for you. Your office absolutely reeks of its style. There's got to be an explanation."

"Of course there is." Todd picked up a morsel of noodle and held it at eye level. "I'm a cultured man, steeped in history, and fascinating as hell." He popped the morsel into his mouth and gave her a cock-eyed look.

The man knew he was irresistible to her and reveled in the knowledge. Regardless, Angela needed to pursue this topic for both of their benefits. "What if there's another cause, something buried deep in your mind, something you're refusing to acknowledge at a conscious level."

"Like?"

"Like a past life memory."

Todd shook his head.

"Would you go to the Regression Portal, just for the sake of curiosity? What do you have to lose?"

"Even if it's possible to remember a past life, and I'd be very surprised to learn it is, there's no way to trust memory. It's one of the most fallible of human capacities."

"My grandfather helps people to remember past lives all the time."

"He gets people to think they do. That's a very different process. Don't get me wrong. Those stories are meaningful. I don't put them down even though I don't accept your explanation. On the contrary, I have a very high regard for such memories because they display people's secret longings and fears...and because they brought you to me." He picked up her hand and kissed it. "I'm very grateful."

When he got into that teasing frame of mind, Angela knew that logic would have no impact. She just knew, from within her soul, what he was like as if she'd known him in this present lifetime for many years. "You're right about one thing." She leaned over and whispered in his ear. "You are fascinating as hell. And just as frustrating."

Twelve

What Thou Dost Earn

In the parlor of the Hyatt Regency VIP suite, Kegan settled back in a chaise lounge and watched Melanie with amused anticipation. Although he remained silent at her request, he promised himself he'd not laugh at her, no matter what silliness she displayed. He felt positive she hadn't a clue about what it took to perform magic.

Attired conservatively for her, Melanie wore a maroon floor length cape. He couldn't see through the material, velvet he guessed. Its hood hung down her back almost obscured by the abundant shaft of her hair. Through the open doorway in the bedroom, one of her day gowns lay tossed on the bed. She might be naked beneath the cape.

In one hand Melanie grasped a bejeweled dagger, more letter opener than weapon, and circumscribed a wide swath around herself and the glass coffee table. Placing the dagger carefully on the glass, she knelt on the plush carpeting strewn with crumpled tissue paper, ribbon, and shopping bags.

An hour earlier she had phoned Kegan on his private line to ask him to visit her. Although she'd surprised him by saying she'd rented accommodations in downtown Phoenix within blocks of the clinic, he enjoyed her availability and discretion. His wife wouldn't find out. Not that she cared. Nor should she. Her public position remained secure.

A small silver cauldron with a built-in incense burner stood on the coffee table. Around it Melanie arranged three black candles and some packages of herbs. Into the cauldron she mixed dried weeds with a pinch of St. John's wort. She dropped in a clump of cat hair, at least that's what the label read. It entertained Kegan to imagine she had pulled the hair out of some unsuspecting feline's tail rather than purchasing it. She could buy anything she wanted. No wonder she had no regard for the value of things.

Melanie consulted a scribbled sheet of paper. "Okay, that's it."

"I thought you said we shouldn't talk."

"Just you. I can say whatever I want, but if you talk you'll break my concentration. I want to be damn sure it's my power, not yours, that's in operation."

Kegan chuckled at her childish seriousness. Melanie glared at him, and his laughter subsided into silence.

Sometimes she confounded him. Two days ago at her apartment, he'd believed he tricked her into thinking she had some telekinetic powers, but obviously he hadn't succeeded or she wouldn't act suspicious of him now.

More and more he thought of her as capable of helping him in a substantive way. Perhaps tonight he would confide his plans to Melanie. They required her to lure Luke into the astral so Kegan could render Luke's physical body useless for return. He had a special drug in mind that left no traces for an autopsy to find.

In Kegan's youth, his grandmother had deluded Kegan into luring her husband out of his physical body into the astral realm. Then she had stabbed the old bastard's defenseless physical body to death. Kegan had feared his grandmother's powers but wanted them for himself.

When he had related the tale to Melanie earlier, she had found the details instructive rather than appalling. He'd left out Kegan's complicity in the murder. Melanie didn't need to know that part.

Would she be willing to work on astral projection? If she agreed, could she become accomplished enough to help him kill his other three enemies? So many uncertainties. Maybe he should keep the whole project to himself. The risks of involving another person might be greater than simply eliminating Todd, Angela, and Luke himself. Slick, neat, and satisfying to his soul alone.

With meticulous care, Melanie poured spell oil up to the brim of the cauldron, far more than she needed. With much fanfare and flickering of long, sharply chiseled fingernails, she spread charcoal granules around the base. She picked up a lighter, lit one candle, then stirred the concoction with a silver spoon. She peered at the sludgy gruel and seemed pleased.

Closing her eyes, she held her arms out toward the ceiling and chanted in a monotone: "Upon the planes in which I live, the gifts of shame and delusion I now give, to Angela Brock with all my soul and heart, to change her and to break her apart. By all on high and law of three, this is my will. So shall it be."

After a nervous intake of breath, Melanie blew out the candle.

Kegan definitely approved of her intention to bring bad luck to the Brock bitch, but the magical spell seemed flimsy at best, unprofessional and sloppy. Melanie glanced at him inquiringly. He didn't want to laugh and spoil the moment but didn't trust himself so he nodded noncommittally and clasped his hand over his mouth to indicate his agreement not to talk.

Amazingly Melanie seemed to take encouragement from him. She lit a second candle and assumed her supplicating position. "Upon the planes in which I live, the gift of...of confusion I now give, to Todd Williams with all my soul and heart, to change him and to break him apart. By all on high and law of three, this is my will. So shall it be."

Confusion? Quite a clever idea for harming a person known internationally as a genius. That curse alone might bring the great and gaudy astrophysicist trouble.

The warnings of his Aurum Solis teacher in England rang in Kegan's head, causing him to remember his magical training. How disapproving the teacher would have been of Melanie and her dabbling. Not only did such wannabe witches give magic a bad name, but also they were dangerous to themselves and others because they unwittingly altered powerful forces. Kegan's conscience tweaked him. He needed to get control of the energy she might provoke.

"Wait till you see what I've got in store for the old fart." Melanie sounded gleeful.

"You mean Luke Brock?"

Melanie gave Kegan an incredulous look. "Who else? I've got this all planned out." She lit the third candle and raised her arms. "Upon the planes in which I live, the gift of—"

"Wait a minute." Kegan chuckled, determined at least to lift the proceedings to a viable basis. "What is the law of three you keep invoking?"

"I don't know what's so funny," Melanie pouted.

"If you're invoking a mystical law, you probably ought to have some idea of possible consequences."

"I found the curse in a spell file." Annoyance in her tone, Melanie spoke while she rummaged around in the shopping bags and pulled out a spell book. "Here, let me read it to you."

"No need. I memorized large portions of Lady Gwen's book. And I quote: 'Ever mind the Rule of Three. Three times what thou givest returns to thee. This lesson well, thou must learn: Thee only gets what thou dost earn.' Do you understand the meaning implied in that incantation?"

"It's just a poem, for Buddha's sake!"

As Kegan suspected, she hadn't a clue. He enjoyed revealing her incompetence, at least to himself, whether she was smart enough to understand. "Why did you inscribe a circle?"

"The book said to."

"Oh, and you do everything without question?" Kegan rose and leaned toward her, intent on turning the subject to sexual innuendo. "Because, if you do, I can write down instructions on another subject that should be quite enjoyable."

"This is not the time for that. It's the time for magical spells." She spoke with ludicrous naiveté.

"Oh, really? Is the moon waxing or waning? Or the year for that matter? Do you even know what the waxing and the waning of the year mean or how they impact magical processes?" Kegan laughed out loud.

"What does it matter?"

"It's dangerous to traffic in powerful magic when you don't know what you're doing." Kegan clasped his sapphire ring and felt the heat from it sear his hand, the power of luck, a mighty protection. He didn't try to keep the derision out of his tone. "I'll show you how this is done."

Leaping toward him, Melanie screamed and grabbed at his cheeks. The cape fell open revealing her lithe body, her skin rich against the velvet folds.

Kegan ducked away from her fingernails, suddenly ready to take her. This time his laugh sounded heavy with craving. "So you want it rough? I can give you that."

"You disgust me." Melanie strode to the door and held it open. "Get the hell out of here."

The beautiful face set in anger turned Kegan on even more. He tried to take her in his arms, but she shoved him back.

"Get out now."

"No, I didn't mean anything. I'll help you learn all the magic you want to practice." Kegan had miscalculated her emotions. It irritated him to feel required to deal with them at all. Their relationship would advance much more satisfactorily if she'd simply do as he said and ignore feelings.

"Which word didn't you understand?" Melanie clenched her fist to close the cape.

"What the hell?" Her nerve infuriated Kegan. Where did she get the notion he could be bossed around in any fashion?

"Get out."

Kegan longed to throttle her, but something cautioned him to refrain. Only fools did murder under the black pall of rage. He would await his chance. He might yet find her useful to his purposes. He forced an expression of contrition on his face, stepped across the threshold into the hall, and turned back to her. He intended to mumble some sort of bogus apology.

The slamming door squelched any retort.

The vacuum lock whistled when the shuttle bay door closed. The melodic feminine voice of the autopilot rose above a symphonic soundtrack. "Please take your seats and fasten your seatbelts securely."

Angela and Todd sat in a double seat with one of the Pinkertons in front of them and one behind. A young couple close to the front of the shuttle chattered excitedly across the aisle to two older women passengers.

The sides of the cylindrical interior bore advertising signs: Eighteenth-Century France Bower, New York in 3000 A. D. Bower, The Jerusalem of Jesus Bower, Shakespearean England Bower. Each travelogue poster depicted the times and places in colorful detail with images of smiling people.

"Thanks for suggesting we go to the Amusement Planetoid." Todd slipped his seatbelt on. "I've always intended to go but never got around to it." He seemed distracted, checked his seatbelt, then tugged at the clasp.

"I'm glad you agreed."

Todd gave her a weak smile. "I'm sure it'll be fun." Somehow his enthusiastic words weren't reflected in his voice.

"No need to thank me. I've got an ulterior motive."

When Todd raised a quizzical eyebrow, Angela grinned and decided she'd not elaborate yet. Teasing could go both ways.

The shuttle pointed its nose in the air, tipping the passengers back so that they almost lay on their backs. Angela tucked her skirt around her ankles as they began a rapid ascent that pulled her against the seat.

When Todd took a deep breath and clenched the chair arms, Angela thought he looked afraid although he averted his gaze so she couldn't read his expression. Earlier at the restaurant, Angela noticed his reluctance to go on the flight even though he eventually agreed.

If he had died in the airplane crash she'd so vividly seen in her dreams, his fear of flying would be completely natural, yet another subtle validation of her intuition. This one she would keep to herself. She had a feeling Todd's ego might become involved. Very masculine men didn't like to admit their weakness. She would protect him by acting like she didn't notice.

"Good afternoon," the autopilot's voice continued merrily. "Welcome to the Disney Amusement Planetoid Air Shuttle. Our flying time will be approximately forty-two minutes. The air is clear. A great day for an adventure. Our bower special for the day is King Arthur's Camelot. You can joust, see the pageantry, and enjoy the triumph of chivalry. The ladies' dresses are replicas of Guinevere's, the men's armor is guaranteed comfortable. You'll eat soup and sparrow with your fingers, all served by wenches in the great hall. Fools will entertain you. Wherever you're going in time or space, have a joyous day."

Taking Angela's hand, Todd leaned toward her. "Sounds like fun. Want to do Camelot?" His cologne smelled heavenly, like cherry blossoms in the spring.

"Not this time." Angela carried on with the mysterious attitude toward her plans.

Todd seemed to enjoy the game as much as she did. If he guessed which bower she wanted to visit, he didn't let on. She settled back and closed her eyes, concentrating on the delight of having her hand in his, even if it felt slightly sweaty, and the warmth of his body against her side. The shuttle hummed as it sped upward.

"You've got to see this." Todd gestured toward the small window beside her. "It's spectacular."

Angela opened her eyes and followed his gaze. The whole of the Pacific Seaboard lay below them, like a vast, winding jewel. Then the curve of the earth emerged. Next the whole earth appeared round and small beneath them, a perspective so splendid she gasped, "Oh my goodness."

"Haven't you ever seen it before?"

"Only on film. It's incredible."

"So are you." Todd squeezed her hand, and she turned toward him. "I don't usually do this sort of thing, but this is as much privacy as we're going to get."

He surprised her with a kiss. Their first.

It was just as she'd known it would be, warm and intimate, their lips a perfect fit. A tremor shuddered through her at the reality of it. All the years of waiting had been worth every minute. She hoped that she had done enough good to deserve him in this lifetime.

The lazy way Todd opened his eyes and smiled at her told her he felt the same pleasure. Now it was more important than ever that Angela convince him of what she suspected to be the truth. She didn't want to miss what she felt she had come into incarnation to do. She believed her previous lifetimes had prepared her to desire a perfect relationship with him. She hoped she knew how to manifest one. Perhaps his time travel explanation would provoke more memories in her and end the doubts about the past life memories.

"Excuse me, sir." One of the detectives tapped Todd on the shoulder. "What would you like us to do when we arrive at the planetoid?"

Angela pulled back from the embrace, feeling embarrassed. She disliked kissing in public, considering it a tasteless display of poor manners. Now she'd done it herself. Her sense of appropriate behavior for a public person seemed to have deserted her. Obviously the kiss hadn't bothered the detective.

"Do you think anyone followed us from the restaurant?" Todd asked.

The detective glanced at the people in the forward part of the cabin. "You can't be too careful, sir. It's hard to know."

"We promised this lady's parents that we'd take the best care of her, so we'll err on the side of safety. Why don't you and your partner go with us to the bower and keep a watchful eye?"

"Yes, sir, be glad to." The detective gave a slim salute and headed back to his seat.

The interruption had broken the romantic mood. Todd entertained her with stories of his days at university. He got so many scholarships that his mom quit her job and rented an apartment near the campus. As a child prodigy he'd been thirteen to his classmates' eighteen. He'd enrolled in graduate school before he needed to shave. Despite his young age, he had great popularity as a lab partner and study team member, accepted as everyone's kid brother. He followed his classmates on dates and learned the facts of life from them.

The other passengers' voices grew louder as the shuttle neared the dock. The autopilot announced the impending landing and gave instructions for return shuttle service at midnight and one in the morning.

After they deplaned, Angela took a quick look around. She'd always wanted to come to the planetoid but hadn't had occasion before to do more than report on its popularity as a day trip or weekend resort. A glance around showed her why.

They and the other passengers stood in an almost empty and very long corridor. Copper gates led off into dozens of bowers. All the entryways looked exactly alike except for their names. The young couple who had deplaned with them entered the Turkish Delight amid giggles and whispers.

"Probably honeymooners." Todd cast an exaggerated expression of envy as the gate closed on the young couple.

Next came the California Cove, a display of many copper gates. The older women who had deplaned with them stopped before the Gold Rush Bower. One said, "Oh, I want to wear a bustle back dress and be a saloon girl."

"Me too."

The two women rushed to the gate.

Angela and Todd continued to walk along, the detectives a discreet few steps behind them. He read the names as they passed, still acting as if he had no idea where they were headed. "1890s, 1900s, 1910s, Roaring Twenties, Depression City, WW II, Fabulous Fifties, Sinful Sixties, Disco Town, Rad Eighties."

"That's us." Angela grabbed Todd's hand, turned, and passed through the gate. Immediately on the other side a blinking neon sign in the shape of a car greeted them.

A turnstile stood between them and a young woman dressed in tight black slacks and tank top. Her slicked hair stood up like a rooster's. She called out, "Welcome to Rad Eighties. I'm a punk rocker."

"That's an old Thunderbird, if I'm not mistaken." Todd waved his ID card before the electronic eye.

Angela pressed the turnstile bar, and they entered the Rad Eighties Bower. She glanced around. "I don't see a bird."

"A Thunderbird is a kind of car they used to make."

"Oh, of course." Angela actually had no idea about cars of the time period.

The punk rocker handed them each a cloth bag and pointed toward doors that read Hombres and Damas. "You can change in there. The entrance to the Rad Eighties Club is through the dressing room. It's a bitchin' place."

"I sure want to see that." Todd gave Angela an imaginary tip of the hat. He seemed in high spirits. "See you in a bit."

"Sir." One of the detectives laid his hand on the door to bar Angela's entry. "I'll just be a minute." He gave Todd an inquisitive stare.

"Thank you." Todd looked more annoyed than worried, but he nodded agreement.

The detective entered the door labeled Damas.

The punk rocker glared at the detective. "What the hell are you doing? You're not supposed to go in there." When he ignored her, she turned to Angela and Todd. "What kind of an airhead is he?"

Returning in less than a minute, the detective said, "Everything's okay, ma'am."

"I'm sure it is."Angela found the Pinkertons' courtly regard for her safety almost as charming as Todd's.

The idea of pretending to live in another time intrigued Angela. She entered the brightly lit dressing room with its row of cubicles. All appeared to be empty, and she took the nearest one. It had a full-length mirror surrounded by theatrical makeup lights. Would the surroundings actually spark memories in Todd? Maybe more in herself? She felt excited about possible outcomes of this adventure.

She set the bag on a wooden shelf, pulled out the contents, and unwrapped a yellow skirt and shirt, so bright they looked like they glowed. Not a color she would ever wear, but she pulled off her blue dress as well as the long underskirt. It wouldn't be appropriate with this costume.

As Angela stepped into the skirt, she realized it wasn't a skirt after all, but some sort of pants that looked like a skirt. The article of clothing barely came down to her knees, but she didn't mind. This was no time for a fashion show. She had more serious business tonight.

Angela donned the shirt, a button-up affair with shoulder pads big enough for a football player. She kicked off her sandals and climbed onto tall, rubber wedge heels. They added four or five inches to her height. She'd be so tall that Todd wouldn't have to bend down to kiss her. This evening could turn interesting in ways she hadn't imagined. She'd like to press against the whole length of his body and experience the way it felt. She thought she knew, but memory, no matter how precious, couldn't compare to the real man. With any luck, they would have the opportunity to dance together.

An envelope in the bag contained a small cardboard box with the word Marlboro on it. It had smelly white sticks inside with brown tips. Angela had no idea what they were. Along with the sticks, she found a comb that had uneven teeth and directions to hold up one's hair and slide the comb back and forth repeatedly so that the hair stood away from the face. After she did so, she gazed at herself in the mirror. The clothes, cut full and unflatteringly, made her look dumpy. She wore similar costumes in some of her dreams, and she found she didn't care. If everyone in the time period dressed like the dregs, she might as well too.

Anxious to see how Todd would look, Angela hung her dress on a hanger, refreshed her lipstick, then hesitated, wondering whether or not to take the Marlboro box. Who knew what she would be missing if she didn't? She stuffed it into her purse, hurried past the rest of the cubicles and through the entry marked Thunderbird Café.

After the door swung shut behind her, the darkness that greeted Angela caused her to stop. Loud music with a lot of percussion and trumpets made her wonder if she'd made an error. The air smelled musty and thick. As her eyes adjusted to the gloom, she saw people standing at tall tables and others sitting in booths shaped like cars around a dance floor. She couldn't tell whether the people were other humans, holographic projections, or automated manikins. She recognized the detectives by the Stetsons as they stood at a table, drinking and chatting. Regardless, everyone seemed to be having a good time.

A different punk rocker, this one with bright red hair spiked out like rays from the sun, carried a tray of drinks. She smiled at Angela. "Welcome to the Thunderbird Café. I'll be your waitress tonight."

Nodding, Angela wondered what had become of Todd. She walked up to a table and laid her purse on it. Perhaps he was having trouble figuring out what to do with the articles in his package too.

"There you are."

Angela heard Todd's voice before she saw him in the foggy atmosphere.

"Let me look at you." Grabbing her shoulder, Todd turned her around, and she stumbled.

Righting herself on the wedged heels, Angela feared she'd sprain an ankle in those stupid shoes. She stood up and held out the tips of the divided skirt that was actually very long shorts. "What do you think? Is it really me?"

"Must be. You look terrific."

They both laughed.

Todd wore a blazer that could be fashionable over a white T-shirt, jeans like he wore in modern times, and soft-sided shoes with laces across the top. By themselves, all of the pieces of his costume seemed tasteless, but on his exquisitely proportioned body, the combination was sensational. He looked so fantastic he could carry off any kind of bizarre costume and cause women to stare.

Angela hadn't realized jeans were such an old style. Perhaps she should do a feature on the history of jeans. If she ever got her day job back, of course. She wondered how the investigation into her car bombing was going. She'd deal with that later. Now she intended to focus on creating a fun memory with Todd in this lifetime.

"You look smashing." Angela glanced around the room. None of the women were ogling Todd, a situation which convinced her they were all manikins or holograms. Any living, breathing woman would be admiring him.

"Hey," Todd raised his arms in a what-can-you-do gesture. "Being comfortable trumps style anytime. I could do the eighties in a heartbeat."

The waitress walked up to them, carrying a tray with drinks on it. "What can I get you to drink?" At least she was human.

"What do you recommend?" Todd asked.

"Love your Adidas." The waitress said.

Todd glanced at Angela. Clearly he didn't understand the word either.

"Your shoes, man."

Todd held up his foot. "This is a style we should definitely bring back."

The waitress blushed as if she took their enjoyment of the Rad Eighties personally. "I recommend a Harvey Wall Banger for the lady and a Bud-Lite for you."

"Sounds great." Todd said.

Angela nodded, curious about a Harvey Wall Banger.

The waitress set the drinks from the tray in front of Todd and Angela.

Maybe they had been taken in by their waitress. Maybe in the 1980s everyone drank the same things, but what did it matter? Angela sipped the drink and it tasted fine, sweet and fruity, like slick bananas with a zing. She wondered how Harvey happened to come up with such a concoction.

The waitress pointed to a selection grid in the tabletop. "Press that when you're ready for the floor show."

Todd took a tentative sip then a big drink. "I could develop a real taste for beer."

Reaching into her purse, Angela pulled out the Marlboro box. "Did you get one of these too?"

Todd took one from his jacket pocket.

"Do you know what we're supposed to do with them?" she asked.

"I've read about it. It was called smoking." Todd pointed across the room to the detectives, one of whom had a white stick in his mouth. Clouds of smoke appeared to be coming off him. "Want to try it?"

"Sure. Why not?"

Flipping open the box, Todd took out two sticks and gave one to Angela. They both put sticks in their mouths. Angela's tasted bitter and flakey, and she wondered how such an activity could turn out to be pleasant.

The waitress, who evidently had nothing to do but tend to their needs, held up a small silver box, did something to the end of it, and fire came out of it. She held it up to Todd's stick and set it afire. "Puff on it." To Angela she said, "Other end. Put the other end in your mouth."

When Angela turned the stick around and sucked in, her throat closed as if she were being choked. She began to cough. Todd joined her, and they both coughed. He handed the cigarette to the waitress, who dropped it on the floor and stepped on it.

"Take mine too." Angela handed hers to the waitress and grabbed her Harvey Wall Banger. She drained it, relieved for moisture to quench the fire in her mouth. "Give me another."

The waitress stepped on Angela's cigarette and walked away. "Be right back."

Are you ready for the floor show?" Todd asked.

"Definitely." Angela pressed the Floor Show grid button.

A loud male voice filled the room. "And now here she is, the material girl herself. The one and only. Madonna!"

"Come on, let's go." Todd picked up his beer can and took her elbow.

The two scurried to a booth in the shape of a red convertible car, a Thunderbird obviously. That she managed to stay upright on the shoes amazed Angela. When they climbed in, Todd sat in the driver's seat, pulled her against him, and wrapped his arm around her. He downed the beer, and the punk rocker set two drinks on a tray attached to the side of the car.

The dim lights faded to black and new music came up, mostly horns. A holograph of a beautiful blonde woman appeared in the middle of the dance floor. She wore a black corset and long black hose with straps of some kind to hold them together. She sang "Give it to me," and moved her loins, flaunting her thighs and breasts in the most provocative moves any woman could ever make, animated or human.

One glance at Todd's expression let Angela know he was enjoying the performance immensely. He laughed and held up his beer in the attitude of a toast to the hologram.

Glad that they were watching a movie, Angela would have been embarrassed for a real woman who behaved like that. The original Madonna was probably sexy in a crude sort of way and she sang very well. That might have been a stage name to thumb her nose at religion. Angela sympathized with that propensity. In the decades around the turn of the twenty-first century religions battled each other constantly. They did more harm than good to anyone.

Thankfully international law currently prohibited religious practices that had led to wars in the past. Those laws hadn't wiped out the religions but had limited their ability to cause widespread harm. Angela wondered if Todd had a religious preference. Not that it made any difference in her desire for him. She would ask him some other time. Right now she wanted to focus him on the 1980s and their previous lifetime together.

When the spotlighted hologram dissolved and dim room lights came on, Todd squeezed Angela's shoulders. "I think I could get off on living in this time. It's so rad." He sounded comfortable with the slang word. It fit his teasing style.

Angela pressed Dance Music on the selection grid mounted in the dashboard. "Let's see what this is about." Mellow piano music began to play. "I would love for you to dance with me," she whispered.

"Absolutely." Todd stepped out of the car seat and held out a beckoning arm to her.

A mellow baritone singer on the taped music began to sing: "Memory. All alone in the moonlight. I can smile at the old days. I was beautiful then."

When Angela moved into the circle of Todd's arms, it felt like coming home. His eyes met hers and he smiled that terrific smile that brought the dimple to his chin. She loved being at eye level and gazed into his eyes.

The singer continued, "I remember the time I knew what happiness was. Let the memory live again."

Angela's awareness shifted in a timeless way.

Todd's face changed somehow into another's. An ancient musical instrument lay across his bare shoulders. Anger and disappointment crossed his face, ruddy with sun exposure. She had let him down in a way that could never be undone. Then his face transformed into another, forlorn one. He tipped a tricorn hat and bid her farewell. Sadness assailed her at the thought that she might never see him again. Had she been the cause of his going to war?

"My dearest love." She put her arms around his neck and he clasped her waist. He crushed her into a long, slow kiss that brought heat to her entire being and her mind back to the twenty-first century.

Maybe his closeness caused memories to stir in her. Or maybe the Harvey Wall Bangers had. Despite the presence of the detectives and the waitress, despite the smoky air, Angela knew what happiness was. Her man, her love, her life. All here in this moment.

Too soon the evening ended. The loud speaker announced the final shuttle of the night would leave in twenty minutes. Angela entered the Damas dressing room and changed into her 2061 clothes. She relinquished the wedged shoes and donned her sandals with some regret. She met Todd and the detectives in the corridor and they all headed back to the shuttle, filled with far more passengers than earlier.

"So," Angela asked as she and Todd slipped into the back seat. "What did you think of the 1980s? Besides that they're rad?"

"It was great fun. I can't wait to try out some of the other bowers. Would you like to try some?" Todd checked his seatbelt and with only a slight grimace released the lock.

"Yes, but specifically the 1980s. Did they provoke any memories in you? I mean of things you didn't already know about the time period?"

"Just Madonna." Todd raised his eyebrows in a conspiratorial expression. "She was hot, don't you think?"

"I was embarrassed for her."

"Why? She wasn't nearly as revealing as many people are today—with see-through clothing and public displays of, shall we say, affection. By our standards, Madonna was absolutely provincial."

"She was out of control. A prisoner of her body, of her desires."

"Precisely. That's why guys love her."

Suddenly Todd's relationship with Melanie made a lot more sense to Angela. Perhaps she'd so fixed on what he was to her in her dreams, and in what she surmised were visions of their former lives together, that she'd lost sight of the kind of woman he chose. Perhaps he would expect Angela to flaunt her body publicly. "Is that what you want from a woman?"

"It's fun. Try it. You'll like it."

Angela couldn't tell whether he was teasing. She had no interest in banter at the moment. Although she didn't recall the details, she knew she'd glimpsed a hint of their previous lives on the dance floor. She had a feeling Todd had been loving and constant in their previous lifetimes. She had been the one to lust after others and to behave disgracefully. She shivered at the possibility. It might take some courage she hadn't imagined necessary to acknowledge her own transgressions. She had to get it right in this lifetime, or what was the point of all these memories? She had to know what she was up against.

"It's not always what you've wanted in a woman. I think you remained true to me...in another lifetime...even when hope was gone of ever finding me again."

"Don't start that. You talk to me like I'm a history book."

"Why don't you go to the Regression Portal with me? We could settle this once and for all."

"No, I don't want to."

Angela resisted the impulse to say that he sounded like a spoiled child. "Would you tell me why you don't want to?"

Todd drummed his fingers on the seat. "It's 2061. I want to live in this time."

"You're the same man you've always been. You've got to stand up and be counted. If not in this lifetime, when?"

"That regression work." Todd rubbed his forehead momentarily, maybe in thoughtfulness, maybe in pain. "It seems to me like an easy out for people who don't want to work on relationships. I don't know very much about you. Are you one of those quick-fix fanatics?"

"You're an incredibly smart man. Why have you got such an opinionated, antiquated—"

"You mean I think like a 1980s guy?"

Angela clung to that thought, remembering his love of old cars and old planes. "Yes, you're the same man you were then. I know it. Just give me a chance to prove it."

"I'm a physicist. I deal in realities. Why can't we have a relationship in this time without all of this woo-woo talk?"

"That would be dishonest from my perspective. It would deny the validity of my experiences. I can't do it. I have to be true to myself."

"I'm sorry you feel that way. I feel just as strongly the other way. We're on a collision course. We may as well end it now before either of us gets hurt."

"You can't mean that. No!"

"I do."

Thirteen

Alone Again

After she returned to her parents' home around three in the morning, Angela lay in bed wide awake. She couldn't sleep. Every time she closed her eyes, an image of Todd appeared as he bid her a strained and formal good-bye at her door. His tone had been so insistent that she knew he meant what he said. Still she called him twice during the day to try to change his mind. She had no pride in the matter because she believed they had both incarnated to be together. His refusal to even consider the possibility caused her to lose hope that their destiny would be fulfilled. A lifetime without Todd seemed a dismal, unhappy prospect.

With nothing else to occupy her mind, she lay in bed, sad and depressed. When her parents encouraged her to come downstairs, she told them she needed rest from the events of the past few days. Regardless of whether they believed her or not, they respected her request and left her alone.

Late in the evening, she fell into exhausted sleep.

Angela flailed in water over her head. Stinky water rushed into her nose. Fishy water gushed into her mouth. Roaring water slammed into her ears. The force drove her down and down. She tried to get her face out of the water to find air to breathe, but her arms failed to propel her through the waves.

Angela awakened in a pool of perspiration, sheets clammy. The digital display beside the bed read 1:30 a.m. Weary and afraid, she wondered how Todd felt right now. Was he as miserable? She hoped so. Maybe then he would relent. She changed into a dry nightgown, put fresh sheets on the bed, and lay back down. She fell into troubled sleep.

The water swirled around her. If she didn't breathe soon, her lungs would burst. She popped out of the water and gulped air. Sharks surrounded her. A hundred of them circled closer and closer. She had no hope of escape.

The horrible scenario awakened Angela at 2:30. She went to the medicine chest and found some aspirins. She felt so overwrought that her hands shook when she held up a glass of water and washed down the pills. Back in her bed, she replayed Todd's words in her mind then turned her head into the pillow and sobbed tears she thought she'd used up. After a while, she dozed.

Angela gasped for air. Each breath rattled in her chest. Pain rippled through her. She dreaded the pain that breathing provoked, but without it she knew she would die. She was dying anyway. How she longed to hold on, but she could not. A distant voice called to her, one she should know but couldn't identify. A sharp pain knifed through her. Blackness absorbed her.

Angela bolted awake. She had to get away. Leaping out of the bed, she threw off her gown and climbed into the shower. The chilly spray failed to revitalize her.

It occurred to her that whoever might wish her harm, car bomber or anyone else, would look for her at her condo, so she decided to take a hotel room in Phoenix close to the television station. That would make her feel a bit safer.

She didn't have to think about what to take with her. She always kept a few changes of clothes in her old room, so she could drop in for an overnight visit without having to pack. She picked up the infamous royal blue dress she'd worn on her first and only date with Todd. Vowing never to don the beastly thing again, she tossed it in the waste basket.

Choosing a black sundress, she brushed her hair into a ponytail, skipped the makeup, and tiptoed into the hall where she retrieved a spare suitcase from a closet. She packed it with her remaining clothes and headed down the stairs through the quiet house.

In the Victorian-styled kitchen she noticed that it was only 5:30. On a Sunday morning, of course her parents would still be asleep. She took down the slate that hung on the fridge door. Since her childhood, she, her mom, and her dad had used the slate for messages so they'd always know where the others were and to keep their busy lives orderly. She wrote with chalk:

Gone back to work. Don't worry.

The Venetian blinds rattled as the back door opened. Vera entered in straw hat and shorts set. "I'm glad to see you up, dear." She set garden shears and gloves on the tile counter and kneaded her back muscles. "Are you feeling better?"

"I'm okay." Angela kissed her mother on the cheek. She smelled of watermelon gum.

Vera gazed at the suitcase sitting on the floor. "You're not leaving?"

"Yes, I need to get home."

"No, you can't. It's not safe."

"Shhhh. You'll wake Dad." Angela hung the slate on its hook.

"I'll go get him." Vera charged through the door into the main part of the house.

"Please don't make a big deal out of this." Angela followed her mother across the rose-colored carpet of the living room.

"Your father will have something to say about that." Vera called up the stairs. "Aaron, Aaron, would you come down here?"

"Look, Mother, I need to get back to work. That's all."

"Ridiculous. The police said you need to stay out of harm's way. You need to stay here where we can protect you."

Aaron appeared at the top of the stairs, pulling a velour robe closed over pajama bottoms. "What's going on? What's the matter?"

"Angela says she's going back to Arizona."

"What? Is she crazy?"

"I will be if I don't get to work. I can't stay around here doing nothing another minute."

Aaron took the stairs two at a time. At the bottom he laid his hands on Angela's shoulders and gazed down at her for a moment. "Tell me what's wrong, little girl. We'll fix it together." He sounded as kind and reassuring as he always had.

How Angela wished he could fix things, but not this time. "I need to get back to work. I don't want to lose my job over this car bombing business. My career's in enough jeopardy already." She hoped she sounded convincing instead of wrung out.

"That's not what this is about, is it?" Aaron tipped her chin up with a sad grin. "You never could lie worth a hoot."

Tears spurted to Angela's eyes, and Aaron drew her against him. She longed to let herself find comfort in his hug. If only his loving kindness could replace the emptiness in her heart.

"I need to go," Angela whispered. "I need to keep busy, or I'll die of a broken heart." She didn't care how melodramatic the words sounded. She might as well be honest about her misery.

"So that's what's going on." Vera moved into Angela's line of vision. "Now listen to me. You hardly know this man, Angela." Her eyes were cool like her matter-of-fact tone. "You're overreacting. Perhaps you're fond of Dr. Williams, but you can't know him that well in so short a time. You'll forget your feelings for him and find a nice man to marry soon enough."

Vera had always been concerned but clueless about what Angela wanted or needed in her life. Even if she explained about her dreams and the past life, Vera wouldn't believe anything other than an overactive imagination at work. Nothing ever went awry in her practical world. Angela and her mother had little in common except short stature and blue eyes.

Through the years, Angela had forged great empathy with her father and her grandfather although she didn't recall any specific details. Probably because of shared lifetimes although she didn't recall specific details. She counted on that connection to persuade her father. "I need to go, Dad. Please try to understand."

"You're in danger. I don't want you to go."

"I know." Angela pulled away from her father and picked up her suitcase. She felt so bleak about her prospects that the car bomber might be doing her a favor by snuffing her out, but she didn't say so. She headed toward the front door.

"Don't let her go, Aaron."

"Angela," Aaron said, his tone sharp. "Be sensible. Turn around and go back upstairs. We'll talk about this later."

"How are you going to make me? By physical force?" Angela knew her father would never lay a hand on her or anyone else in anger.

"Of course not." An expression of frustrated defeat crossed his face.

"I'll call you." Angela gave them both a feeble smile, the best she could muster under the circumstances.

"This being an understanding father sucks." Aaron headed into the kitchen.

"Honey, please..." Vera called, her voice shaky.

Angela opened the hall door and stepped outside. Alone again.

The feelings of isolation persisted through the walk to the subway station and the ride back to Phoenix despite the fact that there was hardly an empty seat. People chattered all around her, but their conversations sounded nonsensical. Their laughter irritated her.

The lobby of the Hyatt appeared equally as crowded with visitors in various garbs—white turbans, exotically colorful gowns, even some aliens in breathing helmets. It seemed that everyone in the known universe wanted to visit the city, now that it had become the capital of the United States of North America. Angela wished she had a magic wand to blow them all away. She wanted to be alone by herself, not in a crowd.

Finally she reached her hotel room, closed the door, and sank onto the bed, relieved to hear only the hum of the air conditioner. She felt dusty from the train station and clammy from the one hundred ten degree heat that invaded her skin.

She wondered what Todd was doing now and imagined him pacing the floor, regretting his words. How she hoped. She should bathe, instead she closed her eyes. Just a few minutes' sleep would refresh her more than anything. Two sleepless nights. Surely now she could rest.

An image flashed full blown into her head.

Angela flailed in the water. Sharks surged around her.

Startled awake, she lunged from the bed. Another nightmare. This had to end or she'd jump in front of the subway engine. In fact dying seemed more and more appealing. Maybe the nightmares were a message from her subconscious to go ahead and end it. Then Todd would really be sorry!

As soon as she had the thought, Angela felt overwhelmed with the sad awareness of how devastating her suicide would be. Todd would feel unwarranted guilt. Her father, her mother, her grandfather would blame themselves because they should have prevented it. Even her brother would grieve and feel he had to return home from far away Biosphere Nine.

Remorse for the fantasy shuddered through her, as if she'd broken some ancient covenant. Although no specific memory occurred to her conscious mind, she felt certain at some time in the past she had made the other decision. She had committed suicide by drowning in some previous lifetime. That's why she experienced the nightmares. They were warning her. Now she knew how wrong it was to commit suicide.

"No, that's not the answer. I can't do that." Angela spoke to no one, but the room didn't feel empty. Someone had heard her.

Fear shuddered through her. Whoever had bombed her car could have followed her to this very room.

Angela dropped to the floor and looked under the bed. No one there. Rising, she stepped into the bathroom and opened the shower stall even though she could see through it. She was completely alone in the hotel room. Perhaps she'd gone a little berserk. Sleep deprivation could cause depression and mental illness.

Ashamed of her fearfulness and despairing, Angela leaned over the sink and cried. She sobbed so hard her chest hurt. She splashed cold water on her face to stop the tears. Patting her face dry with a towel, she glanced at her reflection in the mirror. She saw her contorted visage as she expected.

Behind her was the reflection of a bewhiskered old man in brocade jacket and ruffled shirt. He tipped a riding crop to his forehead, bowed, and smiled at her.

"Oh, my God!" Someone was here. To kill her?

Whirling around, Angela confronted an empty bathroom.

"Angela, get a grip," she said to herself. "You're losing your mind." She closed her eyes and whispered, "I am calm. I am okay. I am all alone." She opened her eyes and saw her own reflection,

The old man was there again. He smiled at her. Whoever he was, she needn't fear him.

"I know you, don't I?" She closed her eyes, trying to remember him, and found him there in her mind and heart.

"You have done well." The old man's thoughts impressed on Angela's mind. "You have the strength to do what you need to do. The Divine Spirit flows through you and operates as you in the world."

When she opened her eyes, the old man had gone, but Angela felt reassured. She had recognized him although she didn't know why. She sensed that she had friends on the other side, ones who had not abandoned her. Neither would she abandon her loved ones here. She would do whatever she needed to do to get well for them.

Energized, Angela sat at a writing table beside the window that looked out over the Civic Center Plaza. From the fifty-eighth floor she couldn't see the fountains below. Government buildings and offices filled the skyline beneath the desert blue vault. She flipped the holophone on so her image would be visible against the backdrop. Flicking lint off the skirt of her dress, she said, "Mom and Dad."

When her dad answered, she assured him that she'd arrived at the hotel, that she would try to get her life back together, and that she would be in touch. "Try not to worry."

"Stay safe, little girl." Aaron signed off, sounding no less worried.

Angela had to get control of the nightmares so she could get some sleep. She would never be able to go hold out until the regular appointment on Friday at the Psi Therapy Clinic, so she called and left a request for an earlier time slot.

In the bathroom she inspected her image. She looked drawn and tired, but passable. She had no one to impress. She brushed her hair, fastened it, grabbed her purse, and rode down to the crowded lobby. Outside she stepped into the air-conditioned causeway of Central Avenue and onto the moving sidewalk that took her past empty office buildings to the television station.

Inside she strode down the corridor and through the sliding glass doors, feeling more alive. She saw people at work in the rows of cubicles. The news never stopped so neither did the news channel. That excitement to find the next unusual event or quirky human behavior had always intrigued Angela. She hoped she could get outside her own emotions enough to enjoy work once again. If she had to continue to live without Todd, and she did for the sakes of the others she loved, then she must find renewed meaning in her work. It had always served her before and would again.

A few of her co-workers called out greetings. She answered, feeling comforted by the camaraderie. She stopped at a cubicle where a young Hispanic man gazed with absorption at his monitor.

"Hey, Carlos, got anything to report to me?"

"Angela, what are you doing here?" Large brown eyes and wide cheeks gave Carlos a cherubic look. "Excuse me. I mean Ms. Brock."

"Any news about the firebombing?"

Carlos shook his head, and a stray lock of hair fell into his eyes. He brushed it back nervously. "No, not yet. I talked with the policeman assigned to the case today. I'll talk with them every day. Mr. Campbell insists."

"Of course, he would." Angela tried to convey their commonality at having a difficult boss.

"Well, uh..."

"You have my number? You'll call me first sign of progress. No matter how small?"

"Absolutely. I'll call you."

Thanking him, Angela tried to speak gently. She didn't understand why her presence made him nervous. She didn't think of herself as intimidating. She certainly wasn't in a position to influence Carlos's career one way or another, or anybody else's, including her own.

The losses rolled through her mind—the anchor slot, the car, the privacy of her home, the luxury of restful sleep, Todd and all the hope for love unrealized that he represented. Did she have anything else to lose?

Angela had to take back her power. How she had lost it she couldn't logically understand, but she refused to go on like this. She would make a new life, in a new place if she had to. Whatever that required of her, she would do what needed to be done. Now she knew she had friends in the Afterlife helping her. A new life she built for herself must include learning to communicate with them. She felt ready to begin.

Preferring not to wait for the elevator, Angela dashed up the stairs. She could see Campbell inside his office, berating the assistant news director. Angela waited for that unfortunate young woman to leave. Poor thing. She didn't have the constitution to deal with her boss, but then who did?

"Angela?" The young woman looked surprised and hurried toward her cubicle.

After turning off her holophone, Angela stepped into the office. "Hello, Mr. Campbell. I need to talk to you."

Campbell glanced at her and thumped a balled fist on the news copy. "What the hell are you doing here?"

"You know just how to make a woman feel welcome." Angela took a sarcastic tone with him. She could act just as tough and impatient.

"Tell me they've caught the bomber. Because, if they haven't, you damn well better get out of town."

"How's Hannah doing? She working out as anchor?"

"Better than you. At least she's awake and on time."

With forced determination, Angela placed her hands on the desk and leaned forward, eye to eye with him. "I want my job back."

Campbell studied her face. "You look like hell."

"Thanks. What will it take for you to reinstate me?"

Leaning back in his chair, Campbell played pit-a-pat on his tight belly as he considered her question. "A name in the field. Public clamor." The man might be a smartass with a corner on rude, but he always said what he meant.

"Have you filled the Alpha Centauri slot yet?"

"Hell, no."

"Send me."

"You?" Campbell pointed a fat finger at her. "You're supposed to be hiding out to stay safe, and you want me to send you to the war-torn outback of the galaxy? Isn't that going from the frying pan into the fire?"

"I'll give you the best reporting you've ever seen. Send me."

"I'll think about it."

"Okay. I'll wait." Angela plopped on the sofa and crossed her arms. "Here. While you think about it."

Campbell's jowls sagged into a smile. "You must be crazy."

"I've thought that myself from time to time. When do I leave?"

"I'll get back to you with the details. In the meantime why don't you get some rest?"

"Thanks, boss. You won't be sorry."

As Angela trod down the corridor, she thought Campbell was an odd combination, gruff and unpleasant as he could be, then concerned about her well-being. She'd noticed the same odd behavior in the parking lot after the bombing. Amazing.

While in his office, she'd been buoyed up by the challenge of convincing Campbell to send her. Now the enormity of what she'd agreed to frightened her. She imagined she'd be physically safe in the reporters' compound, but residing in a war zone had all kinds of risks. She wished she didn't have to go. She wished she could stay here with her family and marry Todd. But with that out as an option, she would make the best career a reporter ever had. She would work on her intuition until she knew the stories before they happened.

At home in Sedona, Luke had just finished a roundedness event when he received a call from Aaron and Vera. Very excited, they talked over each other, and their images skipped around in the static air above his holophone. Luke had to ask them to calm down and talk one at a time—uncharacteristic behavior for both of them but especially for the unflappable Vera.

Luke didn't blame them one bit for being worried. He shared their concern. Angela had staked her whole happiness on winning Todd's love. Luke didn't doubt Angela's memory of her previous identity as his mother. It would make perfect sense for Ty to come back as a man available to her. The toughest duty Luke had was to let their scenario play out, let them each learn in their own way and time.

When the last of the roundedness participants had given him a hug and gone away, Luke packed a suitcase and jumped into his plane. When he got to Phoenix, he verified that Angela had checked in at the Hyatt, as she'd told her folks, but she hadn't returned to her room. She'd gone somewhere, probably to the TV station, but she didn't answer his calls.

Unwilling to take a chance on missing her, Luke sat in an overstuffed, velour wing back chair. He enjoyed the fancy lobby with its huge floral displays, fountains in the walls, and comfy chairs for people watching, one of his favorite pastimes.

Luke loved the vibrant colors of humans, their skin and their clothing, but mostly he liked squinting his eyes and seeing if he could detect their auras. Today he did well, seeing lots of vivid greens and golds. There was so much color in the auras that he wondered whether a medical convention might be in town. Phoenix's new persona, as the capital of the United States of North America, had made it a magnet for all kinds of conventions. Even in the hottest part of summer, people poured in. Of course, federal money had built air conditioned, indoor passageways throughout the downtown area to help build the same international reputation Washington, D. C. had enjoyed before it sank below sea level.

Intending to take Campbell's advice and sleep for a while, Angela went back to the Hyatt and passed through the busy lobby. As she headed up the escalator, she saw a woman on the downward side, a tall, familiar-looking woman with a dark cloak, its hood up. The strangeness of the garment reminded Angela of ancient times and witches praying in circles in the woods.

Their eyes met for a moment. The woman scowled and looked away. It was that damned Melanie Vanderson. What the hell was she doing here? At least, thank God, she didn't have Todd with her.

Luke jumped up and called Angela's name, but she didn't notice him. He couldn't believe he was seeing such an incredible thing—Angela rode up as Melanie rode down. They eyeballed each other in a way that looked more like hate than recognition.

What was there between these two? Lifetime after lifetime. Couldn't they ever relax and give the other a little latitude? Luke squinted and saw traces of their auras, both muddy brown. Not a bit good.

Once in the privacy of her hotel room, Angela turned on the phone, hoping Todd's name would appear as a missed call. Instead the Psi Therapy Clinic showed in the frame. Her stomach flip-flopped with disappointment. It seemed such a long time since she'd seen Todd's handsome face and felt his kiss. Why didn't he want her?

Angela knew she had to get over this grief and move on psychologically. At least she had the people at the clinic willing and able to help her do that. She pressed the phone to get the message.

A hologram of Janice in a smock and slacks stood atop Angela's wrist.

"I'm sorry to hear that your nightmares have returned," Janice's image said. "I've made an appointment for you, Tuesday at nine in the morning. Dr. Kegan will be in at that time, and we can both evaluate you. I'll remind you surgery is becoming more probable as an alternative, but please don't be concerned. We have the ability to resolve your issues and return you to perfect health." The image dissolved.

They'd better hurry with their surgery, Angela thought, since she'd soon be leaving the country. Make that the planet. She shivered as the hair stood up on her arms and the back of her neck.

Intuition told her that she should not go through with the surgery, but she felt compelled to do it. She'd have to be healthy to go to Alpha Centauri. She couldn't risk having the nightmares follow her there.

Fourteen

And It Harm None

"Dr. Williams, Dr. Williams," a female voice accompanied a loud knock. "You've got company, sir."

Todd roused himself, disoriented as to his location or time of day. Pain careened through his brain as he tried to sit up. He unwound his cramped legs and opened the door of a 2030 Bimi with a drop-back seat. Not a comfortable place for his six-foot frame to recline but better than the back seat of any of his other cars. When he couldn't sleep in his bed, he had some insane idea that he might be able to sleep in a car and kick the headache himself.

"Dr. Williams. Are you in there?"

"Uh...huh." Todd's thoughts felt muddled. The row of Mustangs looked shadowy in recessed floor lights. He must have slept into the evening. He headed past the cars toward the side door that opened between the showroom garage and the walkway to the main house. Every step thumped through his head. "Okay. Come."

"The door's locked."

"Damn." Taking a plastic pass key out of his pocket, Todd threaded it through the electronic eye and returned it to his shirt. "You can come in now."

The door opened, and the short, ample housekeeper stood framed in light from the walkway. In a dark hooded cape, and a foot taller, Melanie peered over the housekeeper's shoulder.

"Ms. Vanderson's here to see you." The housekeeper scowled and pulled away.

"Thank you, that's all," Todd said to the housekeeper. He passed his hand over a sensor that turned on a bank of lights at the far corner of the garage. Bright light hurt too much in the midst of a migraine. To Melanie, he said, "Thank you for coming, especially considering our last conversation. You didn't have to."

As the housekeeper closed the door on them, Melanie swooped toward him, throwing back her hood. Her hair fell loose around her face as she gave him a quick, cool kiss on the cheek. "Blessed be."

Todd chuckled and immediately grimaced from the throbbing the laughter induced in his head.

"What's so funny?"

"I've never heard you say that before."

With a distrustful expression, Melanie unfastened the clasp at her neck and removed the cape, revealing a black dress with pointed sleeves and pointed hemline. "I've taken up Wicca."

"Indeed you have." How like her groupie nature to fall into yet another metaphysical organization she knew nothing about. If he hadn't felt so awful, Todd would probably have made a big joke of it and got himself into some real trouble. He left it at a snide "very fashionable."

"May I sit down?"

"Certainly." Todd offered her a seat on the tool bench. "The only other places to sit are in the cars. Would you like to try one?"

"Not really, but I'm glad you called. I wanted to see you and know how you're doing."

Feeling awkward, Todd stood eye to eye with the new witchy Melanie by the bench in the gloom. He could have planned better. He felt guilty for dumping her. He'd have liked to participate in a real relationship, like the one Angela wanted, but he didn't know how to go about it. Angela intimidated the hell out of him. Melanie was a lot less complicated.

"I was hoping we could, you know, get reacquainted. Get back together?" Todd sounded foolish to himself.

"Oh, had we broken up? I didn't realize that." Melanie gave him a casual grin.

Todd felt perplexed by her answer. "Well, maybe not." The sting of the headache hurt so much he sat down on the bench

"You feeling a little confused, are you, Todd?" Melanie crooned and laid a hand on his shoulder.

"It's another damn migraine. The worst one ever. I've had it for two solid days. I've taken every medicine in the cabinet. Done biofeedback, acupuncture. Nothing helps."

"Poor baby. That's what I imagined was wrong. I know my Todd so well." Melanie purred as she reached into the folds of the skirt and withdrew a tiny purple velvet pouch. "I brought these for you." She shook out two purple capsules. "Concentrated healing energy, just-for-you headache potion."

"That's kind of you, but what is it? It might react with what I've already taken." Todd suddenly wished he'd not called Melanie. His reasons were lost to him in his pounding brain. At least he should have waited until he felt better. He had no notion of how to counter her obsessive, cultish behavior.

"Never mind. Just lie back and trust me. You don't have to take any more pills." Melanie shoved his shoulders and forced him to lie down.

Might as well humor her. He didn't have the strength to argue. Todd lay back, his head aching more than ever.

Melanie rummaged in her cape and withdrew a small dagger from the folds. Standing close to him, she traced a circle around them and the bench by pointing the dagger down. She whispered words he couldn't understand or even hear over the pounding inside his head.

The woman had cracked up this time. She'd left the realm of common sense completely behind. And as for himself? Imprudent to get involved with her, to say the least.

Stabbing the dagger over her head, Melanie gazed at it. For a moment Todd imagined himself on a funeral pyre, awaiting death by her hand. It would only take one swift downward motion to do him in.

Just as Todd started to protest, she slit the capsules open and dropped the dagger. Purple powder dropped on his shirt and on the floor around him. Melanie rubbed her hands together spreading the powder across her palms then laid them on his forehead.

Todd felt heat seer through his skin, most certainly from the pressure she applied.

"Now, we wait." Melanie knelt beside him and kissed his lips softly.

Lying there, Todd waited, for what he didn't know. He believed with absolute certainty that her cure was poppycock. Why in hell had he wanted to see her? The reason totally escaped him. She was beautiful, but a nut cake. Angela and her past life stories seemed rational and logical by comparison.

Todd struggled to sit up, hard as it was to do so without throwing up from the ache in his head.

"How do you feel now? Better?" Melanie helped him to a sitting position.

"Not really. Sorry. I guess I'm immune to magic."

"Well, I've done my best. I think it's time you went to see an expert."

That she might know one amused Todd. He would have laughed if he didn't fear the pain it would cause. "Who would that be? I've been to the best doctors in L. A."

"There's a doctor at the Psi Therapy Clinic."

"Not you too!"

Melanie glared at him then composed her face into civility. "There's a neurosurgeon there with a fantastic cure rate. Now I don't know him personally, just by reputation, but...but I think it would really be worth your while to go see him. I'll take you tonight."

"To Phoenix? You want me to go there tonight? No doctors are on duty now except in emergency rooms. Bad as this is," Todd pointed to his head, "it's not an emergency."

"All right, then. Tomorrow. We'll go tomorrow."

"If I'm not better by then, I may have to."

When Luke arrived at Angela's hotel room and observed his granddaughter, he worried more than ever. She seemed distraught and depressed. At least she didn't deny her feelings and told him right off that she intended to have surgery to end the nightmares and then go to Alpha Centauri on assignment for as long as it took to make her a major international star in the reporting world.

"Work is all I have, Granddad. It's all I'll ever have. I've got to make it the best."

"You've got me and your folks. They're worried sick about you." Luke noticed that his words affected her strongly. He feared she might faint at any moment. On the other hand, he wanted her to change her plans, for the good of all of them. He knew just how to persuade her to stay. She always dreaded talk of his death. "But you can't go four light years away. I'll be dead when you get back."

"What difference does that make? You're the one who's always saying we return in different bodies." Angela spat out the words angrily.

"What I said is that death is just a change, a loosening of knowledge and a deepening of knowing."

"And how does that apply to anything?"

Luke had definitely miscalculated her resolve and her angst. "Okay, if you have to go, it's not my place to stop you. I want to support you in all your goals, but I can't forgive you for going away unless you fulfill a wish for me first."

"Oh, I'll miss you so," Angela sobbed. "And Mom and Dad, but I have to do this." She seemed far more volatile than normal.

"Maybe. Maybe not." A glance showed him her suitcase set beside the door. He picked it up. "Come on. I want to take you on a little side trip. To a place you've probably forgotten."

"Okay. If that's what you want." Angela looked so exhausted he wondered if she even knew what she was saying.

They rode up to the launch point atop the Hyatt, a miracle of engineering, perched on top of the rotating restaurant with a runway and hundreds of parking spaces for personal planes.

In the plane, Luke sat at the controls. Angela dozed, yet she started awake several times. He wished he could give her a physical healing but settled for sending her healing thoughts while he kept his hands on the dials and buttons.

Once they left the population hub and headed east, Luke set the plane on autopilot.

The night sky looked unusually lovely. To see bright stars against the blue-black dome in the silence was one of his greatest joys. All the daytime pollution from business, noise, mucked-up thinking, messy auras in everyday life, even the strange, blue quiet of the astral plane, nothing compared to the beauty of the night sky on planet Earth in physical reality.

Luke understood why people continued to reincarnate even after they'd attained perfection. They might say they came to help others, but it would also be so they could enjoy Earth's natural beauty, a special jewel in the solar system. He would be back, unquestionably. He knew he still had things to work on, the physicality issue. Well, okay, sex. His propensity to do good instead of just be good. These were fine points. Whatever he needed to work on Emmons would be quick to tell him once he arrived in the Afterlife.

Refusing to doze, Luke pulled himself up to attention. His charge, this lovely soul sleeping beside him, needed his care for a while longer.

Out of darkness, they flew east into morning light. A magnificent dawn broke over the Mississippi River, fine and rich.

Angela stirred and looked up. The sun's morning orange reflected on her face, lending a surreal glow to the cockpit. "Oh, it's beautiful."

"You got that right, little lady." Luke did his John Wayne imitation to entertain her. His mother had always loved it, but Angela didn't seem to notice. He realized she had no notion of who John Wayne had been. How tricky memory was between and even within lifetimes.

They watched the sunrise together as they flew across Heartland, through Illinois and into Indiana. Luke felt glad that Angela had mended well enough to enjoy the small pleasure.

Luke took control and cut back on the throttle as they neared their destination. Ahead he could see the prison and tomato canning factory that had been turned into museums of twentieth century life. Almost back to his birthplace.

"Oh, my God. I've seen this place before." Angela displayed great excitement.

"Well, of course, you have. I brought you here when you were little. We came to see the monument I bought for my mother."

"No, that was Harlan. You brought him. I was sick with the flu and couldn't come."

"Are you sure?"

"Positive. Your memory has definitely failed you." Angela gave him a suspicious glance.

Luke set the plane down in a parking lot among low-lying public buildings. Only a few people walked the streets. Too early for tourists, he supposed.

"You were kidding about just bringing Harlan?" Angela asked. "You knew I didn't come along, right?"

"I really don't remember bringing just your brother. I thought I brought both of you. Maybe I am getting old."

"That's all beside the point. I recognize this place, Granddad."

"Déjà vu all over again."

"Don't be glib. This is important. I feel so…at home."

Angela opened the cockpit door and dropped to the tarmac. Luke followed her, stepping away from the hot housing.

The air smelled fresh and pleasantly warm, not hot and too dry like an Arizona June. Well-trimmed green hedges grew around the parking lot, and hanging baskets of colorful flowers decorated the shops on the main street. Clouds billowed across the sky.

Closing her eyes, Angela pointed. "There. The cannery is that way. The prison is off in that general direction. And the Methodist church is over there. It's made of brick, not stone. Am I right?"

Luke followed the direction of her arm. "As far as I can tell, you're absolutely correct." He didn't remember the layout of the town, having left it as a toddler, but his mother grew up here and knew it well.

"Come on." Angela strode toward the south, setting a fast pace.

"Wait up for an old man."

"Sorry, Granddad." Angela turned and gave him a genuine smile for the first time since he'd arrived at her hotel room. Despite the dark circles around her eyes, she looked pretty again.

When he caught up with her, she looped her arm through his, and they strolled out of town, past a few homes where some residents nodded at them or stared at them. Luke felt glad that he'd been riding his exercise bicycle. Otherwise the hike would have done him in. After they'd gone about a mile, they rounded a bend and saw many tombstones of various sizes rising in the distance.

"Almost there." Angela sounded breathless, but she wasn't breathing hard like Luke.

Luke felt her tension as her arm pressed against his. He could almost hear her heartbeat. He would have given a lot to know what was going on in her mind, but he'd wait. She would tell him in her own good time.

They turned in at the main entrance with the words *Medfield Cemetery* etched deeply into the stone archway, an improvement over what Luke recalled from his earlier trips when the cemetery needed care. The graves, mowed meticulously, went off in all directions, dotted with wreaths and bouquets, many wilting from Memorial Day a couple of weeks before.

The sun had risen high enough that Luke regretted not having his sun glasses with him. "The graves are over there, to the west." They turned against the sun and strode along in silence. He spied the marble angel, delicate and slim, the highest monument in the section. "That's it up there."

"Okay, good." Angela had an intent expression on her face.

Releasing his arm, she walked in front of him through the grass to the angel, which stood atop a five-foot pedestal on the plot with a red marbleized stone. It read Capt. Wiley Brandon, USAF, born December 14, 1907, died December 20, 1948.

"This was my grandfather. Your great-great grandfather. He was a pilot and a war hero." Luke remembered with forlorn poignancy the cold and blowing snow on the day he'd come here to scatter his mother's ashes over her father's grave.

"I know how proud Angie was of him." Angela sounded reverent.

"And here is her monument." Luke indicated the pedestal with the angel on top. A plaque on the pedestal read *Angela Brandon Brock, 1940 – 1990. A life well lived. May you live again.*

Moving as if entranced, Angela placed her hands on the pedestal and gazed up at the angel. With her long black dress and her flowing black hair she seemed to Luke like a photographer's negative of the statue with its long white gown and flowing white hair. He had ordered the statue especially carved and had sent photographs of his mother. The artist had reflected her likeness precisely. The resemblance between the statue and his granddaughter stunned Luke into humble gratitude.

When Angela touched the cool marble and stared up at the serene image of her great grandmother, quiet settled over her soul. She saw in her mind's eye:

> *Herself in the ocean outside San Diego Bay, being pulled down by the undertow, fearing sharks, but rescued by Ty.*
>
> *The airplane crash in which Ty died as a fact from her past, something that had tormented her but that had been foreordained.*
>
> *Her diseased body coughing and choking for breath in the last days of life.*
>
> *Experiencing peacefulness in crossing over the barrier of death, the joy of reunion with Ty and Emmons.*
>
> *Her work on the other side as an angel to Luke and warning him to stay out of the tower on Nine Eleven.*
>
> *Talking to Luke long before he could hear her from the other side.*
>
> *Watching Aaron grow up and longing to return to these souls she loved so much.*

Agreeing to return with Ty and Melinda to finish what they started long ago.

Studying in her carrel in the Afterlife library in preparation for her return to Earth.

One by one, the images from her nightmares had presented themselves to her waking mind, no longer inducing fear. Now she understood their meaning. Her memories of the Afterlife were so much a part of her she felt amazed that she had not always recalled them.

Angela came to herself and backed away from the statue. Luke caught her in his arms and whispered, "Are you all right?"

"More than all right. I'm home in so many ways."

One glance at Luke's care-worn, beloved face convinced Angela. She recognized him as her son from that lifetime and much more. Although the details didn't come to her, she knew their destinies had intertwined from the beginning. She cherished him in a manner that words could not convey.

Hugging him, she felt his prickly beard and kissed his cheek with a smacking sound. "I love you, Luke."

A startled look crossed his face, and Luke laughed aloud. "That's the first time you ever called me by my first name!"

"Your mother looked out for you. I...she...came to you the night before the towers fell. Isn't that right?"

Luke face worked with barely-controlled emotion. "It was so like her to warn me about danger. She never harmed anyone and always wanted to help. Did she tell you that she came to me?"

"No, she didn't tell me." Angela recalled her frustration in the Afterlife about leaving her beloved child alone on Earth. That moment when she saved him from the burning towers taught her much about her power there and here. It was the same power, and she had to claim it. She did claim it, joyfully. "I know. I remember. I warned you."

Luke crushed her in his arms, and they both cried. When he finally released her, he wiped his tears on his shirt sleeve. "Do you want to walk around and see the graves of your other relatives?"

"Not really. It's time we dwelt among the living for the time we have left together." Angela knew that her time with Luke would be short. She saw death gathering around him, but she didn't fear it. She knew he would be joyful in the Afterlife and that she would see him again one day.

In this twenty-first century lifetime as Angela, she had repressed her powers, thinking of them as small when they were tremendous. She had shied away from her inner knowing out of fear that she would lose everything. Well, she lost it all anyway, but she would get it back somehow. She had confidence in the clarity of her knowledge now.

Angela tucked her arm under Luke's and took one last peek at the lovely visage of her past life self reigning over the graveyard. "Let's go home, Luke. We have a lot to do. If I'm not mistaken, there's a big birthday party for you in the works."

Fifteen

A Rendezvous with Death

Too tired to fly home, Angela and Luke returned to the plane in Medfield. They saw a bed and breakfast built in an 1800s style with purple gables and pink gingerbread decorations on the eaves. Porches ran across three sides with swings and wicker chairs.

"That's so quaint," Luke said, "it looks like a cartoon house."

"Not all of our Indiana heritage is in good taste, but a flop is a flop."

"Spoken like a true Hoosier."

After they rented rooms Angela showered and changed clothes before they went to dinner. She wore her last clean outfit, a lavender sundress with a long skirt. If she didn't return to her condo soon, she'd have to buy new clothes. Using a step stool to climb onto the quilt-covered bed in her room, she sat and called her parents to apologize for arguing and leaving them in a negative way.

Of course, they forgave her immediately. Such sweethearts, she couldn't have picked better parents. During the call, Vera mentioned the surprise party for Luke's birthday, and they agreed to meet at his house in Sedona on Tuesday afternoon.

Angela knocked on Luke's door to collect him. He looked rather tuckered. They walked down the main street. All the shops were already closed.

At an outdoor café, Angela ordered a bottle of wine. "I want to make a toast." After the waiter had poured the wine, they both raised a glass, and she said, "To you, Luke. For insisting I come on this trip. It was the right thing to do."

"I absolutely agree." Luke clicked her glass, drank a sip, and grinned. "There's nothing to compare with being right! I can see the headline now." As if reading skywriting, he traced the air with a forefinger. "SON PREDICTS RETURN OF PSYCHIC MOTHER."

"I talked to Mom and Dad. And by the way, you're having a surprise party. Thought you'd want to know."

"Thank the Divine that I won't have to spend my birthday by myself."

They both laughed at the family joke. They'd given him a party every year as long as Angela could remember. As a small family, they needed some special traditions, and Luke's birthday served as one. She always missed her brother at their parties. Otherwise she enjoyed the only-child attention she received in his absence.

Angela sipped the tangy Chardonnay and marveled at her singular experiences and at how lucky she felt to be able to share with Luke. "You know what was really neat? While I was talking to them and looking at Dad's image on the holophone, I remembered how he looked when he was a baby. Big old cauliflower ears, a lopsided smile, and the blackest hair. What a cutie."

Luke's eyes glistened with sudden tears. He leaned over and kissed her cheek. "How you loved that little guy."

"It's a good thing Melinda didn't abort him."

"At first she wanted to. That was a traumatic time for all of us. I'm not surprised you would remember." Luke shook his head as if he still couldn't believe the events had happened. "You were the one who talked her out of it."

Angela remembered how frustrated she'd felt by Luke's first wife, who was beautiful and talented, but completely self-obsessed. Imagine the gall of wanting to abort a wonderful soul for the sake of a career! Thank God, Angela had won the fight. She had won by the force of her own will. That power resided in her now and would help her reframe her identity to encompass her past life memory. "It's hard to imagine the world without my dad in it. I guess I was doing myself a favor. Otherwise, I couldn't have been born to this family."

Luke stared at her a long time before he whispered, "This is going to take some getting used to."

"Just don't call me *Mom*."

"Okay."

They ordered the house specialty, pot roast, corn on the cob, and biscuits with apple butter. As they ate, Angela asked questions about their lives in the twentieth century. The relationship she shared with Todd was very important and had provoked her dreams, but she wanted to absorb every aspect of her previous life. Luke mentioned people and places from their lives. Some she remembered and some she didn't. Assimilating details proved almost as taxing as reframing her identity.

Although the potatoes and corn tasted delicious, Angela found herself shoving the beef to the side. She noticed Luke doing the same and said, "I just don't have a taste for beef any more."

"Me either. I seldom eat meat of any kind. It dampens my energy, and I don't meditate as well."

"Did Angie eat beef?"

Luke shook his head and gave her a loving smile.

"If I was Angie then and now I'm Angela, who else might I have been?"

"I think I've got some of those answers, but it's better for your soul development for you to remember them in your own time. It won't help you much if I lay historical facts on you." Luke patted her hand. "Don't worry. You'll remember more and more. It's exponential in a way. What you know and understand grows with or without all the history. You'll probably find yourself more psychically attuned as time goes by."

"Did I tell you a premonition kept me out of the car the day it got bombed?"

"No, but I'm not surprised. You'll get better at all the techniques because you're deepening your connection with the Divine."

"Thank God for that." Angela couldn't seem to control her impish spirit. "Was there someone we knew named Emmons?"

"At one time, many years ago he lived a lifetime in the same community with us."

"Was that during colonial times?" Now the clothing of long ago and the riding crop made perfect sense.

"Right, eighteenth century. But now he's our guide."

"I thought that's what you'd say. And a guide helps you make decisions about your lifetimes."

"And reminds you when you've gone astray. He and my mom were very close. She introduced him to me before she passed. It's all there in your memory banks. You'll see him eventually."

"I already have."

"Excellent."

"He scared me half to death."

Luke didn't push her to say more about Emmons. Angela appreciated his wisdom in allowing her time to adjust to her new perspective.

After dinner as they headed back toward the bed and breakfast, they passed a gift shop. Angela said, "I want to stop there in the morning to buy some souvenirs of this town. Maybe some rocks, something sturdy to remind me of my roots."

"That's fine. I'll get the plane refueled and checked while you do that. I won't have time to shop."

"I knew you'd dodge that duty." Angela laughed. "I think I'll buy a gift for Todd too. Something needs to spark his memory. I may not get the chance to give it to him, but then again, I may."

"Think there's a possibility that you'll get back together? What's in your crystal ball for him?"

"Very cloudy right now."

"Hmmm." Luke screwed up his face in a fake, inscrutable expression.

"You know something psychically that I don't know? Tell me, Granddad."

Now Luke really laughed at her. "Wouldn't you like to know, little lady."

Setting her hands on her hips, Angela gave him a stern look. "You can't get away with that. If you know something tell me."

Luke's cocky smile told her she'd get nothing serious from him now. Either he didn't have any intuition about her and Todd or he knew something he didn't want to say.

When Kegan saw Melanie's name as the caller on his holophone, he excused himself from the staff meeting and took the elevator to the seventh floor. The Clinic had progressed nicely with all five counselors busy most of the time. That gave him a few elite cases but not a large work load, a situation that suited his desire to administrate half time and practice medicine half time. The staffing had gone very well, and Janice could finish without him. She had given him further good news, that the Brock bitch had an appointment on Tuesday.

Kegan hurried into his private office with its midnight-blue illuminated walls, slipped into the molded chair behind the desk, and said to the phone, "Melanie Vanderson."

"Hello, Dr. Kegan. Thank you for returning my call."

Kegan recognized her alto voice although not her distant, formal manner. She had turned off the video reception so he had few cues as to her motives or mood.

That she intentionally kept him in ignorance annoyed him, but he'd withhold comment as she might have a reason he didn't discern.

"What can I do for you this afternoon, Ms. Vanderson?" Kegan intended the question to sound polite, or slightly provocative if she were so inclined.

"I'm here with a friend of mine who is suffering from a three-day migraine headache. He's had them for years. In the past, pills, acupuncture, and some other thing have helped."

"Biofeedback," came a male voice on Melanie's end. "Tell him biofeedback hasn't helped either."

Kegan hoped he'd heard the voice of the infamous astrophysicist in the background. If so, Melanie probably had some idea of the extent of Kegan's dislike. But considering they'd not talked at all since Friday when she kicked him out of her hotel room, Kegan couldn't be certain. Perhaps this was her way of making up with him.

"Biofeedback is the other thing," Melanie said. "Would you be able to see my friend yet this evening?

"The Clinic closes in an hour, but—"

"We can't be there before eight. We're flying from L A." Melanie whispered something Kegan couldn't hear. "My friend says he understands the inconvenience of such a late appointment, but I assured him you wouldn't mind." Her voice sounded level as if imparting new information. "If your treatment is successful, he will investigate the possibility of endowing a chair for migraine research at your clinic."

"That would be an important contribution to our staff." Her friend must certainly be that bastard Williams. He had billions to throw around and never missed an opportunity to show off his money. Melanie's formal manner of speech indicated that she had not told Williams she knew Kegan personally. Good work, girl, Kegan thought. "I'll do my best to help. I'll expect you around eight then and look forward to meeting you both."

How much did Melanie understand or suspect of his intentions toward Williams and the others? She shared the same hatred of the Brock bitch, but what did she expect to accomplish from bringing Williams to him? Melanie was too hot for the wimp, but he probably wanted her. Maybe she was going back to him and wanted to flaunt it in Kegan's face although Melanie didn't seem to have any jealousy in her. He would be able to intuit more when he saw them. He needed visual cues to read people. He had many psychic abilities, but clairvoyance had always eluded him.

Kegan gazed at the fluid monitor imbedded in his desktop. He imagined the screen turning on then sent his energy toward it. The selection screen lit up. At least his psychokinesis still worked. By looking at the monitor intensely, he forced it to select sapphire blue, the code for his personal files, and set the order to chronological.

During his training at the Psi Therapy Clinic in England over twenty years before, Kegan had recorded his reincarnation memories. The voice track sounded muffled because of the trance state required for remembrance, and the image track contained brain wave patterns. Technology had advanced in the field in recent years, and he kept intending to re-record his files for the sake of posterity.

The illuminated walls faded to gray, and the first of the files launched. Kegan knew them all by heart but wanted the voice tape to refresh his resolve.

The legend came up on the viewing screen.

Past Life Transcript of Kendall Roberts aka Robert Kendall aka Robert Kegan, recorded November 12, 2035, London, England. Approximately 50 B. C. E. Segment

Brain waves rippled across the wall in front of Kegan as his voice transmission began:

I see myself, a strong, young warrior hundreds of years ago. I wear leather breeches and leggings. I live in a stone hut on a knoll near the great henge. My name is Kegan. I fight bravely in many battles. I have no parents, my allegiance belongs to the tribe. The Goddess singled me out as Her special servant. I pray to Her for wisdom and courage. I intend to be king someday. The Goddess must choose me through the druidess Alma.

Two other warriors rival me for the throne. Morfran is the handsome consort to the druidess. He is a worthy opponent, but Alma betrays Morfran and murders him to avenge the sniveling bard, Taliesin. Alma dishonors the tribe by proclaiming her snot-nosed son, Lugh, king.

I challenge Lugh. It is my right. I fight honorably, but he fights like the hound of hell and defeats me. He should dispatch me to the Goddess to save my honor, but instead he cuts off my hand and banishes me in shame and humiliation.

I curse them all and swear to hunt them down, no matter how long it takes. I die alone in the forest, ravaged by a wild boar.

Kegan no longer went by his birth name of Kendall Roberts. He'd taken the name of Kegan to honor his betrayal in that lifetime. He recognized Melanie as the warrior Morfran, one whose loyalty could be counted on in war, but not necessarily in peace. The brat king Lugh, Luke today, still considered himself superior to everyone around him. He learned nothing through the ages about humility or respect. The bard Taliesin, the troublemaker, was back as Todd, and Angela as the wanton, selfish druidess, Alma.

They would all die by his hand now. Not Lugh, not Alma, not the Goddess, Kegan would be the decider.

The legend read:

> *Past Life Transcript of Kendall Roberts aka Robert Kendall aka Robert Kegan, recorded November 13, 2035, London, England. 1700s Segment*

Brain waves and Kegan's voice began:

> *I see myself at nine. My name is Colin. I live in a mud hut in Ireland. My clothes are rags, not enough to keep me warm in the wind. My father gets drunk and has a go at me. It hurts my back side. He does the same to my idiot brother. He is bigger and younger and dumb as a rock.*
>
> *My father sets us out on the highway. We steal food along the way. We stow away on a boat to England in the time of George the Second. The idiot and I shear sheep and steal when we can. We drink the profits as often as not.*
>
> *We meet a Scot there, MacPhearson, in the woosd. We dodge the sheriff together and run rum. We plot to steal MacPhearson's kid and hold him for ransom. We don't get the money because MacPhearson's wife drowns MacPhearson in the bog.*
>
> *The idiot and I steal the boy ourselves. MacPhearson's wife and her fancy lieutenant lover rescue the kid and blow me and the idiot to kingdom come.*

Kegan despised recalling that miserable lifetime. He'd never had a chance to do or be anything worthwhile. When he tried to take what was owed him, MacPhearson's wife and her lover, those he knew today as Angela and Todd, had murdered him to save the wretched boy, Luke. Melanie, as MacPhearson, had been a real rascal, but a buddy whom Kegan as Colin had understood. Perhaps he could trust Melanie now because of the bond forged then. Honor among thieves, as they say. He chuckled despite himself. He recognized the poor idiot brother in this lifetime too. The son born to him out of wedlock, from whom the Imam had banned him. What a shame that old fart had already died, or Kegan would have him on the hit list.

The legend read:

Past Life Transcript of Kendall Roberts aka Robert Kendall aka Robert Kegan, recorded November 14, 2035, London, England. 1900s Segment

Brain waves and Kegan's voice began:

I attend a meeting in Celestial City. The speaker says this is a time of great chaos and meanness of spirit on Earth. She asks for volunteers to call humankind back from hate into love. I volunteer along with Luke and Melinda. In exchange we will receive great rewards.

I am born into Afghanistan. My name is Karim. My father beats my mother. He takes me to a school and leaves me.

The Imam teaches me to live without alcohol, to control my anger and remain calm. He teaches me to do Allah's bidding. I do not question my masters. I fly a plane into a tower. Melinda dies and Luke escapes.

I return to my soul group. Angie and Melinda try to console me. Emmons tries to talk me out of it, but I demand to return to human life with the powers promised me.

For the first time in a past life memory, Kegan had recalled the interim period, the life between lifetimes. He understood that the dynamics changed in the transition from there to here. Not all emotions or abilities translated into each lifetime.

The life as Karim had been wasted in a sense although through it Kegan had learned never to put his trust in authority. Since adulthood he had lived his life under his own control, bowing to no heavenly or earthly superior. Life had been much more satisfying this way and would get better as he eliminated those who mistreated him. The fact that Luke had avoided the fate forced on Karim and Melinda of dying in the tower enraged Kegan. Luke had again been favored by those supposedly enlightened beings on the other side. They would have to pay for their short-sightedness by the unscheduled deaths of their favorites.

The emotional stress had hampered Kegan's psychokinetic abilities. He shut off the monitor by hand. In the ensuing gloom, he unlocked the safe beneath his desk. There he kept his stocks and bonds, alongside four vials labeled A, L, M, and T for his possible victims. They contained the most lethal medication any lab had ever devised. The beauty lay in the fact that its deadly effects didn't show up in autopsy.

Melanie was a loose cannon. Switching sexes had obviously unsettled her soul. Kegan had no idea what she would do or where her allegiance would lie. If she helped him eliminate Williams, then Kegan would know he could trust her. If not, he needed to be prepared. He took out the vial labeled T because he intended to use it to kill Todd tonight and get one of his enemies out of the way. He stuck the M vial in his pocket just in case Melanie turned on him.

His passion and hatred had cooled. Kegan felt temperate and rational. He had planned his actions and trained his mind to determined persistence. He would do what was necessary to fulfill his destiny. He had no choice.

Sixteen

An Image of Truth

While Luke flew the plane, Angela phoned the TV station and learned from Carlos that the police had discovered nothing new on the car bombing. She was at a loss to know how to proceed, but perhaps her old personal files held a clue. She asked Luke to take her to her condo so she could get the files. Besides she needed her clothes. She sometimes doubted anyone intended to harm her and tried to convince herself she'd been the victim of a random attack, but she always returned to the intuition about the bomb. No coincidence there.

"I'll sleep at home then take the subway to Phoenix in the morning to make my appointment at the Clinic."

"This is a really bad idea, Angela. You're setting yourself up. I'll stay with you and fly you back myself."

"That's not necessary. You need to go home and get some sleep. And clean your house for the party. I'm sure you left it messy." Her attempt to tease didn't seem to lighten his annoyance with her.

"It's probably all right if you go back for sessions with your counselor, but you shouldn't submit to surgery, no matter what."

"It won't happen tomorrow. This is just a diagnostic appointment, but I intend to have the surgery right away, if I need it, so I'll be ready when I get the assignment to Alpha Centauri." The nightmares might stop on their own since Angela had learned so much about the causes for them from her previous life. She would know in a few days whether she could call off the surgery.

"I don't want you to see Kegan at all. Who knows what he'll do to you?"

"There's no reasoning with you on this subject, so let's just drop it."

Darkness fell as they sped over New Mexico. In flickering cabin light, Angela closed her eyes to shut out Luke's troubling glances. The hum of the engine quieted her. *Dear Todd, where are you tonight? Do you miss me? What are you doing?*

Angela entered a profoundly unusual reality, an altered state of consciousness. An image flashed in her mind, bright and still, a picture of truth.

Todd lay on a table in an operating theatre. He appeared to be wearing mechanic's coveralls, not a hospital gown. He looked exhausted and tried to shield his eyes. He seemed tormented. Dr. Kegan stood over him in a surgical gown, a vial in one hand and a syringe in the other. In a cloak, Melanie peered down at Todd from the other side of the table.

"Oh, dear God," Angela cried. "They're killing Todd. We've got to get there right away or it will be too late." Horror swept over her at what he might be experiencing at this very moment. Why would they want to kill her beloved?

"Where are they?"

"In the Psi Therapy Clinic. Hurry."

Luke turned the rudder dial southwest to Phoenix. Angela appreciated the fact that he didn't question her intuition. He simply followed it. She felt terrifyingly confident that her vision showed the truth either of what was happening or would soon happen. She couldn't bear the thought that dear Todd was in such agony. They had to arrive in time. If they didn't...unthinkable.

"Damn." Luke set the speed dial for eight hundred miles per hour. "I feel I'm to blame for Todd's dangerous situation."

"How could you have any responsibility?"

"Sin of omission. I warned you and Melanie about Kegan. When both of you blew me off, I decided not to contact Todd. If only I had—"

"If you had, he wouldn't have believed you either." Fear spiraled through Angela. "I believe you now." She swallowed to quell the bile rising in her throat.

"Divine Spirit," Luke murmured, "you and I are one. You and Angela are one. Together we reach Todd and save him from harm. I see this. I know this. I'm grateful for this. And so it is."

"And so it is."

Angela called the Phoenix Police Department without turning on her video.

"Sorry, ma'am," came the voice of a bored-sounding female," but we have to be able to see you in video. Standard operating procedure."

Pressing on the video despite misgivings, Angela said, "I'm Angela Brock."

"Yeah, and I'm Juan Calderon. And this is the evening news." The operator's tone had turned facetious.

"Please, look at me."

A fat-cheeked woman peered into the lens. "Oh, sorry, Ms. Brock. What can I do for you?"

"I need to speak to the officer in charge of the investigation of a car bombing, my car, that is."

"Do you know his name?"

"No."

"I'll just look it up." A long silence followed, one which Angela thought might actually never end as they sped through the night sky.

"Sergeant Harris. He's gone for the day. Can you call back tomorrow?"

"This is an emergency." Angela lost patience and shouted, "The person who set off that bomb is trying to kill my friend as we speak."

The operator peered around the interior of the airplane with a perplexed look on her face. "In your plane?" She sounded incredulous.

"Not here!" Luke yelled at her. "He's at the Psi Therapy Clinic. Get a squad car over there right away. Uh, seventh floor, probably. That's where his office is."

Angela wondered how Luke knew but didn't take time to ask. "Please. This is an emergency."

"Find Dr. Robert Kegan, and you'll have your man," Luke snarled.

"How could you know what's going on over there?" The operator's words were maddeningly slow.

"We're here." Luke cut the plane's speed to hover.

"Damn it," Angela cried. "Send the squad car!" She left her phone on, hoping the police would listen in.

Luke set the plane down on the tarmac. As Angela opened the door, he said, "Watch out for the security guard."

How did he know there would be a security guard? Angela dashed from the plane. "Let's go."

"Don't wait for me. I'll just slow you down."

Angela took off for the stairwell with Luke lumbering behind her. She ran down two flights and out into the hall, not knowing the exact location of Kegan's office. She ran along the corridor. The carpeting masked the sound of her footsteps. She'd gone the wrong way and backtracked just as Luke came through the door from the stairs with rasping breaths.

"Where's the office?" she asked.

Luke pointed in the direction she'd not taken, and Angela hurried down the hall. Why hadn't she run into the security guard? Maybe they were in luck. Maybe they would arrive in time.

When Angela found the office, the glass panels failed to slide open. The scoundrels must have tripped the locks from inside.

"Stand back," Luke whispered and pulled out a phase gun.

Surprised that he had a gun at all and even more so that he had it with him, Angela stepped aside.

Setting the phase gun against the door, Luke clicked the trigger. A small cut appeared in the glass. He continued to apply the energy in an oval and blasted a hole big enough to step through.

"What in hell are you doing?" Kegan stormed up to the sheared entrance and glared at Luke. "Are you insane?" He tugged up the hem of his surgical gown and stuffed something into his trouser pocket.

A caped Melanie hovered behind him, a stricken look on her face. "Please, don't." She grabbed Kegan's arm.

"Put your hands in the air." Luke turned the gun on them. "Both of you."

As Kegan reached for the ceiling, he yelled, "What the fuck..."

"Shut up. Don't you dare move a muscle."

"Why, Luke, you couldn't hurt me." Melanie moved as if to walk toward him.

"Hands up. You too." Luke looked capable of shooting anyone at the moment.

Certain she'd find her beloved but uncertain as to his condition, Angela ran past Kegan and Melanie, around the desk, and into the back room. There lay Todd on the table. "Have they hurt you?" she cried.

"What?" He propped himself up on one elbow, bleary-eyed. "You?"

"Todd, darling, did they do anything to you? Did they inject you with anything?"

"I don't think so. They're trying to get rid of this headache."

"Come with me. I'm taking you out of here."

Angela grabbed him by the waist and helped him off the table. He must have been working on his cars when they brought him here. With tremendous relief, she heard sirens above the building.

"Why are you here?"

"We came to save you, Granddad and I."

"But—"

"I'll tell you later. Let's go right now."

Trembling, Todd leaned on Angela, and she supported his shaky steps as they moved through the operating theatre into the office.

Jaw drawn down as if he'd just eaten a persimmon, Luke held the gun steadily on Kegan and Melanie. They glowered at the barrel. She might be a victim, too, but Angela would leave that for the police to decipher.

"Stand down. Phoenix Police Department." A shout came from the stairwell, followed by a clank as the door flew open.

Two policemen and one policewoman lunged into the corridor, phase guns swinging in an arc encompassing Angela, Luke, Todd, Melanie, and Kegan.

"Thank God, you're here, officer." Kegan dropped his hands and moved toward the police.

Melanie edged along behind him, holding his lab coat.

"Stay where you are." The policewoman stopped Kegan with the touch of her gun to his chest.

"No, you misunderstand." Kegan gave her a polite smile and backed away. A gray-black strand of hair fell across his face. Blushing, he pushed it back

One policeman relieved Luke of his gun, and he exhaled a huge sigh. "Thanks."

"These people threatened to kill us." Kegan addressed the policewoman as if sharing a confidence.

"That's a lie." Angela pointed a finger at Kegan and said to the policewoman, "Look for a vial and a syringe. They're either on his person or in the operating room. I suspect they contain poison."

"How do you know that, Ms. Brock?" one policeman asked Angela.

Luke lifted his brows in an attitude of dismay. "In a place like this, do you even have to ask?"

"I saw it in a clairvoyant vision." Angela's tone defied anyone to dispute her.

Kegan gave her a quick, murderous glance that changed into a look of long suffering. He folded his arms across his chest. "Please arrest these people, officers. They have invaded my privacy and destroyed my office. I intend to press charges."

The other policeman said, "There's a lot to sort out, but we've got plenty of time. I'll escort all of you to the police station." He looked at Todd, as if noticing his distressed condition for the first time. "And you, sir, you'll go with us too, so we can take your statement."

"Be glad to." With a squeeze of Angela's shoulder, Todd kissed the top of her head. "Thank you."

Despite Todd's illness, Angela felt joyous at being with him. The small intimacy of a kiss on the head felt natural and right.

The policewoman motioned to Kegan and Melanie to walk in front of her. "Come along, folks. I'm sure we'll be able to clear all this up."

Melanie turned to the policewoman. "He made me do it. I'm innocent—"

"Save it for the chief." The policeman waved her gun at a forlorn-looking Melanie and a scowling Kegan, both of whom headed toward the door. Kegan threw his arm around Melanie. She shrugged it off.

One policeman escorted Angela, Todd, and Luke.

As the other policeman walked into the surgery, Angela heard him call for backup. She felt vindicated. They would find the syringe and poison and believe her story, regardless of where she learned the information. She shivered as she recalled their past life.

Back in the 1980s Angela had predicted that her lover's plane would crash. When it did, she came under suspicion by the police and the Navy. Down through the centuries many a poor woman had burned at the stake for lesser deeds. Or tied toe to thumb and drowned. Angela shivered with dread unconquered after so many lifetimes. Fortunately, modern people accepted information gained by psychic means as conceivably correct.

At the station, the policewoman ushered Kegan and Melanie into a separate room out of sight.

Angela, Luke, and Todd gave their statements. The officers acted polite and deferential although they didn't report discovery of the evidence Angela had said they would find. The police released her and her two men with thanks.

They left the police station at one in the morning. A weary-looking Luke offered to fly Angela home, but she insisted on staying with Todd because he'd asked her to.

"Tell me, Granddad, how did you just happen to have a phase gun on the plane?"

"No coincidence to it. I bought it when I found out Dr. Kegan, aka Kendall Roberts, had come back to town. I had to be prepared for anything."

"No one is gladder than I that you were." Angela kissed him good-bye. "Happy birthday, Luke, my dear." She didn't dwell on the fact that she'd born him. Spanning lifetimes and relationships might become awkward were they always acknowledged. Some memories improved from haziness, and this was one of them.

Arm in arm, Angela and Todd walked through the tunnel to the Hyatt. The desk clerk told them there were no rooms available, that all the hotels downtown were full because of the International Association of Visiting Nurses in town. Angela regretted now that she'd checked out to go to Indiana with Luke.

Todd told the desk clerk they'd wait until a room became available.

"I've got to file the story, you know," Angela said. "How do you feel about the use of your name?"

"What difference will it make after the police release their docket? We've only got a few hours of anonymity. Your station might as well have the exclusive." Todd guided her to a secluded section of the lobby, and they sat on a couch facing a painting of a limestone cliff dwelling of the vanished Sinagua Indians. "Actually I like Arizona because the paparazzi have plenty of scandal to cover with the Federal Government here. They don't pester me like the ones in L. A."

Todd looked miserable, like the last thing he needed was someone taking his photo. Angela adjusted her holophone to No Picture so the reporter on the other end wouldn't know her location. She phoned in the story in a brief, knowing some other reporter would get the assignment to talk to the police. She didn't care whether she got credit or not. Protecting her poor darling for a few hours was more important.

Angela sat on the couch, and Todd lay down, his head in her lap. He gave her a smile so small it didn't crease the dimple in his chin. He gazed at her with red-rimmed eyes then fell asleep.

"Sleep well, my darling." Angela felt content to look down on the face and lanky body she'd loved many times over. This would be the best of them. She gently touched his forehead and sent him healing thoughts. Happy, happy day!

Seventeen

Always the Same Sweet Girl

Todd awoke the next morning in the hotel lobby. He still lay with his head in Angela's lap. She slept with her head crooked at an awkward angle, her back against the couch. He hoped she wouldn't have a stiff neck. As he reached up to caress her cheek, he realized his headache had disappeared. The previous day had probably been the most bizarre he'd ever experienced.

Even though he had no idea how, Angela had saved his life.

Everything changed the moment she pulled him off the operating table. His hopes for the future. His belief in the parameters of man's abilities, or woman's, rather. He had a lot of questions and a lot to learn, and he intended to begin right away.

His touch awakened Angela and she smiled down at him, love alive on her face. He wanted to always make her happy. He wanted always to feel so adored.

"Morning, beautiful." A very tousled beautiful, but who cared?

Her phone rang, and she fumbled to touch her wrist. Todd hugged her and stood up to let her move freely.

"Are you feeling better?" Angela sounded sleepy and rubbed her back. How could she have rested at all, holding him as she had? What a selfless woman!

"Much. No more headache."

Angela glanced at her phone. "I'd better answer this." With a smile of apology, she stretched her legs as she flipped the switch. Luke's hologram floated above her wrist.

While she talked on the phone, Todd went to the desk and asked if there were a room available now. The desk clerk said not until three. Todd slapped a thousand dollar bill on the desk top. "I need one now." That's what he'd have done last night if he'd been thinking right.

"The visiting nurses are all leaving this morning. We'll have a room cleaned and ready for you in half an hour, sir." The clerk swiped the bill into his pocket. "Thank you, sir. Room eighteen thirty-two."

"Make sure there's a well-laid out breakfast tray in there, too." Todd passed his identity wrist tattoo over the electronic eye on the counter.

"Thank you, Dr. Williams."

Many women in long white dresses pulled suitcases across the lobby. Todd found the coffee urn and poured himself a cup.

Out of ear shot of Angela, he called his personal assistant and directed him to purchase a set of clothes for Todd and one for Angela and have them delivered to the hotel within the hour. He guessed her size at an eight. He hated to ask. It seemed rude, and he wanted to be perfectly polite and gentlemanly with her. He felt contrite about ending their affair before it even began. He'd been a scared fool.

Angela crossed the lobby to Todd, and he poured her a cup of coffee. He had no idea whether she liked it or, if so, how she drank it. He was fascinated to find out. "How do you like it?"

"Black, please."

Todd filled her cup from the urn.

"My grandfather has postponed his birthday party until tomorrow. One hundred years old, and he's got more important business than to take time to celebrate. I have no idea what he feels he has to do instead, but that's my Luke for you." She smoothed her hair.

Todd handed her the cup. "If you have no plans, milady, I'd enjoy spending some time with you."

"Oh, I've got an appointment with Dr. Kegan and a counselor from the Clinic this morning." A mischievous smile crossed her face.

"The hell you say!"

Angela laughed. "I wouldn't miss it for the world. Would you come with me?"

"I'd be delighted."

"Are you sure your headache is gone?" When he nodded, Angela said, "It's like a miracle."

"One of many in my life lately."

"So, does that mean you're ready to go to the Regression Portal?" Angela seemed far calmer than the events of the past few hours warranted. Where did she get her spunk?

"Well, I don't know." Todd hedged because he didn't relish refusing her outright. She seemed more powerful than she had before. She might deck him.

Angela gave him an indulgent grin. They finished their coffee, and he took her by the elbow and guided her to the elevators. They rode up in silence with several Japanese in military gear. Probably aides to Japan's defense minister, in the capital for talks about wars in the colony planets.

The breakfast spread was deluxe with samplings of every fruit, omelets, all kinds of sausages. Angela took French toast, orange juice, and coffee. Todd loaded his plate and ate enough for three people. His appetite had dwindled in the grip of the headache, and he could almost feel his belly button and his backbone rubbing against each other.

By the time they finished breakfast, the new clothing had arrived. Angela acted appropriately impressed with Todd's consideration in ordering it and retired to the bathroom. When she returned she looked like a fashion model in a gown and bolero of exquisite cut. His personal assistant would get a raise because he'd chosen royal blue for her, obviously remembering that as Todd's favorite. He hadn't seen her carrying a purse or makeup bag, but her face looked perfect. She looked fabulous on the outside and she was fabulous on the inside.

Todd wished he could remove the clothes and see her nude. More than anything, he longed to take her in his arms and make love to her. How would she react? He wondered whether she thought she remembered their sex life from their former life. That's something he intended to ask her after they had made love. That moment would come soon, he hoped. In the meantime, he refused to do anything to jeopardize their future.

For Todd's clothing, the personal assistant had chosen pearl-gray slacks and blazer with a plum silk shirt. Todd would much rather wear jeans, but today he intended to make Angela proud to be with him. He knew from seeing the clothes she wore on the air and in person that she had a very keen sense of style. He liked that in a woman.

As they passed through the sliding glass doors of the busy lobby, Todd knew he'd succeeded. Angela glowed with glamour and confidence and, he hoped, pride in her companion.

They took a taxi to the Psi Therapy Clinic. A security guard manned a barrier that stood beside the name plate kiosk.

In a whisper, Todd said to Angela, "Wonder where that burly fellow was last night? Why he didn't notice anything peculiar, like Luke drilling a big hole in a door with a phase gun?"

"Me, too."

Two police officers had created a bottleneck in front of the elevators. They were checking identity tattoos manually rather than by electronic sensors.

Todd and Angela waited in line while building employees grumbled about the inconvenience. From their conversation they clearly knew little about the events of the night before except that their boss was in jail.

"Excuse me," Angela addressed the guard. "I'd like to ask you a question."

The security guard shrugged.

"Why weren't you here for the excitement last night?"

"What's it to you, lady? Hey, wait a minute, aren't you that reporter?"

"Yes, I am. I'm doing a story on the incident here last night." She lowered her voice so Todd had to strain to hear. "I may have to mention the fact that you weren't here and might have been derelict in your duty."

"No, ma'am." The security guard seemed genuinely offended. "I had permission. Dr. Kegan mentioned it specially. That I could leave early because he'd be working late and would lock up himself."

"Thank you very much."

Angela gave Todd a meaningful glance. The fellow had been warned away, so Kegan could murder Todd. He'd like to kill the son of a bitch.

When their turn came, the security guard admitted Todd and Angela after he called upstairs and verified Angela's appointment. Fortunately none of these professionals considered Todd the victim or perhaps didn't know, and they treated him like everyone else.

Todd and Angela arrived at the fifth floor to find Janice Beatty waiting in the hallway with a trembling handshake for him. "Good to meet you, Dr. Williams." She ushered them inside and seated them on a futon, side by side. The walls glowed a pink color.

Janice coughed and folded her hands. "I'm so very sorry about the unfortunate events of last evening. I'm certain that Dr. Kegan will be exonerated very soon. He's a friend of the governor, you know. In the meantime, I have taken the reins of the organization, and—"

"That's not why we're here." Angela seemed impatient with Janice.

"Yes, I know, but we can't very well do the diagnostic with the doctor...uh, how shall I say it...indisposed. Perhaps we should reschedule."

"Under the circumstances, I don't intend to have any procedure done by Dr. Kegan, now or ever." Angela appeared to be tamping down a fair amount of anger.

"Oh, naturally." Janice glanced at Todd, who tried not to give her any clues about his feelings. He recognized that she probably felt embarrassed, but she'd not been involved, at least so far as he knew. He had no real interest in this woman except that Angela wanted to consult with her.

"I was hoping," Angela spoke forcefully, "that we could use our scheduled time to show Dr. Williams my dream tapes."

"Of course." Janice seemed to suck up something inside herself in order to turn to business. She waved her hand over her desktop, and the glowing walls dimmed. Images began to dance on one wall.

The state-of-the-art equipment impressed Todd, but nothing compared to his astonishment at recognizing the images. Angela ran across tarmac, chasing a Cessna. Then it exploded. He expelled a quick breath and felt her hand rubbing his leg in a comforting way.

The next series of images showed Angela sobbing at a coffin. She picked up a picture that sat on top. A close-up revealed that the photograph was of Todd. "Good God! Where did you get this film?"

"They are my dreams." Angela pressed against him, the scent of her perfume delicate and mystifying, like her. "Do you understand now why I insist we've lived a past lifetime together?"

"I disagreed with her analysis in the beginning." Janice flicked off the tape. The walls turned rosy and soft music began to play.

"Right. You called me star struck." Angela gave the counselor a snide look.

Todd noticed the bad vibes between these two, particularly on the subject of himself. He enjoyed his star status and could be equally as star struck over Angela. More and more he saw how well she complemented him.

"Now." Janice wriggled. Angela obviously made her nervous. "I'm reevaluating my position. I think we should find out what's really going on. With your permission, I'll take you down to the Regression Portal."

"What do you say, now, Todd?"

The day began with Todd's thinking he wanted to please Angela, and going to the Regression Portal definitely would do so. The possibilities intrigued him more every moment. What might he find out about himself? Or about the human experience? What the hell. "I've explored outer space. Now I guess it's time for me to explore inner space."

"Oh, I'm so glad." Angela threw her arms around his waist, laid her cheek on his chest, and hugged him.

Her enthusiasm thrilled Todd. He hoped he didn't disappoint her. Angela seemed to have too much invested in the idea of his remembering something, as if that would validate her memories. But that would not necessarily be the only outcome. In nature different realities co-existed, as in the subatomic world. Why not in history?

Janice escorted them down one floor to the Regression Portal where she introduced them to another counselor. "Magdaleeah will take care of you. I must get back to work." She practically scurried up the hall, whether anxious to work or to get away from them Todd didn't know, but he guessed the latter.

Magdaleeah was a large black woman with golden hoops in her ears, hair about a half an inch long, and a bright orange caftan. "Come in." She moved gracefully for her size.

The portal consisted of a laboratory and control booth with a glass divider between them. The walls glowed lavender, and bells tinkled almost imperceptibly. The scent of lavender flowers carried on the air. In the middle of the lab sat two purple futons. Each had a computer monitor and other electronic equipment lying on a table alongside.

"This is a lovely place to work," Angela said.

"I like it." Magdaleeah's smile inspired trust. "Please lie down and relax. Calm and centeredness are very important to the quality of results we obtain."

Todd and Angela lay down on the two futons. He reached across the space between them. She smiled and squeezed his hand. He intended to hold onto her throughout whatever was about to happen.

Magadaleeah walked around behind them. "The probes I'll attach to your heads will assist you in reaching a theta brainwave pattern quickly. I'll be monitoring the images you produce. That means I'll be able to see what you see. I'll also use a microphone to record your voice and a headset so you can hear me." Magadaleeah attached tiny probes to Angela's head and shoulders, looped a headset over her ears, and clipped a pinhead-sized microphone to her bolero. "How's that?"

"Comfortable. I'm fine," said Angela.

As Magdaleeah attached Todd's equipment, she asked, "Is there any particular time period you're interested in?"

Angela said, "The twentieth century, particularly 1940s to 1980s or 1990s."

"I hope we don't bring up anything too embarrassing." Todd grinned at both women. "Like family skeletons or...indiscretions."

"Don't worry. Nothing shocks me." Laughing, Magdaleeah went into the control booth behind their heads, and momentarily the lights dimmed to half light. Some metallic clicks resounded through the equipment. The computer monitors, positioned so Todd, Angela, and Magdaleeah could see them, began to flicker.

"Here we go!" Angela gave him a glorious smile.

Todd's curiosity grew every minute. He felt ready to experience something extraordinary.

"Now close your eyes and relax." Magdaleeah's voice came through the headset with a pleasant vibrato. "Let the music fill your mind. Go and flow. You are going on a journey back in time. As you go, you will always be safe and comfortable. You will always be able to hear the sound of my voice, and you will respond to me in English."

A pulsing sensation began passing through Todd. He felt like the bones dissolved out of his body, which grew mellow and extremely relaxed. It seemed that he passed over a bridge in his mind onto a plateau of clarity. His head felt healthy as if the origin of the headaches melted away.

Many images seemed to dance in the distance. He was confident that he would be able to grasp them if he chose to and draw them into his awareness. Poised, he remained alert, aware of his surroundings, the futon, Angela, everything. He had thought he would be transported, but he simply felt greater lucidity than ever before.

This was an astoundingly enjoyable state.

"You are going back in time," Magdaleeah's voice said. "The years are flying away—2050, 2040, 2030, 2020, 2010, 2000. We are turning the pages of history. 1990, 1980, 1970, 1960, 1950. We are stopping at 1940. Notice the images from the 1940s. If you lived a lifetime in the 1940s, you will see yourself as you were then."

Todd saw a an image, like a sepia toned photograph of a hospital delivery room, very old, with linoleum on the floor. A woman lay on the table, her body covered by a sheet. A doctor stood forlornly by the table. A nurse held a newborn, who was crying.

"She's dead," Todd gasped although he knew his mother still lived in this lifetime.

The voice said, "You are calm and relaxed and only remembering. You feel no pain, either physical or emotional. Now, move forward in time to a significant event in your life. Notice an image that you can describe to me."

Todd saw an image of a teen boy and girl dancing together. They wore bobby socks and the girl had a long ponytail and a full skirt. They whirled around in a gym with basketball hoops on each end. Other young people danced around them, and a band played. He could hear the music of the recording *Gonna Rock Around the Clock Tonight.*

"I'm dancing with Angie," Todd mumbled. "She's so pretty."

"Are you the same person whose mother died at birth?"

"Yes."

"And what is your name?"

"Tyler." The word amazed Todd as it came out his mouth.

"And your last name?"

"Beckman. It's Tyler Beckman, but everybody calls me Ty."

"I hear music." Angela's voice sounded soft and young. "It's hot in here. I hate it when I sweat because my makeup runs, but I love to dance."

"Who is your dancing partner?

"Angie," Todd said.

"He's a friend of my brother's." Angie's words overlapped his. "His name is Ty. He's so cute."

"Move forward in this lifetime to the next significant event."

"He betrayed me."

Todd spoke over her sobs. "Angie's marrying someone else." He felt guilty and sad.

"Move forward in this lifetime to the next significant event."

"My baby was born. My sweet Luke."

Todd spoke, "I'm driving from Indiana to California. I wanted to stop and see Angie in Arizona, but I can't remember her married name."

"We wish to explore the significance of this relationship to each of you. Go to a scene that makes the significance of this relationship clear. Stop and observe the scene."

In the silence Todd realized how many images he could choose from. He wanted the most important one to come forward. Then he saw himself as he looked in 2061 although he wore white slacks and shirt, like an old Navy uniform. He and Angela stood before a wooden display case. A few visitors milled around. The sign over the trunk read *To Be Opened in 2061*.

"Oh, my God," Angela sighed. "We're at the planetarium."

"Be in that moment. Speak the words you spoke," said Magdaleeah's voice.

"It's sort of a time capsule," Todd whispered, overwhelmed by the scene he had entered. He knew what he had to say. Where did the knowledge come from? "To be opened when Halley's Comet comes again. Every seventy-six or seventy-seven years."

Angela laughed and squeezed his hand. "Did you know Mark Twain was born the year the comet came, 1835? He always said he'd die the year it came again, and he did. In 1910."

"Thanks for the lesson, English teacher."

"When you've got thirty-five wriggling sophomores in front of you, you've got to keep them believing you're smarter than they are."

"How did Twain come to make such an odd prediction? I thought he wrote children's stories," Todd said.

"He had a lot of psychic experiences. He believed in reincarnation too. Said he dreamed of his soul mate in many different bodies, but always the same sweet girl."

"He's got nothing on us."

"What do you mean?"

"I'll meet you here for the trunk opening. In 2061."

"I'll be here. I promise."

After a long silence, Todd heard the clicking of machines.

"You are returning to your normal state of consciousness," Magdaleeah's voice said. "Your body feels lively and energetic. You will remember everything that transpired, and more details may come to you later. Thank you for being very good subjects."

Tension flowed into his Todd's arms and legs. He wanted to rise up and kiss Angela and feel her warmth in his arms. He heard Magdaleeah enter the room.

As she removed the monitoring equipment from him, tears wet Magdaleeah's face. "I want you to look at the monitors before you say anything to each other." She turned and released Angela from the equipment. "You folks are a textbook case. It gets me every time."

Todd sat up and gazed at the monitors. They both displayed the same image of him and Angela standing in front of the Halley's Comet exhibit.

Angela left her futon and stood over him. She laid her hands on his shoulders, a look of amazement on her face. "You said the exact words. The same ones I remembered in my vision. It's incredible."

"I think you've given me my next scientific project. To prove reincarnation empirically."

"It would be wonderful if you could do that, but the important thing for me is that we kept our promise. After all these years. Together again."

"Angie, my love. We'll always be together." Pulling her down on his lap, Todd enfolded her and kissed her lips. She whimpered as she returned his passion.

Magdaleeah sobbed out loud.

Eighteen

Fate Versus Free Will

In a gray prison smock, Kegan sat before a holographic expanse, aware that he viewed the illusion of a library table surrounded by books on shelves to the ceiling. The display masked the presence of the police officer escort, but Kegan would not forget.

Luke Brock appeared to sit on the other side of the table but was really shielded behind a bullet and bomb proof transparent shield. He wore a gold robe, like the one he wore when he taught those infantile roundedness events. He was probably trying to look quaint and saintly but succeeded in looking silly.

Kegan hadn't wanted to talk to the bastard at all, but the police officer had mentioned how favorable it would look in the lawyer's report that Kegan had consulted with a spiritual advisor. He wanted to avoid ending up in prison permanently like his grandmother had for murdering his step-grandfather. With the trial next week, Kegan had much to lose, including his freedom, a scary thought. Had Luke come here to taunt?

"What the hell do you want?" Kegan growled.

"I came to save your soul, asshole. Call me priest, wizard, imam, or whatever you like. I'm not going away until I set you straight about some things."

Luke's irritatingly condescending tone made Kegan wonder if their guide, Emmons, had demanded this meeting. Kegan found some humor in the idea of the old coot as the puppet of forces outside his control.

219

"When did you start to care about my soul?" Kegan didn't wish to hide his derision.

"You've been bent on your own destruction for the past two lifetimes. It's time you recognized that you're hurting yourself far more than you're hurting anyone else."

Lowering his eyes, Kegan focused his concentration, marshaled his psychic energy, and propelled it toward Luke. He wanted to take his old enemy by surprise and push him back just to show him Kegan still had it. This conversation couldn't end positively, a big waste of time.

Luke held out his arms as if to avoid attack. "Cease. Desist."

His comment made it obvious that Luke felt something, but he didn't appear the least bit disturbed. Kegan's energy felt rattled and inconsistent. Maybe because of the plastic barrier. More likely because of his regret and emotional confusion. He relaxed against the chair and rubbed his forehead.

What a hell of a mess he had made of things, getting caught like some incompetent goon. Upstaged by the Brock bitch once more. He'd not foreseen her clairvoyance and her ability to read his actions. She was damned good. Her powers had grown.

"It's about time you stopped comparing your abilities to my granddaughter's and to mine and to everyone else's."

Was it Kegan's imagination or had Luke read his thoughts? Maybe just a coincidence. He intended to monitor their conversation.

"Your psychic abilities were a gift from the Divine, just like all of ours are." Although Luke's voice sounded scratchy, he carried a lot of authority in his manner. "They are ours to use as we see fit. The powers are nothing in themselves. They are merely expressions of our inner natures. It's our souls that are important. The reasons why we use our powers, for good or ill." Luke shook his shaggy head, and his curly gray hair flapped from side to side.

"You've wasted yet another human body. How many will it take for you to start to learn?"

"What would you know about it?"

"I know you caved in to a wrong authority. You could have intercepted that flight and avoided Nine Eleven."

"I was fated to fly that plane into the tower. I had no choice whatsoever."

"Oh, and whose hands held yours to the plane's controls? Right up until the last second, you were making choices. You caved in to the desires of others."

"You were there in the Afterlife. You heard the Eldress tell us humanity needed the lesson. Had to have it, in fact, for the paradigm leap into social consciousness. Fat chance that mankind will ever make that leap!"

"The Eldress and the whole Council hoped it could be avoided. And it could have been if you and others had chosen rightly. You bowed to the petty needs of man, not the higher needs of spirit."

"I couldn't help it. It was my destiny."

"Bull shit. Start owning your power. You've tried to murder me in many lifetimes. When did it ever advance you? We're both always back again. Don't you get sick of the same old hatred? The same old petty view of life?"

The bastard had hit a nerve. Kegan felt weary of the burden of vengeance although he'd never give Luke the satisfaction of saying so.

"And now you try to kill Todd. Someone who has contributed so much to the good of humanity."

"You know why." Kegan snarled. "He shot me and my idiot brother. Killed us in England back in the 1700s."

"Because you killed my foster mother. Because you held me for ransom."

"You robbed me of my birthright! Humiliated me!"

"What goes around comes around. The boomerang theory of life. That's why the Buddhists call it the wheel of suffering. Because it never ends until you end it, man. Get off the carousel."

Kegan was stumped. No retort came to him.

"What about that *idiot brother*?" Luke sounded as if he genuinely cared about Kegan's brother in the previous lifetime despite the pejorative word. "Isn't it about time you atoned to him?"

"How'd you know about him?" Kegan's thoughts flew back to the eighteenth century when he had even introduced the wretched boy as his idiot brother.

"You mean that now he's your bastard son, born out of wedlock? You've never been allowed to know him in this lifetime because you treated him terribly before."

"How'd you know all this? Did Emmons tell you?"

"Just call me psychic." Luke shrugged, and a teasing expression crossed his face. "Actually, I looked up the birth records. You can atone if you want to."

"It's not in my nature." Kegan didn't mention that the son had since died and there was no hope of renewing relationship in this lifetime.

"I'm sorry he's dead, but you can do good work in his honor. You're going to have choice about your punishment."

Did the damned old man read his mind or did he find the death certificate too? Kegan bristled at the invasion of his mental privacy and the assumption of his eventual conviction. "I've not been found guilty yet."

"You will be because you are. You know as well as I do that they found the loaded syringe in your clothes."

Kegan cringed inwardly and lost more hope.

"You can choose to ingest the behavior modification nanobot," Luke said. "It will inhibit your psychic powers, but it will allow you to move freely in the prison environment and practice medicine. You can do surgeries on mentally ill inmates. God knows there are enough of them. You can help them have a more meaningful life. If you do the surgeries, perhaps your son's mother will forgive you. Maybe then you could begin to forgive yourself."

Aching anew, Kegan wished that the Imam had allowed the marriage between Kegan and his son's mother. Another lifetime wasted without love. Although he didn't want Luke to realize he'd made a good suggestion, Kegan thought there might be a real medical challenge for him with the criminally insane. "Those surgeries are hard work, and the success rate is about fifty-fifty. Those aren't odds that interest me."

"It's your choice. Once again. You can choose to sit in a cell instead. Life is always about choices. Let's see, you're about sixty now. With life expectancies being what they are, you can look forward to another twenty-five or thirty years of sitting there. Better take some good books." Luke glanced around at the hologram of the library. "That's a joke, in case you didn't know."

Kegan didn't want to turn out like his grandmother, trapped by her own hatred. She'd taught him to believe in his destiny. He'd bought her whole blasted belief system. The horror of having to live in prison must not overwhelm him. If he controlled his thoughts, his powers would return. He would find a way to escape.

"Don't pretend you have no positive attributes. You're no vicious killer. You're the aching, self-doubting wannabe kind."

"You talk like you know more about me than I know about myself. I don't recognize this weak sister of a man you're referring to. He's not me."

"Oh, is that right? I notice you haven't asked about Melanie."

"What about her?" Kegan felt defensive about involving her and hoped Luke would reveal her fate. The police officers had not volunteered any information about charges against Melanie, where she was incarcerated or if.

"The police let her go."

Kegan would have sighed, had he not been trying to withhold any display of emotion.

"It seems the two of you told the same story. She said you forced her to participate in the attempt on Williams's life, that she had no idea you intended anything other than helping to cure his headaches. There was no evidence linking her to the crime. Who'd have thought you'd turn out to be a gallant asshole. Guess you've still got some surprises in you."

"Watch yourself in the astral plane." Kegan felt so relieved that she'd gone free that he let himself relax and enjoy sparring with the old coot. "Do you still go out traveling?"

"When I do, I always watch out for you. I've still got some forgiveness work to do because of Euphoria." Luke spoke opening and without guile about his own shortcomings. He was as transparent as his wife Euphoria always had been. The two had matched each other in that infuriating quality.

"I told you then and I'll tell you now. I had nothing to do with that woman's death. I wanted to kill her, just because I knew it would confound you, but I couldn't bring myself to do it because she was had nothing to do with your transgressions."

"That's what you said when she died. You've not changed your story one iota."

"It's because I didn't kill her. I didn't harm her in any way."

"That's what she said too." Luke looked moved then pulled himself together. A look of pure contrition crossed his tired old face. "I'm sorry I held that against you for so long. You didn't deserve it."

"Damned straight. I guess we've both got some learning to do. There are some forces at work in our lives that are beyond our control."

"But we decide whether to honor them. Don't we?"

"I never thought I'd say it in any lifetime, but I guess you're right." Kegan chuckled despite himself.

Luke steadied himself against the library table as he rose.

"I'll be out free tonight," Kegan bragged. "Look for me."

An expression of doubt registered on Luke's face. He turned and walked through the door.

"You know what I mean. In the astral!" At least Kegan would be free there.

As the door closed, the projection of the library faded. The police officer stood in the midst of the room's dead monitor walls.

The horror of remaining in prison for the rest of his life assailed Kegan.

Nineteen

Do What Thou Wilt

Weary from the excursion to the police station, Luke flew his personal plane back to Sedona late in the evening. He'd never realized how much playing super hero could wear a person down.

Angela's purse and the purchases she'd made in Indiana lay on the seat. He would return them to her the next day when she arrived for his birthday party. His son and daughter-in-law had grudgingly agreed to change their work plans to come to his home a day late. He couldn't in good conscience inconvenience them again, and skipping his hundredth birthday would never do. Besides, he couldn't wait to see Aaron's and Vera's reactions to the attendance of the redoubtable Dr. Todd Williams at the party.

At the police station, when the officer had separated Todd from Angela for questioning, they gave each other wistful looks and actually kissed good-bye. And this from the reporter who maintained that she was about to leave on a four-year deployment to Alpha Centauri? Not a chance. It didn't take a psychic to know there would be wedding bells in the family before long.

Although Luke had logged into the computer at the global positioning system as soon as he took off, he feared he might fall asleep. The plane could land safely by remote control, but he didn't enjoy leaving his well being in its purview. Some technological advances required more trust than he could muster.

To help keep him awake, he pressed the personal log on the voice recorder and spoke into it:

"Because my birth father deserted Mom and me, I always felt cheated. Even grown men need fathers when they've never had one. I hoped my luck had changed when she hooked up with Ty. I grieved his death as my last chance. In those days I had no remembrance of past lives, but now I know why I felt so bereft. Angie and Ty were my parents in the eighteenth century. I lived a long and valuable life as Lainn MacPhearson in large part because of the home they provided me.

"Euphoria believed their names were Alice and Thomas, but we never found actual records of them. Their names could have been something besides MacPhearson. What I remember is the love they gave me. It pleases me to conjecture that Thomas adopted me, but I don't know for sure. In any case, their union nurtured my soul's growth over the centuries, and I honor them."

The police had a record of Luke's visit to the jail, but he wanted to record a couple of notes to document any testimony he might be asked to give in Kegan's trial.

"The interview with Kegan turned out better than I could have hoped. My ability to read his thoughts is a tantalizing development. The fact that it annoyed Kegan so much amuses me.

"I remember how disconcerted I felt when Euphoria read my mind in the early days of our courtship. Over the years of our marriage that ability of hers made me feel loved and known in a way that surpassed physical or emotional intimacy. Our souls had joined. I'll bet Kegan hates the prospect of such intimacy with a nosey old man like me."

I'm proud of you, my dearest. Euphoria's voice whispered in his mind.

"Me too." Luke laughed aloud, comforted by her nearness. He continued to speak into the personal log:

"There's no doubting Kegan's guilt. One police officer told me they found a syringe and enough poison to kill four people. The victims would choke to death and leave no trace of the cause. Despite his despicable plans for Todd, I sensed the negativity draining out of Kegan as we continued to talk. The rascal came close to confiding in me as a spiritual advisor. Suggesting the behavior modification nanobot had been a long shot, but Kegan hardly resisted. If he didn't volunteer right away, he would before long. He seems beaten by his life choices and wants to redeem his soul."

Luke paused to marvel before he proceeded with the recording:

"Who would have thought that I, Luke Brock, might become the vehicle for Kegan's return to grace?"

You're the perfect person to help him.

"Thank you, my dearest. Heady stuff this soul counseling. I can see how pride might provide more dimensions to overcome even in the Afterlife. I have a great model in Emmons. He takes mellow to a new level with his humility and loving acceptance. I know I'll continue to learn from him even after leaving life on Earth. In the meantime I intend to visit Kegan regularly and keep reminding him that he can change."

Luke sighed. Committing his thoughts to the log satisfied something in him, an urge he'd experienced from time to time to document his life. Once he'd considered writing a memoir but couldn't get past the egotism it evoked. He might as well put all his thoughts down. As much as he hated to admit it, he'd noticed a touch of forgetfulness lately, and these ideas deserved noting.

Relaxing against the cockpit seat, Luke pondered what to do about Melanie. He dictated:

"I'm certain Melanie knows far more about Kegan's plans for murder than she's admitted. She's probably an equal partner and more dangerous because she's on the loose. As to the thorny issue of the gender change...at least the ones I know of...Morfran and MacPhearson on the male side, then Melinda and Melanie. That transformation has hindered her ability to grow emotionally or spiritually.

"I don't know how much help I can give her on a personal level because I don't think she trusts me. At the beginning of this lifetime, I owed her for the time I betrayed her with another woman in the 1700s. She got me back for that one in spades. Now, I'd like to function as a friend and help her think through her decisions so she can get past so much focus on the physical. With her volubility, she's likely to have many rough spots.

"And to be completely candid, I have a bit of personal soul work to finish because Melanie can still strand me between passionate frustration and passionate desire. Maybe I've never forgiven her for being such a despicable father, but I'm not ready to go there. Nothing mellow about that unfinished business. Perhaps I'll make her my new challenge. Maybe I'll learn to read her thoughts, too."

When Luke arrived at his house, the sun had gone down. He parked the plane in the driveway, not caring that it was only eight in the evening. He had to get some sleep. He didn't bother to shut off the voice recorder.

Climbing out, Luke left the cabin door ajar, trudged into the house, and laid his keys on the kitchen counter.

Without turning on any lights, he dropped into his tilt back chair.

He really should have removed his teaching robe and put on his nightshirt...but he didn't.

He really should have turned on the nightlights...but he didn't.

Hopefully, Kegan wouldn't try to provoke any astral projection nonsense. Luke needed restful dreamless peaceful sleep.

Glad to be safely home, Luke sighed and closed his eyes.

Sometime during the night Luke came into conscious awareness in his astral sheath. Through the bluish twilight haze, he noticed many people floating about in their astral bodies, some clothed, some not. Confused, he looked around for a geographic point of reference and realized he had unwittingly wandered out over Coffee Pot Rock nestled among high rise office buildings and condominiums.

Unsettled by not remembering the transit from his physical to his astral form, Luke set off for home near Bell Rock a few miles away.

Ahead, Kegan's astral form beckoned for Luke to go somewhere.

I want no part of this!

Go home. Kegan gestured wildly. *Go home fast, man.* He exuded fear.

Surprised to see Kegan acting so uncharacteristically distraught, Luke found himself even more destabilized. He tried to form the thought to direct himself to head home but could muster no volition whatsoever.

A force greater than his will dragged him toward his house. Momentarily he hovered above it then plunged through the roof.

Melanie bent over his tilt back chair. Her cape fell forward, partially concealing his physical body.

With the utmost effort Luke turned his astral sheath toward his physical body with the intention of entering it. He merged his two forms and became even more stricken. Was he paralyzed?

Despite the shadowy darkness he could see the pointed object Melanie held in her hand.

"What have you done to me?" Luke managed only a whisper.

"I've injected you with a little something." Melanie's voice sounded harsh, her tone bitter. "Call it retribution."

"But why?"

"No man spurns me."

"But you've harmed your soul." Luke's cough rattled in his throat. He didn't want to die.

"You sent my lover to prison. You locked Kegan away from me."

Luke could no longer see her. Blackness suffused his mind. "This is not the end." He felt as if he were suffocating.

Melanie gave a triumphant laugh. "That's for me to say, not you."

Luke gasped for the breath that did not come.

Twenty

A Time to Every Purpose

Angela awakened in her own bed in Anthem. She lay in the circle of Todd's arms, his body touching her length in his sleep. She recalled the frantic nature of their love making the night before, as it had been in the 1980s, trying to catch up for missed moments.

Yet again last night they had made love, that time slowly and easily with care for pleasing each other. She remembered a softness about their life together in the eighteenth century when they'd made love as if they had all the time in the world. Their marriage of many years when their names had been Alison and Thomas set a standard she hoped to surpass in the twenty-first century.

With medical science so much more advanced, Angela and Todd could expect to live longer and have even more years together. She wanted it all this time—quantity and quality. She hoped for many children, three at least. Her family had grown small, providing too few portals into the world for reincarnating souls.

Todd stirred and opened his eyes, lovingly seeking her. The pale wall lighting gave the room a morning glow. She felt his desire nudge her.

"I remember what you like." Angela took his maleness into her and brought him to satisfaction, enjoying his pleasure as much as her own.

They lay for a while, resting and content.

"We need to get ready," Todd whispered, "or we'll miss the birthday party."

"Luke will understand if we're a few minutes late." Angela longed to remain, touched and touching. Todd's body was a miracle to her, one to endlessly explore. "Perhaps we could just move as a unit into the bathroom and bathe together."

With a teasing pout, Todd kissed her cheek and sat up. "You take the first shower. I've got some calls to make."

Angela sighed. She had momentarily forgotten the take-charge, get-things-done fellow who resided inside her lover. Now she remembered only too well. In many lifetimes he had led troops in peace and war. Once a leader, always a leader. She could do nothing but comply.

After a shower, she returned to the bedroom wrapped in a towel, intending to turn her attention to dressing, but the novelty of having a nude man nearby made the chore of choosing a gown seem insignificant. Todd looked stunning, his suntanned body vivid against the lavender walls. As she dropped the towel, he grinned in a taunting way, side-stepped her reach, and hurried into the bathroom.

"You'll not get away next time." Delighted with their playfulness, Angela laughed and turned to the closet. She decided on a low-necked gown the same turquoise as the stone in the silver, Indian necklace her grandfather had given her for college graduation. He always complimented her appearance when she wore the color. She intended to honor him by wearing it today.

On the trip to Indiana with Luke, Angela had bought his birthday gift but couldn't recall what she'd done with it. If she didn't find it, she'd have to give him a rain check. Logic told her the purchases would have been with her purse, but she didn't know what had become of it either. She hoped she had left the purse and the packages in Luke's plane when they landed at the Psi Therapy Clinic in such a desperate hurry. With her house on scan and her money on the wrist tattoo, it was no big deal that she'd misplaced her belongings.

Now that the makeup man at the station didn't have his hands on her hair every day, kinking and curling it, the waves fell softly around her face. Angela stood before her dressing table, brushed her hair, and tucked it behind her ears.

Her face seemed deeper and somehow more mature this morning. Would growing spiritual awareness change her appearance? She definitely felt deep, old, and fulfilled. Perhaps the emotion came from consciously containing the memories of some of her previous lifetimes. On the other hand, having sex might change her appearance, too. Would everyone at the party immediately guess that she and Todd had made love? Oh, well, what did it matter?

Picking up the white coverlet, Angela spread it, plumped the pillows, then sat on the bed, and opened her holophone. Two messages appeared, one from Campbell and one from her mother. She decided to find out what Campbell wanted first and shuddered at the possibility that he might say the assignment to Alpha Centauri had come through. What would she do? Leaving Todd now was out of the question.

After she routed the call, Campbell's portly image resolved above her phone. "Hey, Angela, congrats on the story about the arrest of the Psi Therapy honcho. It ran well."

"Thanks." Angela couldn't recall his ever complimenting her before.

"That item about the missing security guard? Just the kind of detail I like. Plot thickening, you know."

"Glad you liked it." Two compliments in a row? Had her boss undergone a religious conversion or something?

"Well, hey," Campbell beamed a huge smile across the air waves. "I'm thinking you ought to have your old job back. Can you get here by five o'clock. If not, you can start tomorrow."

Angela's first impulse was to shout yes. On the other hand, she'd caught a few minutes of the news a couple of nights ago. Her replacement, Hannah, displayed about as much charisma as a cantaloupe, plus she never looked Juan in the eye when they traded news segments on air. Not a way to inspire confidence in the viewer. The station's ratings might be dropping. Angela intended to enjoy the power shift, if only for a moment.

"Hey, boss, you promised I could go to Alpha Centauri, and I'm really counting on it. The adventure of a lifetime, you know. I'll do good work out there." She tried hard not to laugh aloud at Campbell's look of dismay. A long pause followed.

"Come on, Angela!"

"Oh, all right. I'll come back." Angela faked a regretful tone. She refused to preempt the birthday party, and she had an intuition that she needed more time. "I'll be back Monday."

"But that's five days."

"Sorry, I've got plans."

"Okay. See you Monday. Have a good weekend." Campbell signed off.

An alien obviously had come down and snatched her boss and left a pod person in his place. Angela could barely suppress her amazement that he had made the offer, that he had manners he could use when he needed to, and that she had side-stepped the whole Alpha Centauri thing. Now nothing stood in her way with Todd. She should have held out for a raise too.

When Todd came out of the bathroom, Angela watched him don a sport shirt and jeans with no briefs. How sexy! She related the conversation with Campbell.

"That's great, darling." Todd stepped into his shoes and sat at her dressing table. He pulled her onto his lap, and his expression turned serious. "I've got something I need to ask you."

"Sure, anything."

"You know the plane we rented yesterday so I could teach you to fly?"

"What about it?" She had done very well with his instruction, she thought, and they'd had a wonderful day together.

"I arranged to buy it, and I want to give it to you."

"Good heavens, Todd. That's a huge gift, a million dollars' worth. I can't accept that from you."

"Well, could you if it were a wedding gift?"

His casual question awed her. Certainly she'd hoped he would propose but assumed it would take weeks or months. For a man who'd reached his fortieth birthday as a bachelor, marriage must seem a huge step.

"A selfish gift at that," Todd went on. "You'll need it if you're going to commute between L. A. and Phoenix to work." He gave a naughty glance around the bedroom. "Or did you want to keep living here?"

"I don't care where we live as long as it's together."

"Then you want to marry me?"

"Absolutely. Yes, yes, yes."

Angela took his beloved face in her hands. She hoped her kiss would convey the joy she felt. She'd never been as happy as in this moment.

Todd returned the kiss with quickened fervor. "Are you sure we have to go to the party?"

After she nodded, they both laughed and hurried out to the parking lot in the full blush of a hot June morning.

The tarmac stung her sandaled feet as Angela jumped into the driver's seat of her plane, a charming new model, painted with feathers of gold and red, like an exotic African bird. She knew each step to execute the fifteen-minute flight. She'd had two good teachers in Luke and Todd.

Arriving in Sedona, they hovered above Luke's home and grounds. Police cars and an ambulance with siren lights blinking stood in the street. Luke's plane and Aaron's were both parked in the driveway. People milled around outside the other houses. No voices from below penetrated the sealed plane cabin. Something must have gone terribly wrong.

Dread shuddered through Angela. "Dear God, what's happened?"

"I'll do this." Todd took over the controls and landed the plane down the street. He and Angela clamored out and ran toward Luke's house. As they did so, the ambulance pulled away without a siren. Did that indicate good or bad news?

"Granddad, Mom, Dad," Angela cried as she dashed through the front door of the bungalow.

"We're in here," Vera called in a fractured voice.

Angela entered the kitchen to find her father slumped over the table, his head in his arms. Two policemen stood at the sink. "What's happened? Where's Granddad?"

Vera came around the table and took Angela into her arms.

The stricken expression on her mother's face told Angela the horrid truth. "Oh my God, he's dead!"

Aaron rose, anguish in his manner. "Murdered in his sleep!"

"Murdered?" Angela gasped.

"We don't know that for certain, ma'am," a policeman said.

"His arm had been punctured." Aaron looked old as he draped his arms around his wife and daughter and leaned against them.

Both women sobbed. Todd enfolded the tiny family in his arms, and they cried against his chest.

"Luke rescued me," Todd whispered. "I wish to hell I'd had the chance to save him."

Angela could not imagine the world without Luke in it. Watching her parents cry intensified her own grief. She had to do something.

Drawing himself up to his full height, Aaron spoke to a policeman, "When can we have his body...uh...him back? For the funeral?"

One policeman handed a data chip to Aaron. "We'll be in touch when the autopsy is finished. Thank you, Mr. Brock."

"Autopsy?" The idea that someone would cut her dear Luke open and sift around his insides almost undid Angela. If she couldn't take action soon, she'd fall apart.

After the policemen left, Angela said, "The autopsy will show nothing. I'd bet any amount of money. I saw Kegan with the syringe and vial of poison. Melanie had access to them, too." She didn't understand why but felt compelled to go out to the plane. "I'll be right back."

Uncertain what she would find but certain she should go, Angela dashed outside. As soon as she stepped into Luke's plane, she saw her purse and the shopping bag with the purchases she had made in Indiana.

When she smelled Luke's aftershave, a wave of loss flowed over her. She sat in the pilot's seat and imagined him there beside her, but he wasn't. She couldn't hear his voice and see his smiling face. Now his image would never hover above her holophone. Neither would she feel his arms around her, patting her and reassuring her that she could do anything.

As tears fell she noticed the light blinking on the voice recorder and pressed play.

Luke's hollow voice filled the cabin. Comforted by the sound, she listened to the personal log for the last day of his life. He spoke of her and Todd and the love he'd born them through the ages. How charming that he thought her name had been Alice rather than Alison in the eighteenth-century lifetime. He spoke of Euphoria and their precious bond. Theirs was the model for the kind of marriage Angela wanted to build with Todd, one where they could grow together spiritually.

By now Luke and Euphoria had reunited in the Afterlife. He would probably get to see Emmons too. Home again. Luke must be experiencing bliss, and Angela tried to be happy for him. That was too much to ask of herself at the moment.

Controlling her own grief required all her effort. She had to stop crying and do what needed to be done. Luke would expect nothing less of her.

Next in the log he noted the progress he'd made in an interview with Kegan. So that's the reason Luke postponed the birthday party. He was good to the core, a real saint. Angela felt proud of him on every level and wanted to emulate him. At one point he laughed aloud and seemed to talk with someone from the Afterlife. Angela wondered whether he'd been talking with Euphoria.

Then Luke spoke of Melanie and his intention to rescue her from herself. The messages on the tape sounded like directions telling Angela what she needed to do. He wanted to retrieve the souls of Kegan and Melanie. Maybe Angela wanted that too.

What had Luke meant about the early years of his marriage to Melinda? How did Melinda get back at him? Did she take a lover? Very believable if she was anything like the Melanie incarnation today. Such details might be lost in time. Darn.

Feeling more connected to Luke through hearing his notes, Angela grabbed her purse and the shopping bag and returned to the kitchen. Todd stood at the counter, fixing a pot of coffee. Vera and Aaron sat at the table, holding hands.

"Luke and I went to Indiana last weekend." Angela set her purse and shopping bag on the table. "He took me on a roots trip to see my great-grandmother's grave. He had built a statue to her. She looked just like me. She was me." She hoped Todd and her father might understand. It didn't matter that Vera probably couldn't. "Luke's birthday just can't go by unnoticed." Angela opened the package and set a potpourri basket on the table. "Here, Mother, I brought this for you."

Nodding her thanks, Vera looked confused as if she didn't know quite what to say.

Neither did Angela, but she felt it best to let each grieve in his or her own way without laying judgment. For herself, giving the presents was a healing act. "Dad, this is for you." She handed Aaron a paperweight. "A relic of a bygone time. They used to be popular when people kept their windows open, I guess."

"It's Bedford Stone, very famous." Aaron examined the stone. "I wish I'd had this for my collections as a kid."

Angela unwrapped a cardinal cut from a ruby. "Here's what I bought for Luke. The state bird of Indiana. He'd want you to have it, Dad."

Aaron set the glass statue next to the stone. "Dad would have loved it." He bit his lip and turned away.

Angela set two miniatures of astronauts on the table and managed a wistful smile. "These are for you, Todd. Know who they are?"

"Frank Borman and Gus Grissom, astronauts from Indiana." Todd hugged her and kissed her in front of her parents. They didn't seem surprised.

Angela felt relieved that they knew of the love between her and Todd without her having to announce it. She sat at the table, squeezed her father's hand, and opened her holophone. "I need to do this now. For Luke."

While they listened she called the Phoenix policewoman to whom she had given the tip to look for the syringe and poison. She learned that the investigators had found both items, as Angela expected. She gave the police another tip, to search Melanie Vanderson's room at the Hyatt in Phoenix for more of the same. "You'd better hurry. My guess is she'll leave town fast since her boyfriend's in jail without conjugal privileges."

The next few days passed in a haze of grief and love from friends and family. Aaron invited all the people Luke had known for years, including the students from his roundedness events, old law buddies, as many of Aaron's Hispanic cousins as he could contact. Even Euphoria's daughter, Psyche, attended with a granddaughter. How like Aaron to want to make the funeral a grand testimony.

The guests at the memorial service filled the largest church in Sedona to capacity. The people who wanted to honor Luke included Governor Goldman, who attended herself, rather than send a representative. Perhaps she feared her name had been tarnished by linkage with Dr. Kegan. In any case, Angela and her family considered the governor's presence fitting for a citizen who had lived over ninety years in Arizona and contributed so much to the community.

The constant presence of her husband-to-be nourished Angela. Internationally known physicist slash celebrity, notwithstanding, Todd knew what it meant to support a loved one in time of need. He bonded with both of her parents in ways unique to their personalities. Love grew among them out of this sad time.

The evening after the memorial, the Phoenix policewoman called Angela. Her image stood crisply atop the holophone. "It's not really procedure, ma'am. We're only supposed to use information from psychics as corroborative evidence, but you helped us solve two crimes, so in my opinion we owe you."

"I don't want any money." Angela felt vindicated that her psychic abilities were being honored by this policewoman and perhaps by others on her staff.

"That's what I figured, but I wanted to tell you what we found...because of the circumstances...your grandfather, I mean. We owe you at least that."

"You found the poison, didn't you?"

"We got a court order to search Melanie Vanderson's hotel room and discovered two vials of poison and two syringes labeled A and M for reasons unclear. Also, we found bomb-making materials that matched those used to destroy your Bimi."

"You mean she firebombed my car too?" Angela had never even suspected Melanie, but of course she could have known about Angela's appointments at the Psi Therapy Clinic through Kegan.

The policewoman said, "Melanie Vanderson is facing charges for the murder of Luke Brock and the attempted murder of Angela Brock."

"Thank you for telling me...and for believing me. It's made all the difference." Angela didn't know whether she might see visions that would help the police in the future, but a bridge of trust had been built through these awful circumstances.

One bright spot in all the events for Aaron and Vera happened when Angela told them she would soon return to L. A. to marry Todd and live in his home. Vera worked hard, packing Luke's books for the book museum. Aaron insisted on taking as many personal items as he could pack, as if he could preserve his father's memory by carting home his things. Angela chose photographs, some dating back to the 1970s and the brass Tibetan bell. They decided to give Luke's old plane to the aeronautical museum in Balboa Park, so Todd arranged to fly it to San Diego.

On the driveway, Angela kissed Todd good-bye with the promise that they would meet at his home the next day after work. With so much change, Luke's death, her impending marriage, acceptance of her psychic knowledge by the local police, she should try to keep a few things unchanged, for ballast in stormy water. She intended to return on Monday, as she'd told her boss. In all the confusion, she couldn't remember whether she had asked Todd an important question.

As he started to climb into Luke's plane, she pulled him back. "One thing I want to ask. You want children, don't you?"

"As many as you're willing to bear, milady." Todd gave her his wonderful smile, climbed in, and waved from the cockpit. Once before he had waved like that then died before her eyes. She forced herself to put away her fears and no longer let the past haunt her. She and Todd lived a new life. She trusted that he would return to her this time.

One last task remained for Angela, something she'd requested to do. She had brought Luke into the world alone and considered it her sacred obligation to scatter his ashes alone.

Late in the afternoon, she changed into the jeans and tank top that Luke had said made her look like the original Angie. The original was very much alive in her today as she drove her personal plane to the entrance to Boynton Canyon, one of Luke's favorite spots in Sedona. He'd often reminisced about meeting Euphoria there for the first time.

Angela strapped on a backpack that contained water and Luke's Tibetan meditation bowl and ringer. She carried the precious urn so nothing would spill out.

The sun stood high in the sky, the air sticky and breezeless, the temperature over a hundred. As Angela trod into the canyon, her tennis shoes kicked up dry red dirt. Coppery slate broke through juniper shrubs and aspen trees, the blue-green of Sedona's flora deep against the desert sky.

Thick hot air and sharp colors of nature intensified the passion within Angela. She had an intuition that she would find the perfect spot to stop and perform a ritual. As she trudged higher the air did not seem to thin out, the heat did not diminish. The water failed to quench her thirst.

Perspiring, Angela walked around a bend bordered by shrubs, climbed over some rocks, and slid down into a clearing with a rock-face cliff on one side and a gorge of evergreen shrubs on the other.

This is the place, Angela thought or heard.

She set down her belongings. Walking around the clearing, she gathered small rocks and arranged them in a circle on the ground. She knelt before it, emptied Luke's ashes into the center, and picked up the brass bowl. She panned the inside of the bowl with the ringer.

The vibrant tone sang through the trees and bounced off the rocks. The mellow gong reverberated through the canyon, clarifying the air.

"I consecrate these ashes." Words came to Angela out of an infinite knowledge from ancient times. "Blessed be, my son, my grandfather. Out of darkness into light. Out of pain into joy. Out of many into the One. And so it is." She felt attuned to the ritual.

Entering a quiet place in her mind, Angela saw herself as Alma, a druid priestess, administering last rites to the dead. She'd learned then the words so meaningful today. She knew she had been selfish and had harmed others in that lifetime.

Generations later she had been low born as Alison to atone for her arrogance and ruthless acts as Alma. Reborn as Angie she overcame selfishness of spirit and learned to love without expectation, but Angie had not trusted her gifts.

In this lifetime as Angela she would honor her psychic abilities and they would grow. She would find a way to forgive Melanie for murdering her beloved Luke, no matter how difficult the task, and help Kegan and Melanie as Luke had intended to do. By doing so, Angela could clear her karmic debt and honor Luke by following his lead.

No longer a beginner mystic, Angela intended to gain conscious control over her psychic processes. The force of much learning stood behind her. She would incorporate more and more learning from her past lives but still live the present lifetime with zest. Her soul memory would improve in this incarnation and help her mature spiritually.

During the time between her lives Angela remembered watching over Luke, speaking to him, and warning him to stay out of the tower on Nine Eleven. She believed he would want to help her in return, especially with the rehabilitation of Kegan and Melanie.

Angela intended to remain alert to hear from Luke. He would surely try to contact her and watch over her because he loved her. They were always connected in a fine web of the past, the present, and the future. Both teacher to each other. Never absent from each other's hearts.

The sun set and a breeze blew across Angela's face. The ashes drifted and shifted, swirled, and blew away.

A comet streaked across the darkening sky, trailing glory dust. Halley's Comet gone for another seventy-six years. Angela wondered if she'd still be around when it returned or if her days on Earth would have ended.

It didn't matter somehow. Whatever happened was in perfect order.

Angela would journey back down the mountain to a new life with her beloved. She and Todd would have children and give Luke a portal into the world, if he chose to return.

Epilogue

From a great distance, Luke heard tinkling bells, clear and bright. A breeze stirred the air around him. He felt contented, unwilling to open his eyes, and relaxed against what felt like a bed of rose petals. From long habit, he thought to himself his morning affirmation—I arrived a conscious being in this world, and I will leave it a conscious being, awake and aware of my transition.

His surroundings glistened a white so bright he could see it despite his closed eyes.

"It's good to have you home, darling." Euphoria spoke, the sound of her voice as beautiful and welcome as a bird's song.

Luke might have been mistaken about awakening. Otherwise how could her voice originate outside his mind? "Am I dead or is this a dream?" He knew the answer as soon as he asked. Moments ago, Melanie had given him a dose of poison. It was fatal.

"Welcome, Luke, you have done well." The unmistakable timbre of Emmons's voice brought Luke to full alert, and he opened his eyes.

The whiteness around them became more subdued. Euphoria shimmered in golden light and Emmons in pale blue, their substances ephemeral but their identities unchanged.

Euphoria moved toward Luke. Waves of auburn hair framed her lovely face. She smiled in the same vibrant way she had when she lived on Earth.

"I've missed you so," Luke murmured. Then he recalled that he needn't speak aloud. Everyone here communicated telepathically.

"And I you." Euphoria's smile thrilled him. "We can be together more, now that you're back."

"I'm glad to see you," Luke thought, "but I wasn't ready to die. I had so much to do. Is anyone ever ready to die?"

"Not really, I suppose. Now relax and take comfort." Effervescent streams of light radiated from Euphoria. Love pulsed from her fingertips as she embraced Luke. Her aura surrounded him. Their energies merged in a rainbow spray of light, more intimate than physical love.

When she released Luke, he felt restored, rested, and young again.

Bells in the distance rang with a majestic sound.

"It's time to go." Emmons stepped closer.

The spires of Celestial City gleamed golden against the whiteness. Souls moved about as pinpoints of light.

Luke could see around himself in all directions as he trod the jade green grass toward the busy city with Euphoria on one side and Emmons on the other.

Ahead stood the Doric columns of the auditorium where he'd volunteered for this journey a hundred years ago. He had listened while the Eldress explained the Plan to fill the great need Earth had for volunteers to return and make a sacrifice. The Plan would give the whole world a chance to learn to love each other and grow together spiritually. Luke, Melanie, and Kegan had volunteered gladly, willingly, freely. Now he knew they had played roles in the event that became known as Nine Eleven.

The city vibrated with light, a hub of harmony. Innumerable souls glowed with individual energy patterns of color as they went about the business of preparing to be reborn on Earth or returning from it. A few early stars appeared in the twilight vault.

The complex, constructed to look like Earth, had been idealized to represent what souls would encounter in the real world, a way station to help them adjust to the great change of awareness and loss of memory that birth into or withdrawal from a human body entailed.

Luke remembered his most recent birth with Angie as his mother and what it had been like to feel confined in a tiny body. Soon after he had begun to forget the Afterlife. It had taken many years and much effort on Earth to remove the layers of forgetfulness and restore his soul memory.

Near the embarkation portal stood an amphitheatre, screening rooms, and consultation alcoves surrounded by gardens with fountains, trees, and flowers of many varieties.

Water trumpeted from porcelain tiger lilies and splattered on gold nuggets piled on the fountain's floor. Fragile scents of rosemary floated in the silky air. Trees swayed, their boughs heavy with pink leaves.

"Follow me." Emmons entered the portal with tall doors.

Striding across the golden floor, Luke and Euphoria followed Emmons down a hall and into a council chamber, the same one where Luke had been counseled after other lifetimes. He wondered who might be present because the members of his council varied from lifetime to lifetime.

Five elders, all glowing in soft purple light, sat at a curved conference table. The Eldress who had proposed the Plan honored Luke by sitting on his council. The seventh member on the reviewing panel was new. She gave off a rich yellow light and radiated love to Luke. Her display of affection touched him although her identity eluded him. He should know her.

"Catherine, is that you? Caitlin? What should I call you? You're an elder now?"

Her laughter floated toward him. "An eldress."

Luke laughed too, delighted to see one from his own soul group had earned a place on the council. He felt proud of her and cherished the love they had born each other through many incarnations.

With a full heart, Luke took the seat in the center reserved for the returning soul. Emmons remained behind him to his left and Euphoria to his right. They would both be available to give support, but Luke doubted he would need it. He felt excited, ready for his life review.

"Welcome, Lugh." The Lead Elder in the center wore a large medallion signifying leadership. He addressed Luke by his soul name. "How do you feel about the life you've just completed?

"It was a good life. I think I made some progress. I wasn't ready to return though. Kegan and Melanie need me."

The Lead Elder gazed deep into Luke's mind. It was impossible to lie to him. "You bear Melanie no animosity for the murder? Or Kegan for attempting it?"

"Well, I can't go that far. Forgiving Melanie won't be easy, but I have to admit it will be easier to forgive her here than if I have to live another lifetime with her. As for Kegan, he somewhat redeemed himself. After all, he did try to warn me that Melanie was about to kill me. I think there's hope for him if he has the right guidance."

"Does it have to be yours?" Caitlin asked.

"I understand them better than anyone, and they won't fare well on Earth without me. Also, I hoped to spend time with Angela and Todd, to finally enjoy the loving relationship I knew I could have with them, now that I'm aware of our eternal connection. I waited many years for Angela to come into her own. Now just as she has emerged as a soul of power, I have to leave. Why?"

"Your number was up, as they say on Earth." Emmons smiled but his tone was solemn. "The elders extended your stay for reasons having to do with the needs of your son, Aaron, not of yourself. They didn't want him to become an orphan. It would have been too much for his soul to deal with. You benefited greatly from the additional time on Earth and grew spiritually, far surpassing your hopes and mine."

"Thanks, I guess. I thought you had more confidence in me."

"I'm very proud of you."

"We are all proud of you," the Lead Elder said. "You were able to achieve what Kegan and Morfran have failed to accomplish, despite the fact that they received their rewards for Nine Eleven and you did not. Kegan incarnated too quickly without processing his learning, and Morfran became stuck in physicality as Melanie."

"That's why they need me now," Luke said. "I thought we had agreed I would get an extra boost on my spiritual development from volunteering for Nine Eleven. Why did you make me do the work the slow and tedious way on Earth?"

"Don't argue with success," the Eldress said.

Luke remembered the anticipation with which he had volunteered after hearing the Eldress speak. His reward would have been great spiritual learning had he died on Nine Eleven rather than remaining alive for another sixty years. Kegan and Melanie had also volunteered. Kegan had been promised enhanced psychic powers in his next life, and Melanie would receive great physical beauty.

Addressing the Eldress who had proposed the Plan, Luke asked, "The Plan to create a viable habitat on Earth didn't work out too well, did it? You really can't jump start spiritual development, I guess."

"Opinion is divided here as well as on Earth," the Eldress said. "It was a very difficult assignment."

"Mankind is surviving." Caitlin sounded optimistic.

"But damaged." Emmons seemed to brood. "Earth has so depleted its natural resources that raiders from other planets aren't even interested in plunder. There's been so much violence that residents of other planets steer away from Earth as too dangerous a place for habitation."

"It will be all right." Luke found it odd to comfort Emmons instead of the other way around. Even though he wanted to go back, he wanted to stay too. He glanced at Euphoria, uncertain how she might react. She gazed at the council members, perhaps lost in thought or perhaps allowing him space to make his own decision. "I'm willing to go back and help straighten things out."

"You may have to, but I hope not, for your sake." Emmons looked toward the council members.

Silence settled over the chamber as the elders conferred telepathically. Luke had complete trust in their wisdom. Councils had watched over his development throughout centuries and lifetimes. They would know what was best for him to do.

The Lead Elder gazed at Luke with kind eyes. "We find your lifetime as Luke Brock satisfactory. You no longer need to reincarnate unless you wish to."

The news overwhelmed Luke. He had no idea he'd done that well. Alleluia!

"However," the Lead Elder said, "you may return if you wish. A body will be available soon to return appropriately placed to rise to a position of political leadership in the United States of North America. You would be able to achieve great positive change on Earth by accepting this lifetime. If you do not wish to return, we will appoint you as a guide to new souls just embarking on incarnations. Or, you may choose to remain here as a companion to Euphoria and an angel to those in your soul group still on Earth— Angela, Todd, Melanie, and Kegan. Which would you prefer?"

Luke felt torn. He longed to help his soul group on Earth. He could do that here while also experiencing the life of the soul with Euphoria for a companion. Their abilities and their love would flourish.

On the other hand, there was great honor in being chosen as a guide. Shaping and guiding younger souls would be far more gratifying than teaching metaphysics on Earth and he had loved that. He would do important work as a guide and get to learn all that Emmons had to teach him.

Unfortunately, his duties as a guide would prevent him from reincarnating very often, if at all. Luke wasn't sure he could give up Earth with its compelling beauty and its excruciating experiences. If he went back in a new incarnation, he would be able to do much more good than he had so far. He could have a positive impact on many more souls. The Earth needed a great deal of help.

The entire council, Emmons, and Euphoria—all watched him with anticipation.

"I'll need some time to think about this."

Acknowledgments

Over the years while I have imagined and written the *Alma Chronicles*, many people have influenced my life and thought. Some have given me support, encouragement, and love. I would like to thank these people here and tell them how grateful I am for their presence in my life. Even though a few have died, I trust they know I appreciate them.

Aaron Heathcotte, Annette Lewis, Barby Heathcotte, Betty Joy, Beulah Fesler, Brandon Heathcotte, Brock Heathcotte, Bruce Heathcotte, Bryan Heathcotte, Carol Gibson, Chip Myers, David Perez, Dean Gordon

Emily Heathcotte, Greg Williams, Howard Fesler, Jacque Beatty, Jim Green, Joe Perez, John Bergman, Josh Heathcotte, Judith Lynn-Perez, Larry Crosley

Maggie Perry, Martha Davis, Mary Livingston, Mike MacCarthy, Mike Murphy, Nancy Brehm, Noonie Crosley, Pat Kennedy, Phil Shirley, Rick Aynes, Rick Williams

Rita Heathcotte, Robert Meya, Sharon Atkins, Sonny Crosley, Stephanie Heathcotte, Tearle Dwiggins, Ted Moore, Tom Brehm, Tom Franklin, Tom Larkin, Trena Aynes, Vijaya Schartz

I thank these authors for their books:

Deepak Chopra, Dick Sutphen, Ernest Holmes, Jane Roberts, John Edward, Judith Orloff, Ralph Waldo Emerson, Richard Bach, Walt Whitman

Toby Fesler Heathcotte is both mother and grandmother. A former teacher, she now serves as president of Arizona Authors Association and lives in Glendale, Arizona.

tobyheathcotte.com and outofthepsychiccloset.com

Write to her at toby@tobyheathcotte.com

Books by Toby Fesler Heathcotte

The Alma Chronicles

- *I Alison's Legacy*
- *II Lainn's Destiny*
- *III Angie's Promise*
- *IV Luke's Covenant*
- *V The Comet's Return*

Out of the Psychic Closet: The Quest to Trust My True Nature published by Twilight Times Books

Program Building: A Practical Handbook for High School Speech and Drama Teachers

Seeds for Fertile Minds: Eight Curriculum Integration Tools with Betty Joy